Sara Alexi is the author of the Greek Village Collection.

She divides her time between England and a small village in Greece.

http://facebook.com/authorsaraalexi

Sara Alexi

A Handful of Pebbles

oneiro

Published by Oneiro Press 2014

ISBN-13: 978-1500295929

ISBN-10: 1500295922

For Sophia

Chapter 1

In truth, the whole place looks like it could be abandoned, a ghost town. Everywhere greying whitewash, peeling paint and dust.

Sarah hopes it is the wrong village.

A central palm tree offers dappled shade to the village square. Laurence is not visible; he is paying and asking for directions under the awnings of the kiosk. Rolling the chilled water bottle, still wet from the fridge, across her forehead, Sarah stretches the journey out of her legs by walking over to a small, lifeless fountain. A crisp packet and a drink can lay still in the dry bottom. Around the fountain, abandoned in the heat, clusters of metal chairs are casually arranged around circular metal tables as if they have spilt over from the rather grim-looking café across the road.

Cracking open the water, she takes a long sip, the iced liquid chilling down through her chest. Her clothes, which seemed so flimsy when she bought them, cling and weigh her down. She lifts the neckline from her throat.

'*Seira sou.*' The meaningless sounds float as a window opens at the charmless café opposite. Laughter and gruff voices are punctuated by a sharp thwack of wood on wood, the sound of a board game enthusiastically played.

Sarah wanders around to the other side of the palm tree for a better view, to see the people who inhabit this world of unlimited sunshine, who have time to play games.

The laughter and voices merge into a hum: relaxed, warm, inviting. Sarah takes a second drink of water.

Inside the café, shapes move, men come into focus; tall, short, rounded, thin; some white-haired and some dark. Age and hardship etched on their faces. Uniformed in dark trousers and sagging, baggy shirts. Some talk with animation as if addressing everyone, others turn to their neighbour, exchanging quiet words, smiling, scowling. A man in a crisp white shirt with a halo of frizzy hair strides between tables, brandy glasses on a tray.

'*Yia mas*!' someone shouts, and drinks are held high.

She rolls her water bottle down her neck. The café actually looks quite charismatic, engaging even, the stark walls and hard edges somehow appropriate in the heat.

One of the men looks out and stares at her, and smooths his impressive moustache. She turns away and puts her back against the palm tree.

'We are in the outback of nowhere surround by dimwits ...' Laurence appears and strides towards the car. A donkey brays from somewhere on the hill behind the kiosk and Sarah looks up the rise behind the village. It is topped with a tuft of pine trees that sway ever so gently by an unfelt breeze.

'For pity's sake, why have you left the door open?' Laurence breaks her stare. 'It'll get hot. Get in.' Before she is fully settled in her seat, the air conditioning is on full blast. The hairs on her arm rise up in protest.

'Here.' He throws the map towards her. 'The woman had no idea how to read a map. All she could do was giggle.'

'Did she speak English, then?' Sarah asks.

'Not a word. I pointed to the village on the map but I might as well have been showing her Chinese hieroglyphics.' He snaps his seat belt on. Sarah's brow creases and a condescending smile tugs at the corners of her mouth. Hieroglyphics are Egyptian, not Chinese. Part of her would delight in pointing this out, but, then again, she searches her memory, perhaps the term applies to more than just Egyptian writing and Laurence is correct after all. The smile fades.

'Did you try just saying the name of the place or the names of the people?' she asks.

His eyes narrow, and before they turn on her, she offers, 'Shall I try?'

'If she doesn't understand then she doesn't understand.' Laurence checks the mirror and puts his hand on the gearstick.

'I'll try.' Pushing the door open, the heat, like a wind, rushes into the cold car.

'No,' Laurence states, but Sarah is out and across the square. She doesn't pause to close the door. As she ducks under the awning, the woman in the kiosk grins and raises a hand of welcome. Sarah's fists unclench.

'Hello,' Sarah begins.

'Hello. English.' The woman laughs, her perfectly coiffured hair stiff with lacquer.

'I am looking for ...' Sarah's eye is drawn to the rows of lighters, stacked packs of cigarettes, boxes of condoms, individual wrapped chewing gums, and endless other colourful piles that hem in the woman. Sarah pauses and pulls folded papers from her back pocket. Someone approaches; the man with the moustache from the cafe. Sarah shuffles around, turning her back towards him as she fumbles with the printouts. No one speaks or moves.

'Please.' Sarah half turns to wave him ahead of her to be served.

'No, no,' he replies in an accent strong enough to imply these are all the English words he knows.

He stands with feet apart, his barrel chest stretching his shirt, a gold chain around his neck, and his thick, long moustache twitching. His eyes sparkle and Sarah is momentarily held in his gaze before snapping herself back to her papers.

She skim-reads the printed email, self-conscious now and half wishing she had left this to Laurence after all. 'Do you know Michelle or Juliet?'

The woman looks blank but then starts to laugh; an embarrassed chortle. The man now grins, one hand in his pocket, the other swinging some beads on a loop of thread.

'Michelle?' Sarah persists. The woman stops laughing. 'Juliet?' Sarah tries.

'Ah,' the woman exclaims, raises a finger to indicate Sarah should wait, and turns her back. Going through the small door at the back of her protective hut, she emerges between stacks of bottle crates and newspapers to link Sarah's arm. The man with the moustache steps aside as they march past the fridges and beyond in the direction of the palm tree. Eyes from the café are upon them. The smell of hairspray mixes with something fresh and chemical Sarah cannot identify; fabric conditioner, perhaps.

The woman taps Sarah's arm and points frantically up the street, saying something very loudly that sounds like 'A key'.

'*Ti ginetai?*' The kiosk lady spins round at the sound of another woman's voice behind them and as she does, she unlinks arms. A string of sounds spills from her matte-coloured lips and she pats Sarah's shoulder before walking away back towards her kiosk with a brief wave.

The approaching woman, petite, in a sleeveless floral dress, walks with loose limbs, a slight sway to her hips.

'Tell me,' she says in English. The sun is behind her; it is hard to see her face

'You speak English?' Sarah asks, squinting to make out her features.

'Better than your Greek, I am thinking.' The words are soft, her head tilted slightly to one side.

'Oh well, I am looking for Michelle's house, but the person I need to find is Juliet.'

'Ah, you have come to stay, *kala*. I am Stella.' She offers her hand and they shake. Stella is slow to loosen her grip, and Sarah is touched by her warmth and has an odd sense of belonging. Blinking a few times, she regains her sense of reality. A car horn sounds twice. Sarah looks back towards the kiosk where Laurence, in the car, is out of sight. Stella doesn't seem to have noticed.

'So you know where Juliet or the house is?' Sarah brings her attention back to Stella's face. Warm dark eyes, messy hair. She tries to age her.

'Of course. We can walk together.' Stella takes a lazy step.

'Oh, actually my husband is waiting in a car.'

'Ah, the man who sounded his horn.' She draws her foot back.

Sarah looks at the ground and finds it hard to meet Stella's eyes. When she looks up, she searches for judgement in the woman's face.

There is none.

'So you go here, turn left, take the low road, very sharp right, and follow the lane to the end,' Stella announces directly.

‘Sorry, thank you,’ Sarah says.

‘Why to be sorry? It is to be happy.’ Stella’s hair swings as she trots across to the cafe, skips up the two steps. The door opens and a tall man resting on a shepherd’s crook leans out to talk to her. She is not invited in. The smell of smoke drifts to Sarah along with carefree laughter. She can almost remember the feeling, the lightness in her chest of such a laugh.

The car horn sounds again.

‘Belt,’ Laurence says before Sarah has fully closed the door.

A fly buzzes furiously between the windscreen and the dashboard. Others lie dead and dying in the acute angle. She presses the window open. Taking the road atlas and pushing some of the pages down between the glass and the hot plastic, she sweeps along, hoping to dislodge the living and dead alike. With a brisk final movement, one carcass flies out through the side window, another drops towards her lap and she quickly moves her legs, the half-dead creature twitching on the carpet.

The remaining fly, still full of life, continues its assault on the window. Laurence buzzes her window closed.

They turn off the square and drive a short distance.

'Left here,' Sarah announces. He brakes suddenly.

'It can't be. It looks like a river bed.'

'The woman said left here.'

'She can't have. She didn't speak English.'

'Another woman.'

Laurence looks dubiously down the lane.

'What, up that sloping road?' He shifts into first.

'No, no, the lower road and a sharp right at the end of that wall, I think.'

'We're just going to get even more lost. I suggest we go back to Saros and start again.'

'Just try it.' Sarah can hear the sharpness in her voice and quickly follows with, 'It'll save going back all that way if it is right.'

Laurence looks again, his hand on the gear stick. The car remains stationary.

A dog runs towards them, shaggy, with a bouncy gait. Sarah opens the window.

'Here boy.' She clicks her fingers. It seems to catch her scent and lollops towards her, its tongue hanging out to one side. Sarah reaches, her fingers almost touching its nose when Laurence revs the engine and turns into the lane. The dog bounds sideways in alarm.

'You scared it.'

'It's a dog.' He buzzes the window closed again.

'You still scared it. Right here.'

'What, up there? It looks like a road to nowhere.'

'That's what the woman said.' Sarah folds her arms and looks out of the window. The air conditioning is giving her a headache. They have turned into a steeply sloping little square, a house on each side and an opening in the top corner that leads to a lane just wide enough for a single car.

Up this narrow, unpaved lane, there are low cottages on the left and a whitewashed wall on the right. The cottage on the corner seems abandoned, the garden overgrown, dried leaves on the porch. The road narrows even more and Laurence slows to a crawl. The next house has a garden full of brightly coloured flowers.

'Oh look at the colours,' Sarah says.

'This can't be right.'

The next cottage has a chain on the gate but the yard looks swept. The building after that has a long, sloping roof that nearly touches the ground by the lane, and Sarah recognises it from the pictures the owner sent. There is a cutaway where they can park. Laurence's silence suggests he recognises it, too. Sarah takes out the printed email again.

'Go past the parking space to the end of the lane, to Juliet's house, where you can turn your car around. Juliet will welcome you and show you around,' she reads aloud.

Sarah looks at the sloping roof as they pass and glimpses the sparkling blue strip beyond an orange tree behind the building.

Laurence drives beyond the building they recognise and crunches the car to a stop on what is, presumably, Juliet's gravel drive. A low L-shaped, whitewashed stone house faces them with a tiled roof, freshly painted blue shutters, pots of flowers, and on the patio stands a woman waving, barefoot, her hair loose, no makeup, and somehow decidedly English.

'Hello, Sarah and Laurence, I presume.' She laughs and holds out her hand, first towards Sarah. From the corner of her eye, Sarah can see Laurence has bristled and he retracts his hand in response to being greeted second. When the woman turns to him, he seems reluctant to shake.

'Hi, I'm Juliet,' she announces. 'Long journey from the airport. Can I get you some water, or juice, a frappe?' She indicates a rather sagging-looking sofa on her patio covered with a white throw. A cat is curled in one corner next to a brightly embroidered cushion.

'I think we'll just ...' Laurence begins. Sarah edges towards the cat.

'Oh but you must be tired after your journey. Please, sit. I am having a frappe myself. Sugar?' Sarah nods in answer to Juliet's question and sits tentatively on the edge of the sofa. The cushions give and the cat rolls into her, stretches, and offers its stomach to be stroked, purring in anticipation.

Laurence jiggles the car keys in his pocket. From inside the house come the sounds of cupboards opening and closing, taps running, and Juliet soon reappears with three froth-topped coffees in glasses, ice cubes knocking the sides.

'You must be so excited, you have two sons, right, and it's the younger one that's getting married did you say in your email?' Juliet passes a frappe to Sarah. 'It's metrio, just a bit of sugar, but I can put more if you want it.' She turns and holds out a glass to Laurence. 'Same with yours.'

'I don't take sugar.' He does not take his hands from his pockets.

'Oh.' Juliet looks at the glass and disappears back inside.

'Why?' Sarah hisses as soon as she is gone. 'Just say thank you and try it. There was no need to be rude.'

'There is no rude about it. She assumed, and she was wrong. I know how I take my coffee.' Laurence makes no effort to lower his voice.

'Oh for the love of God, how many cold coffees have you ever had?' Sarah hisses.

'I hope you are not starting with one of your moods.' He fiddles with his keys and then takes his hands out of his pockets to pull his trousers up by the designer belt Sarah gave him as a present when he returned from his last long trip.

'I just think ...' But she stops and smiles as Juliet returns with another frappe.

Chapter 2

'Here you go, Laurence.' Juliet hands him the chilled glass and indicates a chair. She sits with grace, her litheness belying the age that the smile lines around her eyes suggest. Laurence remains standing.

Sarah shifts her weight, clears her throat, and looks down into her own glass.

'I get the feeling that you would rather be in and settled.' Juliet addresses Laurence, narrowing her eyes against the sun as she looks up at him. 'Would you like me to show you round or ...' Laurence shakes his head. 'Okay, here's the key. I'm sure you can tell the difference between the kitchen and the bathroom. If you want to put the air con on, you will need to put the card attached to the key in the slot by the door. Anything else, just ask.' She looks over to Sarah, who makes no move to leave. 'Sarah do you want a biscuit, or a sandwich even; are you hungry?'

Laurence hesitates, looks at Juliet and then at Sarah, who busies herself stroking the cat, who stretches in response to her touch before it jumps down. Laurence puts his glass on the table and crunches back across the gravel. He looks almost unrecognisable in his new polo shirt and off-white trousers. Sarah tries to recall the last time she saw him not in a shirt or uniform but gives up and sinks lower into the sofa.

'So, Sarah, it's good to put a face to all those emails. How was your journey?' Juliet's words come unrushed, as if she has all the time in the world. She moves slowly, too, and blinks slowly, as if the heat has sucked all the haste from her life. How wonderful it must be, living out here in the sun in such a beautiful spot. The flowers in the pots dot colour here and there, the trees against the wall bear some sort of unripe fruit; it is idyllic, hard to believe it is really someone's life.

'It was okay. It's glorious here.' She tips her head back to face the sun that finds its way through the vine leaves that shade the patio. 'Why is travelling so tiring?' She gives a little laugh; the sun on the inside of her eyelids glows red.

'It is, though, isn't it? Did your friends find somewhere?'

'Liz and Neville? They booked the villa you suggested, just outside the village, I think. I can't remember its name.' She may never move again, spend the rest of her life motionless here on Juliet's sofa with the sun on her face, listening to the distant sounds of dogs barking and the cicadas rasping love calls across the village.

'Ah, they took Villa Katerina then?'

Sarah reluctantly opens her eyes so as not to appear impolite.

'Yes, that's the one. Is it far?' Somewhere in the village, a goat bleats and Sarah retracts every condemnatory thought she had about the place when they first arrived. No wonder the shutters on the village houses have peeling paint; why would you want to do anything but sit and enjoy the moment here?

Juliet points over the whitewashed boundary wall. 'You can't see it sitting down, but just over there is a hill—well, two actually, one topped with pines and another behind it with a rocky outcrop. The house is in the scoop between the two, five minutes' walk.' She takes another sip of her coffee and rattles the ice cubes around the glass; Sarah doesn't bother to stand to look for the house, content instead to stare at the endless blue sky above the wall.

'So are all the arrangements made for this week?' One of Juliet's gold hoop earrings peeps through her long, reddish-blonde hair, catching the light. Her hand lazily trails a course down the soft, furry spine of the cat who now sits on her knee, making no complaint as Juliet stretches out her legs, pointing her bare toes.

'Her family is doing everything as far as I know. All we need to do is turn up on the day and then we are away the day after; Laurence had work.' The blue sky forgotten, Sarah sucks in her bottom lip and bites gently. There's that feeling again. If only the emotion would come with words, then at least she would know what she is dealing with. Her free hand crosses her chest to rub the side of her neck and she rotates her head.

'The perfect wedding, then.' Juliet chuckles and closes her eyes as she leans her head back. Sarah does not reply but glances briefly toward the gate. There is no sign of Laurence.

'I could sit here all day, but I suppose I'd best go help Laurence to unpack a little.' Sarah gives up rubbing at her neck; it is not helping.

'You can sit here all day if you like. After all, you are here on holiday.' Juliet opens her eyes and smiles, and her warmth brings a tightness to Sarah's chest, a rushing in her ears, and she is suddenly struck by threatening tears. She clears her throat and swallows hard.

'No, I don't want to hold you back. I'm sure there are things you need to be doing.' The words are brisk, hoarse even as she battles the unnamed cause of her panic. She struggles out of the low sofa, fighting heavy limbs. Maybe this holiday will help her pull herself together, stop these silly attacks.

'Not really, but it's up to you.' Juliet remains lazing in her chair.

'I'd best give Laurence a hand.' Sarah stands, looking at the cat to avoid eye contact with Juliet, her legs trembling. The journey and her lack of sleep must be catching up with her; it is bound to make her emotional. Her fingers pull at the waistband of her skirt to relieve a knot of tightness deep in the pit of her guts. A wave of nausea sweeps over her.

'Let me know if you need anything,' Juliet murmurs, tipping her head back and closing her eyes.

Putting her empty glass next to Laurence's untouched coffee on the table, Sarah steadies herself to crunch across the gravel. Walking helps.

Laurence has taken his suitcase from the car, but Sarah's is still in the boot. She tries to lift it out but it is heavy and she scrapes the material on the boot lock, leaving a black mark. Then the luggage strap catches and she gives up. Laurence can do it later, but for now, she unzips the front pocket and takes out her flip-flops. The cat comes to help, biting at the ankle straps of her relinquished shoes, then jumping on the coloured leather flowers that adorn her new summer flip-flops. The flat leather feels cool to her soles and the cat's antics help to relax the tightness in her chest and her breathing slows. She'll be fine after a few days' holiday.

The animal accompanies her through Juliet's arched gateway, which is crowned with wild roses that Sarah had not noticed on the way in; so pretty, it lifts her heart. The fence of the holiday cottage next door hangs heavy with vine leaves and grapes no bigger than a fingernail, green and hard. A butterfly is darting around them, its white wings never settling. A bee searches the leaves and the cicadas' song fills the air. There seems to be more nature here somehow. The world seems more alive and, as suddenly as the tears and tension that sprang earlier, a feeling of lightness, possibilities, as if anything could happen, a sense of hope and freedom engulfs her. Energy returns to her limbs. Laurence is right, her moods are becoming unpredictable.

The cottage is a restored old, low stone barn with an equally old but carefully restored lean-to, the roof of which slopes almost to the ground. The area between the lean-to and the barn has been paved with weathered stone flags shaded with a pergola that is all but taken over by vines. Under the dapple of this greenery are two loungers, a table with four chairs and a hammock strung from the building to one of the pergola supports. A traditional, domed bread oven and an orange tree all but block the view to the garden behind, where a shimmering blue streak indicates the pool. It's perfect.

A shadow passes across the inside of one of the patio windows—Laurence. No doubt unpacking, laying out his ablutions, filling chests of drawers, lining up shoes. When all is perfect, he will, no doubt, check his emails. He strides past again. Her hand on the gate becomes motionless. The house looks inviting, the pool even more so, but she needs space, time, just a little, for herself.

Down the lane, a movement catches her eye. The dog, nose down, lurches this way and that, sucking up smells. She glances again at the blue, the hammock, the darkened windows before deciding there is time to walk to the end of the lane to see the dog and then hurry back to help Laurence.

Turning on her heel, she marches briskly, arms swinging, but her haste only lasts a few steps before her speed is ground to a snail's pace by the intensity of the sun, and in her lethargy, she has time to look around her, to observe the details of her world in all this bright, beautiful sunshine. The sun has dried and browned the central grass strip up the middle of the lane. The angular stones of the wall on her left have softened and smoothed under the years of re-applied paint, and now the wall appears to have dribbled down the lane and frozen in time. She exhales slowly through puffed-out cheeks. The long wall is the back low building, roofed with terracotta tiles, age-worn and discoloured, dipping in places. The variation in colour is limitless.

A lizard stands motionless on one of the hot tiles, one leg raised, blinking, rolling its eyes. It lifts each leg in turn, in sudden, sharp movements. Sarah comes to a standstill to watch as it twists its head on parched skin, tongue darting out to taste the air before scuttling away, tiny nails tapping on ceramic.

At the end of the lane, the dog scampers across the sloping square towards the village. Everywhere are whitewashed walls and houses, blue shutters and pots of geraniums. If the dog doesn't stop to be petted before the square, Sarah decides she will turn back. The sloping square speeds her steps and she turns, hoping to see the mutt in the road. It is there, sniffing at a stone. Sarah holds out her hand to approach; if she startles it now, it will run off into the village centre.

Her hand reaches out, stretches. The animal hesitates, sniffs, making up its mind. It edges towards her, nervous. Sarah stays motionless, arm extended. It stares, sniffs, lifts a paw to take the final step to make contact.

'No way! Sarah, is that you?'

The dog scampers away. Sarah looks up, startled, and is engulfed by arms that wrap around her. The years drop away, her head drops and tears fall.

Chapter 3

'Oh my God, it's not that awful to see me, is it?' Liz wipes away Sarah's tears, then wraps her arms even more tightly around her friend, rocking her as they stand.

It's dark against Liz's dress with her eyes closed; Liz's perfume is dusky and aromatic and reminds her of baked apples. Liz has worn the same fragrance for years, ever since she married Neville and could afford it. Sarah has smelt it so seldom since Neville's work moved them, and his mother, to London, it's like a dream remembered.

'It's brilliant to see you.' Sarah's laughter mixes with the lump in her throat and they pull apart.

'So stop crying then, you silly moo.' Liz pulls her in for another hug.

'Your accent's changed.' Sarah sniffs as they break again and brushes up the end of her nose with her finger and raises her chin. 'I heard it on the phone, but it's more noticeable in real life.'

'Yours hasn't,' Liz retorts, lifting her own chin and looking away.

Sarah's laughter chases away the last of her tears. They stand looking at each other, confirming that nothing has changed.

'You look great for forty-nine,' Liz announces.

'Says you!' Sarah always knew Liz was going to age better than her; she has always had a slight roundness to her face, giving her a youthful look. When they were teenagers, Sarah's angular looks had been to her advantage and she was often mistaken for being older than she was. Liz, of course, at the time, hated her own youthful appearance, but now she looks amazing. People would never believe they are the same age.

They stare into each other's eyes, the years disappearing, the children within surfacing.

'Where's Laurence?' Liz asks, her head sinking into her shoulders, her eyes narrowing as she looks left and right.

'He's back at the house. Shall we go up?' Sarah points the way she has come.

'Better idea.' Liz picks up a plastic bag by her feet, which clinks with the sound of glass. 'Let's avoid Laurence and go to mine. I have the cure for all ills in these bags.'

'Well, I don't know. I didn't tell him ...'

'Come on; he'll manage.' Liz raises her hand as a sun visor.

'Yes, but he won't know where I am, he left me ...'

'Oh, text him as soon as we get to mine. Come on. We have wine, we have sun.' She lifts her face to the sky. 'What more can a woman want?' Sarah feels the return of the knot in her stomach, that same old familiar feeling. Her smile grows watery. Steadying her breathing, she induces calm. The feeling does not grow.

'I sometimes wonder, you know, if, perhaps we possibly made a mistake all those years ago,' Sarah says.

Liz sniffs. A moped putters past them. The farmer has a dog across his knee, and he is texting as he drives. 'Different world here,' Liz says, watching his progress before slinging an arm around Sarah's shoulder, forcing her to walk. 'God, it's good to see you. Come on, it's this way. It takes us through a really steep olive grove and you can see the whole village from the top.'

The lane divides and they take the right fork, which is lined with single-storey houses, the dust on the road kicking up with each step. Red tiles all but slip from the roofs of whitewashed houses, each with a swept concrete yard in the front, most boasting tables with chairs, and all with potted flowers, bursts of colour, bougainvillaea and geraniums. There is a smell of cooking: tomatoes, herbs. Sarah gets the strange feeling of belonging again, but it is brief this time, like a whisper.

'Where is everyone?' Sarah asks, 'I've seen so few people.' She takes a hanky from her pocket and mops her brow and under her chin.

'It's that time of day, you know, like a siesta. Here it's called *mesimeri*.' Liz laughs. 'Messy Mary.' She laughs again. 'Talking of messy, how is Finn? Any cold feet yet?'

Sarah snorts a chuckle. Finn, her impossibly tidy son.

'Like he would tell me if he had. He would talk to Joss.'

'I always thought he would come out one day, surprise you with a good-looking boyfriend,' Liz muses.

'Who, Finn? With his track record?' Sarah looks at Liz, whose freckled skin is reddening in the sun.

The houses peter out and the lane here is edged with irregular fencing made from mismatched wire and various props, a metal bed frame, some planks of wood, make-do arrangements that look like they have remained for years, rust blending them together.

'It's like Ireland was when we were kids, isn't it?' Liz points to some oven racks that have been joined together with twists of wire into a gap between hedge and chicken wire. 'Do you remember that time we walked to the cliffs and tried to find the short way back past Dinni McMahon's house?'

'It was your idea to climb the walls.'

'But not that fence.'

'But what other way was there?'

'I did say to hold it down.'

'Holy Mary, my ma was furious. She'd just bought me that coat ...' Childhood accents return.

Sarah's eyes shine. Her walk develops a spring.

The fence ends and on the open ground to the left is a long building, barely the height of a man, set back a good way from the road. The roof undulates, tiles missing here and there. In front of the construction, a tightly fenced area devoid of all vegetation is bisected by a trough nearly as long as the building. The smell hits them before the sounds. The sheep are audibly different from the goats.

‘There’s another reminder of our childhood. I bet your London friends would not have been so keen to befriend you when you smelled the same yourself.’ She sniffs the air, enjoying the pungent aroma of the animals.

‘You just remember who has the wine before flinging your insults. Besides, we neither of us smelt so sweet back then.’

‘Do you miss Ireland even more now you are in London? The Isle of Man is just across the water but London! It’s like once more removed again.’ Her voice is soft, slow.

Liz doesn’t answer. Sarah knows not to ask twice, but after a minute, Liz says, ‘It was thirty years I lived on the Isle of Man, which was longer than we were alive in Ireland. But you know, it never really felt like home there. I don’t miss Ireland either, really. I just miss, well, you know, how life was before ...’ They both fall silent.

A large dog by the animal enclosure lazily raises its head to look at them, trying to muster some interest, move in the heat, as it wakes from its *mesimeri*. It eventually gets up and, once on its feet, barks excitedly at them. Gaining energy, it runs full-pelt towards them, only to be throttled to a standstill by the chain around its neck.

'Here, up here, it gets steep,' Liz says. They climb a dusty road and just as Sarah thinks the gradient will defeat her in the heat, Liz continues. 'Hey, not that way. We cross and then up between the olives the other side.' Sarah follows Liz with relief into the grove. The patchy shade is delicious and when Liz turns to climb the hill again, Sarah declares she's had enough and sits on a rock under a dense clump of branches. Liz is quick to join her.

'So tell me what's new, apart from the wedding.' Liz is fishing around in her material bag, which has some designer label stitched on the outside.

'Nothing much. You?'

'Ah,' Liz pauses, deep in thought. 'But no, I'll tell you that later. Da dah!' She pulls out a Swiss Army knife from her bag. 'No, tell me about you now. I know you were weeping with joy at the sight of me.' She chuckles. 'But I also know you only cry when your emotions are near the surface, so come on, what's going on? Is it the wedding?' She levers the corkscrew from the army knife and pulls one of the bottles from the plastic bag.

'I think I'm just tired from the travel. We didn't get much sleep.'

'And?' There is a satisfactory pop.

'And nothing,' Sarah replies. Liz offers her the bottle. 'So much for your posh London ways.' Sarah takes a swig; it is cool, which seems odd as it is red, but then, the day is so hot, after a second swig, she feels tempted to empty the bottle by herself.

'Okay, I'm not buying it. How is Laurence anyway, a proud Father-in-law-to-be? Does he approve?' Liz takes the wine back and drinks.

'Oh yes. Big family, wealthy, half of them live in Australia. There's a whole bunch from Germany and the Father and Mother, and Grandmother I think, are in America. A lot of her cousins are with Helena in London. I think Finn originally met her through a cousin.' Sarah takes a breath. With words more languid, she adds, 'In construction, most of them. And they have some company that designs artificial limbs or something ... Would you look at that!'

Liz follows her gaze across the land laid out before them, stretching to the blue-tinted hills at the feet of pale purple-hued mountains that encircle the plain. A spread of deep green orange groves and silver-blue olive trees, dotted red-roofed houses, and a lacework of dusty roads lays before them. The colour soaked out by the sun, a heat haze over everything. Just visible to the left, a slice of blue in the distance, hints that the sea is hidden round the end of the hill they are climbing.

'I think you're burning.' Liz puts her hand on Sarah's shoulder. 'Come on, it's two minutes from here and we can sit on the veranda with the same view and air con.' Liz heaves herself up and offers Sarah first a helping hand and then, once standing, the bottle, which Sarah declines. Liz takes another gulp, rams the cork home, and true to her word, in a couple of minutes, they are on the patio of a very large stone house.

'I'll get glasses.' Liz disappears into what looks to be a very grand interior, with white gauze floating curtains, plump sofas facing each other, glints of polished glass and silver in the shadows. Sarah takes out her phone. Her intention is to text Laurence but instead, she texts Finn.

'We have arrived. Shall we come to you, meet up, what?' She waits; there is no instant response.

'Liz, is that you?' a light voice calls. Hairs on the back of Sarah's neck prickle. Swallowing, she steps back onto the patio, vaguely wondering if there is somewhere she won't be seen. 'Who are you talking to? Oh Sarah, oh my dear, how are you, how lovely to see you. Is Laurence with you?'

'Hi Neville, it's good to see you, too. I'm sorry to hear about your mum.' She links her arms loosely across her chest. His hair is entirely white now.

Laurence, three years younger than his cousin, appears years and years his junior. Although Sarah is aware that this is in part at least thanks to the dye bottle, she nonetheless experiences a strange sensation of momentary relief that Laurence does not look Neville's age. Neville looks like an old man, but then, sixty-eight seems a lifetime away from her forty-nine

'Oh thank you, Sarah, you always were so kind. She passed quickly, thank the Lord, so we have to be thankful for small mercies, I suppose. And she was ninety four.' He walks towards her.

'It's a good age. Everything else alright? I hope you have been spoiling Liz?' Sarah shows him her cheek to receive a kiss but Neville embraces her. Her arms unfold. He smells the same as he always has, clean, always so clean.

'Of course.' He breaks away but his fingers trail down her arms and take her hands, which he holds as he looks at her. Sarah pulls away gently, looking him in the eye.

'Here you go, Sarah. Ah Nev, you want a glass?' Liz reappears.

'Oh, no thank you dear. A little early perhaps?' He looks at his watch just a little too long.

'It's a holiday,' Liz retorts and Sarah catches Liz's quick glance at Neville, her face like stone.

'So, good journey?' Sarah breezes.

'Yes, it was eventless, which I always think is good. Where did you say Laurence was?' Neville asks.

'Oh, well, Liz sort of kidnapped me. He's back at our place.'

'Oh, okay. I'll call him; he has his mobile with him, I take it?' It's a rhetorical question and Neville leaves them without waiting for an answer.

'Come out here,' Liz says. The large room is open on one side onto a spacious patio with grand stone arches that provide shade and support for the balconies on the upper floor.

Liz flops onto a sun lounger with a hood, which seems redundant in the shade of the stone arch. Sarah lowers herself into an egg-shaped chair, which is much more comfortable than it looks.

'So you're free!' Sarah says. 'It must be brilliant now that, well since ... How long has it been since Miriam died?'

'Six months.' Liz sighs deeply and takes a long drink of wine before reaching to top herself up. She swings the bottle towards Sarah, who has to lean to try and reach it. They both lean, they giggle, they lean some more until the exchange is made, Liz slapping her hand on the floor so as not to fall over.

Once settled again, Sarah asks, 'Six months? You guys must have painted the town red several times by now? Wining and dining, Neville taking you to shows and all the other things you guys have been planning for so long?'

'Yeah, right.' Liz looks across the village roofs spread out below them.

'What, has he too much work on?'

'You won't believe what's happened now.'

Sarah scans Liz's face, searching for clues as to the severity of what she is about to say. 'Tell me,' she demands.

'Ah, there you are, girls. I just rang Laurence. He had no idea you were here, you know, Sarah.' He pauses and looks at her, chastising with his eyes. She turns to look at the view. 'Anyway, I've told him where we are and he says he'll join us after a shower and a change, so I suggest when he arrives, we go into Saros town, have a coffee, look around, and find a good restaurant. Sarah, you can use our shower here. Shall I ring Laurence back and tell him to bring some fresh clothes?'

Sarah looks down at her cotton shirt and calf-length skirt. Not evening wear exactly, but they are on holiday. She's presentable.

'No, I'm fine. Thank you Neville.'

'Oh, okay then, if you are sure.' Neville sounds almost disappointed.

'Nev, can you see if you can get that back door to unstick, or will you call the owners to tell them to come and sort it out?' Liz asks. Sarah has seen it many times before, since the first, or maybe it was the second month of their marriage, when she gained stature with a change of her surname and a bank account bigger than she could ever have imagined. Even before Neville's mother was taken ill, Liz had become the master of getting Neville to leave the room on some pretence and Neville, always one to oblige, never made a fuss.

'So tell me what's happened,' Sarah says as soon as he is out of earshot.

'You know, I'm so tired with it, I can hardly tell you. Twenty-four years I nursed Miriam.' Poor Liz, it wasn't what she bargained for. Sarah nods her compassion. Liz swings her feet from the recliner and, kicking off her shoes, slaps her bare feet across the marble floor to the kitchen, returning with a second bottle of wine.

'What we really need is a gin and tonic, but the corner shop down there is very limited in the booze department.'

'I don't suppose they have much call for it.' Sarah remembers the café with the old men. The man with the moustache comes to mind and sends a shiver down her spine.

'Someone walk over your grave?' Liz asks.

'No, no, a creepy guy in the village. Well, not creepy. Intense, the way he stared at me.' She shivers, shaking her head. 'One minute I was by the kiosk alone and then next, I look up and he was there. Big guy, puffed out chest, really masculine.'

'Bit of a change from Laurence, then.' Liz laughs.

Sarah stifles her own. 'That's breaking the rule.'

'I didn't say anything negative about Laurence. I just said it was a change.'

'Slippery slope, Liz. We agreed, we do not make comments about each other's husband. It was part of the deal,' Sarah hisses looking into the shade of the house, just in case.

Liz uncorks the bottle, nodding in agreement. 'But I bet you won't stick to the rule when I tell you what Neville's suggesting.'

'Let me guess. You're not moving again, are you?' Sarah takes a refill even though she can see her hand is no longer steady. 'Oh, or are you moving back to the Isle of Man?' She almost shouts, her delight evident.

'No, nothing to do with moving. Why would you think that?'

'Because the last shock you gave me was your move to London. Oh, it is good to see you, Liz.' Her tongue struggles around the words, slurring the sounds together. Liz's return smile does not reach her eyes. 'Oh Liz, what is it?' Sarah can feel her own tears welling in response to her friend's sad face. Wine on top of being tired was a bad idea maybe.

The both turn sharply as a car scrunches to a stop in the driveway.

Chapter 4

Sarah has been watching the light gradually change to dusk over the last couple of hours, getting slowly drunk at the harbour café. She receives a text from Finn saying he has been asked to collect one of Helena's relatives from the airport. He will be back late and will see her tomorrow. Her heart sinks a little and the clawing darkness in the pit of her stomach tries to oozes up into her chest, but looking up from her phone, the sight before her is like a balm. The light on the sea is ever changing and a small fishing boat put-putts its way across the bay to moor up against the harbour wall. Once the ropes are tied, the fisherman takes a polystyrene-lidded crate from his vessel and strides off with purpose into town. The sea is mesmerizing; the blue has darkened to a turquoise green and imperceptibly loses its transparency to become silver as the sun dips behind the mountains across the bay, the sky paling to a yellow before burning orange and then red above the hills as the globe of fire is sucked from view. The hills take on a two-dimensional quality, flattened dark blue at the water's edge, the colour fading and blending them into the sky the further they are in the distance. Laurence and Neville are laughing loudly. Sarah hasn't been listening and has no idea what they are talking about. She rolls her eyes at Liz, who tuts and nods before Sarah returns her attention to the view. Laurence is saying something about his hire car. Neville is teasing him about being too old to be a boy racer and they compare their hire cars, Laurence bragging with his upgrade, Neville boasting that he forked out for the top of the range.

'I could just sit here all night,' Sarah sighs, addressing Liz.

'So could I if it wasn't for the fact that I am starving,' Liz replies.

'Yes, now you mention it.' Sarah rubs her stomach. It growls in response.

The lights on the square behind them come on one by one and new shadows are cast.

Finishing the last of his coffee, Neville suggests, 'Shall we go and find a restaurant?' His hand is in the air for the bill.

'Taverna,' Liz corrects, standing and offering her hand to Sarah to help her stand.

Sarah feels no inclination to move.

Adjusting the straps on her impractical dress, Liz's unharnessed bosom seems just a little too ample for the sheer material and the diamante straps cutting in, just slightly, to her now-sunburnt shoulders. But she still looks beautiful to Sarah's eyes. The darker, underneath red of her hair is dominating as she has pinned it all loosely on top. She does dishevelled very well. Sarah watches Liz's manicured hands as they pinch up the dress at the front so as to walk more freely. She seems a little uncomfortable, as if in seizing the occasion to wear finery, she has overdone it. Next to her, Sarah feels short in her flat shoes and under-dressed, but the ease it affords her mixes well with the residual heat of the day. Her arms swing loosely. Laurence takes her hand. She looks up at him but he is staring straight ahead, pretending this action is natural, usual even.

Back from the waterfront, the streets narrow, impassable for cars but not for the mopeds which weave between the pedestrians, driven by tanned and reckless youths, bumping on the cobbles.

In the dusk, the shops and tavernas are gaily lit. The orange glow localises around its source, each a pocket of promise, a cache ready to give up its treasures. Bougainvillaea is strung from balcony to balcony above their heads, purple, crimson, and white. Sarah's spine straightens, her chin lifts, her hips begin to roll as she walks. She slips her hand from Laurence's to feel free.

'What about this one?' Neville suggests. A waiter greets them, tells them the food is good. They have fish, he adds and reels off a list of Greek food.

There is nothing to distinguish it from the last; wooden tables covered with paper cloths, waiters rushing backwards and forwards with arms full of plates, the smell of onions and tomatoes mixing with herbs and wine.

'Why not?' Laurence says. His hand hovers in the small of Sarah's back, guiding.

Inside, the taverna appears almost empty of furniture; most of the tables that normally occupy the space have been arranged outside, on the pavement, but by the open window, one table remains, and sitting at it, leaning back with a glass in his hand, is the man with the moustache.

'Shall we look at the next one before we decide?' Sarah suggests, turning away. The man has not seen her yet.

'They're all the same. Let's sit here.' Liz puts her hand on the back of an empty chair by a table for two. She has had a brandy with her coffee and she is unsteady.

They look around, but there are no tables for four.

'Never mind, let's move on,' Sarah says, but as the words leave her mouth, a waiter approaches with an upturned table held aloft which he lowers next to the table for two, making it big enough for four. He makes an exaggerated welcoming gesture with a smile and a wink. As this is happening, the man with the moustache looks up and catches Sarah's eye. He raises his glass and nods, grinning at her. Sarah looks away. Trying to find something else to focus on, she misses her opportunity to choose a seat. Laurence draws a chair back for her and waits to push it in. She is diagonally opposite Liz and facing the open window. Head bowed, she lets Laurence push in her chair and busies herself with a napkin.

'Isn't this charming?' Neville flourishes his serviette.

The taverna is on a corner from around which drifts the sound of live music. A pair with bouzouki and clarinet stroll into view.

'Did you ever get to see Nigel Kennedy, Neville?' asks Laurence.

'Oh yes, a true musician. He opened with Bach and then improvised to the basic themes. It was wonderful. Such charisma.'

'Bought the CD,' Liz confirms. She has taken a tube from her evening bag and is sticking a false nail back on.

'Not here, dear,' Neville whispers.

'It's done.' Liz holds out her hand, fingers spread to look at them.

Sarah loves Liz's disregard for all the finery Neville is constantly trying to teach her. She has sat through opera and ballet, Shakespeare and recitals, unfailingly able to rate each performance 'boring' or 'fantastic,' buying all the merchandise or declaring it a waste of time. When they were both still dating, the four of them would fly from the Isle of Man to London for short weekends to see a play or catch an act. Then Neville had asked Liz to go to an opera with him one weekend, impressing that it would be just the two of them. Sarah and Liz presumed he wanted to finally have his way with her. But ever the gentleman, Neville had made no move in that direction. Instead, he had surprised her.

As soon as they touched down at Heathrow, Neville, Liz reported, had marched her straight to another plane bound for Rome. 'Best place to see it, and in the original Italian,' Liz had said, mimicking Neville's accent. She and Sarah rolled on their beds in their bedsit, laughing as she recounted the details, laughing till their sides ached when Liz said he had even booked separate rooms in the hotel.

Sarah closes her eyes at their behaviour, so long ago. So much has changed. The dark weight inside her shifts as if to let her know it is still there.

'I am going in to choose the fish.' Laurence stands, as does Neville.

'I guess it will be fresh this morning,' he states.

'Yes, from my brother boat.' The waiter's English has just the hint of an accent.

'I wonder how much time he spends on his brother's boat,' Liz murmurs.

'Sorry, dear?' Neville pauses. Liz is eyeing the waiter.

'Nothing.' She dismisses Neville. 'Can we have some wine?' She looks up at the waiter, almost fluttering her eyelashes.

'Liz!' Sarah chastises with a smirk.

'Red, rosé, or white, madam?' The waiter smiles.

'Do you have a wine list?' Neville asks briskly. This seems to confuse the waiter.

'We have the wine from Nemea if you want a bottle.' Neville and the waiter continue their conversation, walking into the taverna.

Sarah glances to the window but the man and his moustache are not visible; leaning back, he is all but obscured, just his knees and a hand playing with a string of beads are visible. She draws her attention back to her own table.

'So Liz, come on tell me or it will never be told. What is Neville up to now?'

Liz's slumps in her chair and her smile slips from her face. 'Oh Sarah, he is only suggesting Agnes moves in with us.'

'What!' Sarah knows it came out too loud; everyone is looking at her except the waiter. 'You mean as in Agnes his first wife?' she repeats, hissing.

The bottle is uncorked next to them and two glasses are poured with no prerequisite tasting. The men are still inside, examining the fish. Sarah can see them in the narrow passage that leads to the kitchen at the back.

'It's sad, I mean really sad. She has been diagnosed with cancer. Their children are beside themselves, and all of them on the phone to Neville all the time.'

'Well, I can understand that but ...'

'Well, apparently she has no one to look after her. She can get Macmillian care, but to be left to die like that on your own.' She sighs and drinks the wine as if it is water.

'What about a hospice? What exactly is Neville saying, that she move in with you and you start caring for her where you left off caring for his mother!'

'That's about it.' Liz pours more wine.

'You're kidding me?'

'No.' Liz gulps down another glass and hitches up the neckline of her dress.

Sarah sits back and looks through the open door to the back of Neville, who is being shown a metal fridge drawer, presumably full of fish.

'Liz, you can't. I thought Neveille had all these plans and ideas of what you guys were going to do once his mum was gone. You told me about them—the trips, the weekends, the concerts you have been planning for years. What will happen to you two learning to sail and going around the Indonesian Islands?'

Lis shrugs and fiddles with her earrings; diamond drops, no doubt bequeathed to her by Miriam or passed on by Neville.

'But for her to move in.' Sarah shakes her head, her mouth open.

'What can I do?' Liz puts down her glass, sits up straight, and fixes a smile. 'Did you find a fish?'

The men sit.

Sarah's bottom lip quivers as she stares at her friend, who is flirting again with the waiter. Sometimes, life just seems too unfair, too much like hard work to keep going. Her gaze wanders. Between her and the window are several tables, and at one, sitting sideways to Sarah, is Stella, the helpful woman from the village, in a different sleeveless floral dress. Opposite her is a man who is listening to her every word, the man she had watched Stella talking to in the café doorway. Stella uses her hands to gesticulate as she talks, but when they come to rest on the table, the man slides his hand over hers and she smiles. Their faces are close as if they share a secret until, with a rich peal of laughter, she throws her head back and pats his hand to gently admonish him. He grins.

Plates that are placed in front of them are no interruption. Sarah watches as Stella cuts up everything on her plate, but it is only when she exchanges it with the man's that she notices he only has one arm. Sarah's bottom lip quivers again. Why does Finn have to get married? She hears the words in her head but has no idea why she has thought them, or what it has to do with watching Stella and her man. Helena is perfect for him and they are so in love.

'You alright?' Laurence's hand is on her shoulder.

'Yes, what? Right, oh. I will have ...' She looks down at the menu, 'your recommendation.' She looks up at the waiter and hands back the menu. He smiles and says her dish will be the best.

Liz is picking out the middle of her piece of bread and rolling it into balls.

They made a mistake all those years ago—well, Liz definitely did. Sarah's been lucky, or rather luckyish. Shaking her head, she takes a sip of her wine. They will need to break the deal of not talking about their husbands if Neville persists that Agnes moves in, How can she avoid expressing her opinions on Neville then? To have his ex-wife move back in, the mother of his children, to choose that over the plans he and Liz had made, plans that were promises to Liz after years of care for his mum, is just plain wrong. Neville has been wrong in so many ways.

'Oh, that looks nice,' Laurence greets his starter.

The food is good.

'How do you ask for more wine?' Sarah asks everyone at the table.

'*Krassi*,' the waiter says as he passes with a tray of food. On his return, Sarah lifts her empty glass and says, '*Krassi*.'

'You want bottle or would you like local wine?' The waiter addresses her.

'Oh let's try local.' Liz nods. Neville frowns. The wine comes in a jug. It is light and very palatable. One jug follows another and the husbands revert to Manx accents, Liz's London twang being usurped by her mother's Irish. Sarah's mind floats on alcohol, She has a stomach that is full and the air is warm. Her worries fade and it begins to feel like a perfect evening.

No one wants dessert; besides, there is no dessert on the menu. The waiter explains that it is traditional to go on to a café for baklava and coffee.

'The food was excellent. Please give my compliments to the chef and thank you for your recommendations. I will only drink local wine from now on!' Sarah slurs as she looks in the waiter's eyes. She can see why Liz is flirting with him, such long lashes. A few minutes later, a plate of sliced watermelon appears, as do apple pieces dripping in honey, all with the waiter's compliments.

Neville is dripping honey over his lips when a child, not much higher than the table, with matted hair and huge brown eyes and dirty clothes pushes a bunch of individually wrapped red carnations under his nose.

'How much?' His words slur. The child continues to hold out her hand, unblinking. 'How much?' he repeats, but there is no answer. Liz's eyes grow wide.

'None of them speak English,' Laurence says, 'Not here and not in the village.' He stifles a hiccup. The child is waved away and Sarah watches the trace of a smile on Liz's lips fade. She is not sure if it was there for the possibility of the gift of a flower or the sight of the young child.

After the fruit is eaten and belts undone a notch, the bill is called for. It arrives with a carnation, which is presented to Sarah. She raises her eyebrows and the waiter points. Sarah follows his finger past a big American woman, beyond her the villager in the sleeveless dress and behind her is the open window into the taverna. The man is still there. She can see his knees and a hand slowly rotating a string of worry beads.

'Who?' Laurence asks, his chin jutting forward. Neville is counting out change for the tip. Liz is looking over one shoulder and then jiggling around to look over the other, trying to work out who is the admirer.

Sarah can feel the heat rising up her neck. She fans the menu to create a breeze, forcing her actions to appear relaxed as she hides her colour.

'Who?' Laurence repeats, still searching the faces of the customers.

Liz is mouthing 'Who?' with a big grin on her face.

'That is Stella,' Sarah finally whispers to Laurence loud enough for Liz to overhear, and points. 'The lady who gave me directions to the house today. She wished me welcome. She was very friendly. I guess it is from her.' But Stella is engrossed in her own conversation with the one-armed man and does not look their way. Neville chucks a few coins on the table and stands and pulls Liz's chair out for her. She is unsteady on her feet, and he offers his arm.

Laurence does the same for Sarah and as they stroll away to find another café to savour a dessert and drink brandies and ouzos until the small hours of the morning, Sarah leans across to Liz and hands her the carnation.

When Sarah wakes the next morning, the other side of the bed is empty and everything around her is unfamiliar. She uses the toilet in an unknown bathroom and steps out of the bedroom to an unknown hall with a dark wooden staircase. Holding tightly to the rail, she descends to find she is at Liz and Neville's.

'Morning,' Neville breezes. 'Laurence has gone already; he said he had some emails that need his attention. There is pancakes and toast.' He waves a spatula over a laid-out table.

'Liz?' Sarah asks.

'Mother of all hangovers. I don't suppose we'll see sight of her till this afternoon.' He chuckles and shrugs as if it is a regular occurrence and Sarah wonders if it is—or has become so since the death of his mother, Liz now free of responsibilities.

'Coffee?' Neville begins to pour a cup.

'No, no. I'll just get off. Thank you.' Nothing will persuade her to have a *petite dejeuner* for two with Neville. She needs a bath and a change of clothes and he needs to focus on Liz.

'Okay.' He wipes his hands and pulls off his apron, moving towards her. 'I'll drop you.'

'No! No, thank you. It's a beautiful day and a walk might lift my headache.' She backs to the patio window before turning and walking away calling, 'Tell Liz I'll call.'

Once through the garden gate, she is in an olive grove where she stops, hangs her head backwards, lets her jaw hang open, and huffs a sigh.

She could, maybe, draw the walk back out a little. A stolen hour just for herself.

Chapter 5

She deserves a worse headache. Already, the throbbing is subsiding, but the sun is piercing and she wishes she had brought her sunglasses.

The twisted olive trees look timeless, the leaves fluttering silver-blue, and Sarah wonders how many other people have strolled between them, what sort of lives they have led, what sort of love they have given and received. In amongst the trees, goats and sheep nibble at the vegetation which is still green in the shade. Their occasional throaty bleating echoes down to the village.

Joss is due to arrive today with Pruella de Ville. She giggles with the thought. She has never said it out loud.

She misses Joss. Of course she misses Joss, but the positive side of him moving to the States is she does not see Prudence very much at all. Joss comes back to visit occasionally, but she cannot even recall the last time she saw Pru. She can remember the first. Joss brought her over from London to the Isle of Man for a weekend. Sarah thought that tea at Tynwald Mills would be a nice day out for Pru, seeing as Laurence had taken Joss off to the golf course.

'What do you think of these?' Sarah asked, holding up some earrings and looking at herself in the mirror.

'Oh, I can remember a time I would have worn something like that, but then we all go through strange styles in our teens.' Pru walked away to look at something else.

Sarah put the earrings back, her hand over her stomach; the undefined dark weight inside her was her companion even back then. To divert her thoughts, she went to look for some gloves for Laurence; goodness knows he needed some. The ones she coveted were sheepskin with the seams on the outside, warm and practical.

'I am thinking of getting these for Laurence.'

'Oh right, yes. I forgot you're from Ireland, aren't you,' Pru replied with a lopsided smile before turning to look at some impossibly high heeled shoes.

Pru's comments tipped back the years and Sarah remained motionless, feeling like a young country girl from Ireland, as if she had made no progress in life at all.

But time has passed since then. Pru's been promoted and they have moved to New York. Maybe she's changed. Pru is Joss's love, and she will treat her kindly and civilly even if such basic manners are not returned.

'Why the sad face?' The thick accent is both Greek and Australian at the same time. Sarah looks around. Sitting on a rock, chewing on a grass stem, is a familiar stranger. Scanning his face, her brow creases. She knows she knows him but then again, she does not.

'Did I look sad?' Sarah buys herself a little time, hoping it will come to her. Some sheep eat their way towards them, the grinding of their teeth audible in the silence. She hopes she doesn't look as bad as she feels. He stands, the width of his chest and the gold chain rushing her memory and before she can stop herself she says, 'You've shaved your moustache off!'

'Is it better, or worse?' he asks, the fingers of one hand exploring the exposed skin. As no answer is forthcoming, he draws his beads from his pocket and worries at them, still holding her in his gaze. 'You walking down to the village?'

There is no other way to go so she nods with a final glance back to the house.

'May I have the pleasure of walking with you?'

He seems pleasant enough, gentle, easy-going, but you can never be sure. Sarah tries to judge his age. He is no older than her but more solid somehow and, although he has a weather-beaten ruggedness about him, she feels confident that, thanks to her gym sessions, she would be the faster runner if need be. As they begin to walk, she nevertheless keeps her distance, an arm's reach away, better safe than sorry.

They silently fall in step, but only for half a minute before he veers off the footworn path and crouches to pull back a spiky bush, revealing buds of colour beneath.

'Wild bee orchids,' he says, brushing them with his fingertips. The intense purple flower, no bigger than his little fingernail, sings against the surrounding green leaves, and under the petals is a bee-shaped lip patterned in yellow and a very dark red.

'I can see where they get their name from.' Sarah bends to look more closely, aware of the closing distance between them.

'The plant produces a scent similar to that of the female bee, which attracts the male bee to copulate with it, ensuring pollination.' He lets the gorse fall and they both straighten.

Sarah is lost for words; any reply could be awkward. She steps back to the track, saying nothing.

'Greece is a good place for flowers.' He begins to stroll on. 'The carnation is another flower that grows very well here.'

'Look ...' Sarah pauses to consider how she is going to phrase what she needs to say. 'You obviously want me to say something about the flower last night. I don't think "thank you" is appropriate, nor honest, as I don't thank you. With my husband sitting right next to me, it could have been a lot more awkward than it was. And while we are on the subject, I would like you to explain how you knew I would be here today. It makes me wonder if I am safe.' She widens the gap between them.

'Sorry?' He chortles and stops walking, his hand raising to his jaw, his fingers rubbing, feeling the stubble.

'Last night, the flower?'

'What flower?'

She looks him in the face, searching for sincerity, the heat rising on her neck, reaching her cheeks. Maybe it really was Stella. But even if he didn't give her the flower, it doesn't explain him lying in wait for her today.

'The flower at the taverna?' she says.

'Oh, did you get one from the chef?'

'What?' Sarah replays the events in her head, the waiter's pointing finger, past the large woman, past Stella, to the window and his knees. But the picture continues through the empty taverna to the kitchen door. 'The chef?' It is more of an exhalation than words.

'My guess is you sent him your compliments?' He is giggling to himself now. 'Five a night he gives out, keeps people coming back and the restaurant full.' His smiling eyes seem to mock her, or is she being uncharitable? He begins to stroll on, giving Sarah some space. All she can hear are the goats munching and a rushing in her ears. Her cheeks feel on fire. She watches the sheep gnawing the scant grass back to the soil, the goats, their front feet tapping against the bark as they stretch up the trunks to graze on the tops of bushes and foliage beyond the sheeps' reach.

How much easier life must be as a goat: mindless, unaccountable and with no ability to form words and dig themselves into bottomless ditches. Bliss, to roam these hills all day doing nothing but eating. Her stomach rumbles, reminding her that she has not had breakfast.

He is further along the path, waiting for her. She would rather go back and deal with Neville than face this man now, but to turn and walk away would be to add insult on top of injury. She cannot do it.

'Look.' He is pointing through a break in the tree branches. She doesn't quicken her pace. He lowers his hand and waits until she has caught up. 'Look,' he repeats, pointing again. Beyond the trees, the fields stretch out across the plain and one burns bright orange, on fire with light.

'Oh my goodness, is it a fire? Should we call the firemen?' Her hand goes to her throat, her blunders forgotten in view of the potential disaster.

'No, it's a photovoltaic field.' He puts both hands in his dark serge farmer's trousers, his beads clicking in his pocket.

'It's what?'

'Photovoltaic, solar panels, electricity,' he summarises. 'We are just at the right angle to see the sun reflecting off the panels. Impressive, isn't it? Only at this time of day is it so.' He sighs contentedly.

Apart from feeling a little silly that she thought the field was on fire, Sarah is just glad the focus has moved on from her earlier mistake. What an arrogant presumption it must have seemed, but, and the feeling creeps upon her slowly, what is even more disconcerting is the trace of disappointment that the flower last night was not from him.

'So come on.' He begins walking again. 'Tell me, why so sad?'

The change in topics is too quick for her. She cannot recall what she was thinking when he first saw her. The ever-present feeling of weight sometimes in her chest and sometimes in her stomach darkens and nestles deep inside her, hiding from inquiry.

'Am I?' is all she manages. She cannot deny that something dark sits in the pit of her stomach, making itself known every now and again, but she is not sure she would call it sadness. To be honest, it has been there so long, it just feels like part of her.

'From the first time I saw you.'

'Really?'

'All I could think was why is a pretty lady so sad?'

He has a good profile, with a really straight nose, and he just called her pretty. He called her pretty and, somehow, he knew she was going to be here today.

'You are on holiday, yes? So leave your worries. No?'

'I'm here for my younger son's wedding.' There it is, that black weight in her stomach again.

'There.' He points a finger to her face. 'There is that sad look again.'

Looking away, she rubs the tightness at her stomach.

'You don't want him to marry?'

'No, no, not at all. Helena's lovely, perfect for him. They're in love.'

'But ...'

'No buts.'

'That's good then.' He grins, a wide mouth and so many teeth.

The track winds around olive trees. Here and there, they duck under low branches and Sarah's hand drops from her stomach. He stops again, this time to show her wild asparagus. 'They are young shoots at this time of year. It is the best time to collect.' But he leaves them unpicked and they continue to walk. The gap between them closes as they come to a flat part of the track.

'You have an Australian accent,' Sarah says. It's almost a question.

'Yes, many years in Australia. Perth, Melbourne.'

'Ah.' She is not sure what else to say but as she thinks of this man in Australia and then Joss in America and, soon, Finn starting out with his own family, Liz in London, her life spins away from her, a momentary rushing that she recognises as panic which is quickly replaced with nothing. A strange blank nothing.

'There's that look again. What are you thinking?' His words are spoken like a song, rising and falling, slow, soft, and warm. She is glad the tear that escapes runs down the cheek furthest from him. 'You know we have no access to the past, nor to the future. There is only now. And now you are under the olive tree.' He reaches up and picks a leaf and hands it to her. 'One side blue-green, the other silver. The wind blows and we see both sides. But you, the wind cannot blow you, you get to choose.' He stops walking. They have reached a wide track that leads out of the olive grove and down to the tarmac road. The leaf flips blue-green to silver as she rolls the stem between her finger and thumb.

'So, see you,' he states, planting his feet and pulling his trousers up from where they have settled around his hips.

'Oh.' Sarah looks up and then down the track and then back at the olive grove. 'You are not going to the village?'

'I think my sheep may get lonely without me,' he grins, teasing.

'Oh.' No words will come to mind, just a sea of feelings. He twists his hand in a half wave and turns around, his measured pace taking him back into the trees, back to his herd.

'Arrogant, self-centred, just plain stupid,' she hisses, criticising herself under her breath, marching down to the road. 'How could he have known you would be walking there? Why would he follow you? Arrogant, craziness.'

The tarmac has no give; her flip-flops flap against her heels as she steps. The sun is gaining strength and the village seems very active. The deserted porches of the houses she passed yesterday with Liz are now populated with women in house coats as bright and gay as the flowers in the pots. Some sweep, some mop, some tend the flowers. A man sits at one patio table drinking coffee and smoking cigarettes; in another yard, a small dog has its lead tied to the table leg. Mopeds hum and zip past her. It all feels very busy.

Up the side road that leads to Juliet's and the cottage is a large battered van with its back doors flung open. Two women are talking and peering into the depths of the vehicle. Boiler suits and floral dresses on hangers are hooked over its doors. Buckets with mops in front of them, baskets of tea-towels and something else Sarah does not recognise, and in the centre of this cornucopia, leaning into the van, rummaging for something, is a man whistling a happy tune. The scene feels at odds with how she feels so she looks away, to the bins; big industrial metal bins on wheels, the green plastic lids flipped back and nervous cats tearing through the contents.

Despite the growing heat, Sarah quickens her pace up the lane, eager to be somewhere alone, safe. She has no idea what is happening to her, but it does not need an audience. She barely looks at the holiday home as she pushes open the gate. She does not take in the stone-walled sitting room where Laurence sits, peering at his laptop.

'Morning. A little worse for wear are we?'

'Where's the bathroom?'

He points to a door in the corner.

'You okay?' he asks, looking back at the computer screen.

'Fine. Need a bath.' The door closes solidly behind her. She locks it and exhales.

Chapter 6

The water threatens to slosh over the edge as she lowers herself into the metal bath. A small square window has been placed so she can look out over the garden whilst soaking, and it offers a view of a huge cascading fig tree with a slice of sparkling blue pool in front. She knows she should be thrilled to be here. She slips down, and the water covers her face. All is quiet except a hollow ring as her heel hits against the bottom. Opening her eyes under water, the blue-painted boards that are the ceiling smear and undulate. Blue. Everything is blue. Letting out a bubble, she wonders how long she can hold her breath. She begins to feel a tightness in her chest, the building of pressure, her body fighting, her reflexes kicking in. The blue is all-absorbing. What if she were never to breathe again? What if she were to breathe in the water? She lets another bubble escape. They say it is pleasant after the first breath—dreamy and calm. Her leg jerks as her lungs demand air. Kicking down with her heels, she pushes off, explodes out of the water gasping, the brilliance of the sunlight startling, and the water now slopping over the edge and onto the tiled floor. She is hit with how beautiful everything is in the sunlight, the white of the walls, the blue of the window frame, the green of the fig tree. But it is an academic beauty that leaves her unmoved.

'What's wrong with me?' The words float over the water. She is answered by a multitude of feelings, each jostling for attention.

The dominant one does not surprise her. With Finn married, her role as mother is all but gone. Finn and Helena will probably stay living in London, although Finn has seen possibilities of taking his work to America, to be near Joss and even further from her. His clothes will then always be washed and ironed by Helena, or, more likely, by a housekeeper. His meals will always be cooked by Helena. But then, hasn't that been happening since he moved to London anyway? It is not that her role is officially being relinquished to another, it's not jealousy, it's ... Sarah struggles to define it. It is a feeling of uselessness mixed in with a pointlessness mixed in turn with an *it-doesn't-matter-ness*.

'Not your average doesn't-matter-ness,' Sarah whispers to herself. It is more than that. It is a nugatory feeling, a space, a void, and there is nothing she can do to alter that.

'You want coffee?' Laurence shouts through the door.

'When I come out.' The squeakiness of her voice catches her by surprise and she coughs.

He doesn't help. She is not sure she would go so far as to say he is a control freak—she does have a theoretical say in their lives—but the reality is that the things that come about in their lives are the things Laurence wants or suggests. Her ideas remain just that, ideas. But he always leaves room to argue it is not so. Like the move when the boys were so small. She suggested that they needed a larger house when the boys got bigger. Somewhere with a garden where they could run around, let off steam. Laurence's salary was good, they could afford it, and it could be a family home, a place that was theirs, and not just his bachelor pad that she had moved into. It didn't happen; the boys continued to bounce off the walls, she continued to be surrounded by relics of his single days until, one day, she was called back home to County Clare, to an uncle's funeral, and Laurence stayed home with the boys. After her week away, Laurence met her at the airport full of *his* idea that they needed a bigger home, with space for the boys, and within the following week, they had seen four houses and Laurence had put an offer in for one of them—but not the one she liked best. The house move was his ever recurring example, both in private and public, as to the equality he gave her.

'Everything.' Sarah sinks beneath the water again. It's like that with everything, right down to when he takes her clothes shopping. Now she has a wardrobe full of so many dresses that she only half-likes but Laurence loves.

'I don't matter. Nothing I do matters.' The garbled words create pockets of air that jettison to the surface.

She pushes herself up and reaches for the shampoo. Laurence, true to form, has laid everything out in order: shampoo, conditioner, shaving foam, deodorant, contact lens solution, toothpaste.

'Coffee's going cold,' Laurence calls.

'Alright.'

She slips under the water again to wash off the soap before grabbing at the conditioner bottle. It's light; it doesn't occur to Laurence that packing a nearly empty bottle is a bit pointless. She makes a mental note to buy more. Shaking the shaving foam and the contact solution bottle, she finds that at least they are full. She needs to go to a supermarket anyway, get some staples in, something for breakfast; coffee, milk, sugar.

'I matter for that,' she sneers. 'Keeping the cupboards stocked.' Which is almost true, although, at home, she uses a delivery service that brings the same stuff every week. It is only the special things that she would buy herself from specialist shops. It fills her days.

But here, there will be no delivery service. She will have to go shopping. There is bound to be a supermarket in Saros; she could pop in when they go in to to meet Joss and Pru. But then, Finn had said they should meet up today.

She pulls herself from the water, stepping out of the bath and, drying her hands first, reaches for her phone.

'Have you arrived?' she texts Josh.

The heat is drying her more quickly than the towel, which she wraps around her to go and find some fresh clothes. The reply comes before she leaves the bathroom.

'Meeting Finn and Helena for lunch, join us?' it says.

'Where?' She drips water from her hair onto the phone as she replies.

'One minute,' is the answer.

Laurence is still on his laptop. She looks around the room for another door that will lead to a bedroom, but there is only the door that she came in by which went through the kitchen.

'Where's the bedroom?'

'Another door on the patio.'

'Oh, not very useful if you need the toilet in the night.'

'It has an en suite.' He doesn't look up.

It feels odd to walk outside in a towel and nothing else, but the sun kisses her skin through the vine leaves and she feels a distant promise that everything could be alright here in the sun.

The bedroom is also stone walled, with a really big bed and is exquisitely furnished in creams and pale blue.

Her phone peeps. The message this time is from Finn.

'Hey! Meet us at café "Kendrikon", main square, Saros, midday.'

She taps her message back. 'Ok, xxx, mum'

She likes sending *x*'s and hopes he feels loved by them.

'Is that coffee still warm?'

'It's in the kitchen.'

'Joss and Finn say to meet them for lunch. Midday.'

'You've spoken to them then?' He looks up, surprised.

'Text.'

'Oh.' He is back in his computer.

Sarah strolls out onto the patio with a cup of barely warm coffee. Everywhere she looks, the place has been beautifully finished, the details considered. She steps onto the neatly mowed lawn and wonders who waters it to keep it so green in this heat. Her simple shift dress is a lot cooler than was her skirt and top. She ducks under the orange tree and the garden opens up: on one side, a row of flowering bushes marks the perimeter and on the other, the lawn merges into what must be Juliet's garden next door, which has a more rural feel and is dotted with trees; long rushes grow from a natural pond by a solitary, twisted old olive tree. But Sarah is mesmerised by the blue of the pool in front of the fig tree, the water so clear, the sun reflecting from all the facets. The temptation to jump in fully clothed is almost irresistible.

She chuckles, a dry humourless sound as she imagines what Laurence would do or say if she were to do such a thing. Her coffee all gone, she still continues to move from bush to plant, taking it all in, looking at the details of nature, as she falls into a place where she thinks no thoughts.

'Darling, time's flying. We'd best be off, I think,' Laurence calls from the patio.

'It must be really early yet,' she calls back but she knows it is not a discussion and the last thing she needs before seeing Pruella de Ville is a moody Laurence. All these people who annoy her. Maybe, she thinks, and it is not a comfortable thought, but maybe it is not them, maybe it is her. Her stomach grumbles. She still hasn't eaten. She will have to wait for lunch now.

Lunch with Joss and Finn, both of them, at the same time, for the first time in she cannot remember how long. Joss and Finn, her lovely boys. Well, not really boys anymore. They are men now, and Joss perhaps a little too like his father ... But Finn is still her baby. If only she could have kept a younger version of them at the same time she let them grow up.

'Sarah!' His tone is sharper this time.

'Okay, okay. I'm coming.' She bends and dips her hand in the water. It's not that cold; by late afternoon, it might even be positively warm.

The car engine starts up.

'Oh for pity's sake.' She puts the coffee cup down on the table on the patio. The main door is shut and she cannot be bothered to go through the process of getting the key from Laurence to go inside for her bag. Besides, Laurence has the money, so really, all she is missing is her lipstick.

They park where they did the night before and head straight up a paved pedestrian street. Laurence has Googled the *Kendrikon* and leads assertively. Sarah tries to loiter, look in the shops, one selling seashells and inflated puffer fish, jewellery and postcards. Another sells cheesecloth shirts and loose trousers. On the corner, more shops sell art pieces in ceramic, felted items, and hologram bookmarks.

Sarah lingers, but not too long, so as not to lose Laurence. They have reached the town's main square. It is bigger than she expected and has a vaguely Venetian feel. The perimeter is lined with cafés and tavernas, their seats and tables spilling out onto the smooth marble. In the centre, a colourful jumble of people stroll around boys who are engaged in a frantic game of football. In the corner is a wide-spreading plane tree, with some of its branches supported by wooden struts, and in its shade are plump, white-cushioned wickerwork chairs arranged around marble-topped tables.

'I guess this is it,' Laurence says. Sarah begins searching for her boys' familiar faces, for that first glimpse that will pull her heart into her mouth and make her lose all sense of self.

'There!' She points and moves at the same time.

'Joss! Finn.' Finn stands and flings his arms around her. He looks so well and so happy. 'Wow, you look amazing, Finn. Joss!' She turns to her eldest. His arms are slower but the hug is more powerful. Finn is shaking hands with Laurence, and Joss breaks his hug to do the same.

'Hello Pru. Hi Helena. How are you feeling? Are you nervous?' Sarah asks.

'Hello Mrs Quauyle.' Pru holds out her hand to be shaken. It seems overly formal and Sarah wonders if she should suggest Pru call her Sarah. Pru is so groomed, finished.

'Hi Sarah.' Helena interrupts and pulls her into a hug and kisses her on both cheeks. She smells of suntan cream and her embrace is warm and heartfelt. Sarah is aware of her own stiffness and awkwardness in comparison.

They pull up chairs and sit, Joss enquiring about some shares suggested to Laurence, Finn asking Helena if she is comfortable.

'How was the trip?' Sarah asks Pru, stealing glances at Joss, scrutinising for any changes, marks of struggle or bliss.

'Long.' Pru takes out a packet of cigarettes and lights one, blowing smoke above everyone's head.

'*Ti thelete paidia*?' A white-shirted waiter stands loose limbed at Sarah's side. She looks from Pru to Joss to Finn to Helena to find someone who understands.

'Okay, what do we want, guys?' Helena asks. They all look blank and the waiter steps away and returns with drinks and snacks menus.

Sarah's hunger is forgotten, replaced with such joy at seeing her sons. Finn looks so happy, energised, Helena by his side. They order, and Sarah drinks in the conversations that buzz around her. Joss teasing Finn with his dry, straight-faced humour about how easy it is to establish yourself in Britain compared to the US. Laurence is asking Pru how her work is. She has recently been promoted again in her company; she is explaining what she does now.

Helena turns to her. 'I am so glad you are here. When are you coming up to the house? It's chaos. My *yiayia* wants to do all the cooking herself and is driving us all crazy with tasting spoons of this and spoons of that. Mama says she is too old, she has never catered for five hundred and she shouldn't start now. Some second cousins from Australia came last night, and my uncles come today from America.' Her words almost slur, she speaks so fast and with such energy.

Sarah feels out of breath just listening to her.

'The flower people are saying there is a problem with the flowers and we may have to use Ruscus leaves instead of Smokebush, but to be honest, I really don't think it is a deal breaker.' Helena pauses to take a sip of her frappe. Sarah has also ordered a cold coffee, this time trying it *glyko*—sweet.

'Have you got your dress yet?' Sarah squeezes the question in just as Helena is about to say more. She can see why Finn is attracted to her, with so much energy but, really, she is almost too much.

'Oh, it is to die for.' Helena's hand raises to her chest. She sucks in her lower lip and looks to the skies.

Pru's head turns.

'I saw a shop with wedding dresses in the window on the way here,' Pru says. 'Greek taste is very, um, interesting,' She inhales on her cigarette and then her jaw pushes forward and bottom lip extends as she blows smoke above Helena's head. 'The one in the window was all net bodice and diamante. It was so, how shall we say,' she pauses for effect, 'bold.'

Helena's eyes flash, perhaps hers is net bodice and diamante. Sarah wants to say, 'Have you met Pruella de Ville?' but instead pours herself some more water as her heart goes out to Helena, who is some years junior to Pru and with a fragility about her.

'It's possible that they could look too 'bold,' as you put it,' Helena replies with a calmness that impresses Sarah. 'Few could wear them, as you really do have to have the figure.' Helena's focus flicks from Pru's eyes down to Pru's ever-so-slightly spreading waist. Pru looks away. Helena stands and excuses herself, smoothing her dress over her slim hips and, with slinky movements, extracts herself from the group and heads indoors, presumably to the toilet.

Sarah wants to shout 'Touché.'

'Isn't she amazing, Mum?' Finn leans over and whispers.

Sarah smiles at the closeness of his face. 'Somehow, I think I'm going to like your Helena.' She smiles and brushes a stray hair from his face as if he was eight years old again.

Chapter 7

When Helena re-joins the group, the conversation moves onto the complexities of living in different countries.

'I miss so many people back in Ireland,' Sarah joins in, and Laurence raises his eyebrows as if this is news to him.

'But the world is getting smaller. I mean, I was born in the States and I am back there now, but I have lived and worked in Hong Kong and London. It's no big deal anymore to keep up. Sure, my friends in Hong Kong meet me halfway, usually Paris, but all you need is a long weekend.' Pru lights another cigarette, tipping her head to one side behind the lighter, the sun catching its gold, a momentary dazzle, hiding her face

'I think you have to like flying,' Helena answers. She seems to bear no grudge from the previous encounter. 'I mean, even though I was born here, we moved to Australia when I was six months old and we stayed till I was seven and then moved to the States. When I settled in London, it seemed a long journey to catch up with old friends. I've only been back to Oz four times.' This explains why she has no

Greek accent. Finn is holding Helena's hand under the table.

Sarah can count the times she has been on a plane on her fingers.

'I haven't travelled much,' she feels compelled to say. 'I mean, we holiday two or three times a year, don't we?' She turns to her husband. 'But with Laurence traveling all over the world with his work and golfing, he prefers to ...' she pauses, looking for the right word. '... explore the UK. Less travel, more relaxing.' The words ring hollow in her ears. She looks from Helena to Pru and back again; her jury wears a slight frown. She would like to add that they have plans to travel, but they don't.

'So you're a golfer,' Helena chimes in, taking the focus from Sarah. 'It must be handy being a pilot. You must play in some of the best clubs in the world?'

Laurence shuffles his feet. 'Well, the golfing's enjoyable of course, but it's also a tool for business. I mix with pilots from other airlines, and it has paid off, as shown by my recent move. But also with the suits on the ground, the decision makers, it's good to spend time with them.' He casts a fleeting look sideways to Sarah. 'But mostly, it just kills time between turnarounds.'

Laurence has had long stopovers in America, Mexico, the Bahamas, Puerto Rico, Jamaica. All places Sarah would like to visit, all places with golf courses. The first time he had a long stopover, they had just got married. She had been so young, hadn't even turned twenty. He sat on the bed with her, holding her hand, explaining how it was just a turnaround, how boring it would be, how he would be filling in his paperwork, playing a round of golf with someone from the airline, and really, he would have no time for her at all. She would be left alone. Sarah had pointed out that she would be left alone at home anyway and that she would be rather be left alone in the sun. Surely the hotel would have a pool?

Laurence had sighed and explained kindly how it would not look right if he were to bring his wife along to his work. It just wasn't done. He seemed so much older than her in that moment; he had a certain gravitas at thirty-four compared to her nineteen years. Sarah suggested that she just take his flight, once they were at the hotel, he wouldn't even have to acknowledge her. His hands had un-entwined from hers and he had stood up at that point, dropped his kind tone and asked why she was trying to make his life difficult when he was trying to be so considerate. This was his work they were talking about, not playtime. That was the first of the golfing stopovers at far-flung, beautiful-sounding places with people (he said) it was important he mixed with. Her holidays with him were in five-star hotels in Dublin, or Bath, or Edinburgh. One time, they only got as far the Mount Murray Hotel, a ten-minute drive from their home in Ballasalla, and that had a golf course where he met up with friends and she spent her time in the spa.

'I tell you what I find tricky about having a foot in so many countries—the tax. Because I have a house here in Greece, I must file a return even though, officially, I am a UK resident for tax purposes,' Helena says.

'The same for me,' Laurence rejoins. 'I did live in London once, just briefly when I qualified. Bought a flat; thought it was the right thing to do. Rented it out when I moved back home, but I seem to get endless letters from the letting agency, and I have the rental income to declare. Get a tax accountant, that's my answer. All the post goes to him now.'

Joss says something about his Green Card and Sarah's gaze drifts to some people watching. Families with small children sit nearest to the open area in the square, their children tentatively venturing away from them with balls or tricycles. Round the back of the plane tree sit couples absorbed in the moment. She is aware that she is vaguely looking for the shepherd, but as she becomes aware of this, she rebukes herself, firstly because there is no reason for him to be here and secondly, what is it to her where he is? She lets her thoughts drift. It is strange to see no variation in hair colour; everyone's dark, the women with the occasional gleam of red, dark and shiny. Men and women alike seem to have a dress sense that screams confidence in their appearance, the women coordinated, high heeled. If they walked down Strand Street, they would look, well, very overdressed. A bit tarty perhaps, but here in the sun, they look like birds of paradise.

As if on cue, a sparrow flies down from the tree and hops along the ground. Now, she sees, there are many of them busy clearing crumbs, some bold enough to sit on the backs of seats, others waiting expectantly under the tables. A cat lazes under a chair with no interest in either birds or leftovers.

A dog barks and Sarah turns to see a Husky at the feet of one of the coffee drinkers. The owner is leaning over, his shoulder-length hair flopped forward, his hand on the back of its neck pushing down so there is no choice but for it to lay. The poor thing must be so hot in this weather. The owner of the dog talks to it before straightening and just for the briefest of seconds, as he flips his hair back, Sarah sees Torin. Her thighs tense and she sits up straight. His dark hair, the straightness across the shoulders, the way he moves his head to settle his hair. And then, as quickly as it arrived, the illusion is gone and the dog owner is a Greek stranger again.

It's been a while since she has thought of Torin. She is not sure if that is a good or a bad thing. They don't talk of him. She doesn't want to upset Liz, and Liz probably doesn't want to upset her. But really, it has been twenty-nine years. They should speak of him with ease by now.

'I saw someone today who reminded me of Torin.' The pool is deliciously warm by the time the sun disappears behind the fig tree. She is drying now in the evening's residual heat, which is warm enough for her to lay there in her bikini. The husbands have gone for a walk, the boys have left for a *mesimeri*—siesta—before heading out with a young group of Helena's family to the nightclubs along the coast road out of Saros town that open late and don't close till dawn. Sarah and Laurence have not been invited.

Liz spins the lilo around to face her.

'Just for a moment, I thought it was him,' Sarah muses.

'I see him all the time.' Liz pushes herself away from the edge with her toes. Her retro swimsuit really suits her.

'Do you? It's an odd feeling. Inside, my love is exactly the same for him. I suppose it's because he hasn't changed. He is still twenty.'

'Mine too,' Liz replies.

'It's funny, well not funny, strange maybe, that if it wasn't for Torin, our lives would be so different.'

'If it wasn't for Torin, we would probably be married to some dead-end bartenders in Cork or somewhere.' She refers to a time when Liz was proposed to in one of the new bars in Cork. They took the bus there one Saturday as schoolgirls. 'To get coloured paper from Bowen's for an art project,' they told their mums, and then spent the day trying one licensed place after another until they returned worse for wear with the bartender's number, and his friend's, but without any purchases from Bowens.

'Well, you might be, but I would be married to Torin. Do you want a G & T?' Sarah replies.

'Do think we would have been any different if you had been my sister-in-law all this time?' Liz asks.

'No, you would have irritated me just as much,' Sarah teases. 'Do want a G & T or not?'

'Yes, of course. Do you need to ask?' Liz grabs the pool side and pulls hard, sending herself spinning toward the fig tree.

Sarah returns with two tall glasses filled to the brim.

'You want this on the lilo or are you coming out?'

'Here.' Liz cups one hand and rows herself to the edge.

'You would have been an aunt to Joss and Finn,' Sarah muses.

'It wouldn't have been Joss and Finn, though.' Liz is now paddling with one hand and going around in circles; her other hand holds her drink.

'True.' Sarah watches her. She stops paddling to take a sip of her cold gin and tonic, closes her eyes in appreciation, and the lilo drifts off to the other end of the pool with the current from the water filter.

Joss and Finn or Torin? But of course, she would never have known Joss and Finn to miss them, and the truth is she would never have swapped Torin for two people she had never met. She tips her head back and looks up at the fig tree behind her. Torin would have climbed the fig tree rather than sit under it, discovered all the streets of the village rather than sipping gin and tonic, and probably made friends with a few of the villagers, make everything in their lives seem like it matters.

Or to be more accurate, he had made her feel that she mattered, and no one has done that since he died. Well, the boys when they were young, maybe Liz before she moved to London, but not ever, if she is honest, Laurence, and definitely not, and it stings to admit it, herself.

The gin percolates into her bloodstream, distancing herself from her surroundings.

Other than her boys, the things she has filled her life with since have just been meaningless. She had joined a string of groups after the boys grew up and first Joss and then Finn went off to university. The organic farm helped for a while. Getting her fingers into soil had been so cathartic. She would go along and spend hours digging and weeding, planting and pruning, listening to the hum of insects. The other people were enthusiastic, but no one seemed to understand the marketing side of the business. The women who were just filling in time had annoyed her, which was so hypocritical. The men her own age seem to be directionless; she had very little to say to them. The lack of anyone taking control of the business side of things had the project doomed from the start, and none of them were surprised when the co-op broke up with finger pointing and blame and the land was bought by developers.

But she kept trying. The beekeeping night course mixed her in with a new set of people and for a while, it was something she looked forward to each week, but as the course neared its end, her fellow students began talking about what they would take next year: lace making, painting, learning Spanish, and the reality that she was finding substitutes for any real meaning in her life closed in on her and so she quit and became almost reclusive.

'Finding substitutes for any real meaning.' She didn't really even know what she meant by that. Life had no meaning and nothing she could do could give it meaning.

The thought takes her right back to the party to celebrate the eighteenth of a friend of Torin's. She and Liz had spent hours getting ready at Liz's house. Torin was out taking his driving test and they could tell by the whoops and cheers he had passed.

It was as if he had changed whilst taking his test from an awkward best-friend's-brother to Torin the man. Sarah was transfixed by the transformation as he admired her dress. At the party, he told her of his plans to move to Dublin, where there was more to life than there ever could be in county Clare, and it felt exciting. In that one evening, Torin brought relief from the thought there was no meaning, to a future full of possibilities. He entertained her, made her laugh, and turned life into an adventure. He said they would take bites out of living together.

Then all too quickly, he was gone and without him, she was left without power and the questioning re-emerged.

Sarah blinks against the sun at the sound of voices.

'Hey girls, have you had a good time? We walked all the way up the dry river bed to an ancient pile of stones. It didn't have anything to tell you what it was, but it was clearly ancient.' Neville wanders into the garden.

'It says here ...' Laurence comes up behind him with a guide book Sarah saw on one of the shelves in the bedroom earlier. 'That it is Mycenaean, so 1500 BC. Can you believe it? And what a relief from the usual oversell. There was not a plaque, not a tearoom, not a gift shop in sight.'

'Anyone getting hungry? Shall we go into Saros again?' Neville asks.

The thought is too much effort. It would be less exerting to cook.

'Or I can do us omelettes.' It is the easiest thing she can think of that Laurence will consider a proper meal.

'Oh, good idea,' he says.

'Good for me.' Liz pushes herself off from the end of the pool. She has left her empty glass on the side.

'Oh, you don't want to leave that there.' Neville strides over and picks it up.

'Laurence, why don't you get Liz a top up and something for Neville?' Sarah pulls her wrap around her and heads for the kitchen, marvelling at being outside in nothing but a bikini and a wrap at seven o' clock at night and for it to still be warm. Laurence pours drinks and leaves one for Sarah on the side before returning outside.

The place is well equipped and she wants for nothing. Nothing but eggs. She never did make it to the supermarket, but, she guesses, they are bound to sell them at the village shop. Undoing her sarong and crossing it to tie it at the back of her neck converts it into a presentable dress. Grabbing her bag, she hesitates at the gate. Perhaps she should tell them where she is going, but then, she'll only be a minute or two.

Chapter 8

Sarah walks slowly. Why not; it is her first holiday abroad in the sun since they got married. Somewhere, a dog is barking; another answers it and a chain of howls fades into the distance. In the garden next door but one, with the masses of flowers in pots, there is a lady with a watering can, her back turned to the lane, black skirt and jumper, a blue misshapen hat for shade, and pink slippers. Sarah walks past quietly, not wishing to disturb her, her footsteps more sure as she reaches the abandoned house at the corner. It looks forlorn even in the sun, and she wonders if it is for sale. There's no sign.

The dog is there again. It runs past her towards the main road, and she follows, turning the corner.

A voice startles her.

'Hi.' Sarah jumps.

'Oh Stella, hello. You surprised me.' Today, Stella wears a belted floral, sleeveless dress. Sarah instinctively likes Stella. Her countenance is open. She moves as if she is capable of hard work, but there is a softness about her.

'Are you settled in now? Everything good?' Stella asks as they fall into step, heading towards the village centre.

'Oh it's lovely.' Sarah replies.

'It is a beautiful house. Michelle, she came for a holiday and now she lives here,' Stella says. Her skin is darker than most Greeks Sarah has seen, her eyes almost black, and there is a childlike quality about her that is not just to do with her size, but somehow conveyed by her energy.

'Michelle, oh yes, the owner. Did she know Juliet before she came?'

'Oh yes, they are old friends. That is why she came here on holiday. *Yia sou Stavro*.' She waves and calls to a boy who passes them on a slow moped, a partly filled crate of oranges gripped in his fist, which is disconcertingly balanced on the foot of one extended leg.

'So if she lives here, does she have more than one house?' Sarah wonders where Stella has learnt such fluent English but then reflects that many foreigners speak two languages. It is the English who only speak one.

'She has a guest house on Orino Island. Have you been there?' Stella shields her eyes with her hand to watch the moped negotiate the turning past the square ahead.

'To the island? No.' Sarah cannot help but wonder if there are any age limits on driving mopeds and motorcycles, as it certainly doesn't seem so.

'It is very beautiful,' Stella continues. 'No cars, no bikes, just donkeys. *Yia sou Maria pos paei*?' Stella greets a woman brushing her front steps.

The thought of no cars or bikes sounds like a slow and ponderous life. 'I suppose there is a lot of tourism on such an island?' she states.

'Many tourists, many tavernas and hotels. Also, many houses belong to foreigners,' Stella chirps. 'But you are here. You like our village?' She gesticulates to everything around them with an open hand.

A man in overalls is on his knees with a bag of tools by the fountain. The men from the kafenio have now spilled out onto the square in the relative cool of the evening, drinking coffee and watching a big screen television propped in the open window of the café. In the dusk, the lights are on inside, creating an inviting glow. The shepherd is not there.

'This is my husband, Mitsos.' Stella points to the one-armed man as they draw near to one of the tables which is crammed with glasses, cigarette packets, and ashtrays.

'Hello, very pleased to meet you.' Sarah offers her hand to shake. Mitsos gently takes it but instead of shaking it, brushes it lightly against his lips. It is the action of a content man.

'He does not speak a word of English,' Stella laughs. *'Afti einai i gynaka apo tis Michelle.'*

Sarah wonders what Stella has said, recognises the word Michelle and figures she is explaining who she is.

'Where are you going?' Stella asks. Sarah is still making eye contact with Mitsos and his companions but breaks her gaze to answer.

'Oh, just to the shop.'

'Come, I go there too. It is new,' she says proudly, and for a moment, Sarah is not sure what Stella is talking about. 'Well, not new. The old shop, it was hit by a tree, so they built it again. It looks the same but it is new.'

'Ah.' Sarah's understanding comes as a sigh, her attention still drawn by the villagers in the square. 'Everyone here seems so, oh I don't know, content?'

'Most of them sit and argue or complain when really, they should be happy drinking ouzo in the warm evening surrounded by friends. *Yia sou Damiane.*' She taps a man on the shoulder as they pass his table before crossing the empty road. She seems to know everyone, but then, of course, it is her village.

Three steps take them onto the raised forecourt of the village shop. A woman sits on a chair by the door with her feet up on an empty crate.

'*Marina afti einai*. Sorry, what was your name again?' Stella turns to Sarah, who answers her. 'Oh yes, *afti eiani i Sarah pou menei sto spiti tis Michelle*.'

Sarah hears her own name and picks out the word Michelle more easily this time.

'Ah, welcome, welcome. I understand but no speak. Welcome. Marina.' The woman says in broken English before she pats her ample housecoated bosom as she says her name.

'How do I say hello?' Sarah asks Stella. She is not sure if the feeling in her stomach is excitement or hunger.

'*Yia sou*.' Stella tries to say it in an English accent, enunciating clearly.

'*Yia sou Marina*.' Sarah smiles into the shop owner's face. The woman stands and waddles into the shop. Behind the counter, from floor to ceiling, are shelves piled high with different brands of cigarettes. To the right is a little window that looks out to the raised forecourt with its three drinks cabinets and a rack displaying soil-clogged loose vegetables. A Spanish omelette would be nice. Everything looks so fresh.

Marina settles in behind the counter. To her right on the top shelf is a row of bottles of wine. Below that is a shelf of knitting needles, dolls, plastic flowers, and playing cards; under that, boxes of stockings and shower caps. Sarah cannot take it all in; the whole place is lined with shelves, including a row that stands back to back down the centre of the narrow space.

'How many days you here?' Marina's accent is so strong, Sarah can barely understand her. The sounds sink in and she filters out the words.

'It's my son's wedding. He is marrying Helena Plusiopoulos. Do you know her?'

'Ah yes.' She resorts to her mother tongue. *'Poli kala, kali ikoyenia me ta hrimata. Poli kala yia to yio sou.'*

Sarah looks blankly at Stella. 'She says they are a good family.'

'Now what did I come for?' Stella asks herself and then turns to Marina and they speak fluently for some minutes.

This gives Sarah time to discover shepherds' crooks leaning in the corner, dog collars by the biscuits, red and yellow boxed mousetraps on the shelf below the pasta, and a glimpse through a back door onto a flower-filled courtyard across which is a house, presumably Marina's. A chicken pecks away in the middle at the weeds between the thick flagstones.

It all seems so much more real here. Closer to nature maybe. She doubts there will be co-ops growing organic vegetables or evening classes on lace making. By the looks of what she has seen, everyone grows vegetables. Every garden seems to have something planted between the flowers; even the lady with the garden filled with potted flowers on her lane has a border of lettuce and some other things growing. There'll be no time for night courses, what with chickens to feed, courtyards to sweep, and glasses of ouzo to drink.

'She says what do you need?' Stella touches Sarah's shoulder.

'Oh, er, a dozen eggs please.'

'Do you want village eggs or for the town?' Stella asks.

The question feels like liquid gold to her spirit, it pulls her so far from her life back home. Not graded for size or colour, instead whether they have come from someone in the village or a place just a few miles away.

'Oh village, please. Do I just go and choose vegetables or do I ask?'

'Either.' Stella slides her plastic bag up her arm. 'I go now. Bye.' And with no more said, Stella swings her bag as she heads down the steps and across the square towards what looks like a basic taverna with tables outside and unlit fairy lights wrapped around the tree that arches the door.

The vegetables smell of the ground; the tomatoes are not an even red but have a strong, warm smell; the lettuces are wet, and one has a tiny slug near where it has been cut from its roots.

'These please, Marina, and a bottle of wine.' She takes out her purse.

'*Kokkino, lefko, rosé*?' Marina asks, her toe tapping a long line of plastic bottles arranged up on the floor beneath the lowest shelf. Sarah had not noticed them before, with so much else to look at. She glances at the glass bottles of wine on the top shelf. There are not many of them and they are dusty, and Marina could not even reach them up there without standing on something.

'Sorry?' She looks back at the plastic bottles.

'*Kokkino*.' Marina taps a red plastic bottle with her toe. '*Lefko*.' She taps a pale yellow bottle. '*Ee rosé*?' She taps a pale pink one.

'Oh.' Sarah laughs with the relief of her comprehension. 'One,' she holds up a finger, '*kokkino* and one,' she tucks her purse under her arm and holds up a finger with her other hand, 'Rosé.'

Marina bags the bottles. 'Finish?' she asks.

Nodding, Sarah pulls out some cash, examining the notes. Marina rings everything up on the cash register and points to the numbers. It is cheaper than Sarah could have imagined, and she counts out her coins to find she is twenty cents short in change and will have to break a fifty Euro note.

'Sorry.' She passes the note across. Marina pushes it back and cupping her hand she mimes that Sarah should tip up her purse.

'I am twenty cents short.' She tips the change out. Marina's fingers are swift to count.

'Okay, okay.' She pours the change into her till.

'But it is short,' Sarah insists.

'Ah, tomorrow.' The word almost becomes lost in her thick accent but her smile makes everything clear.

'Thank you so much.' Sarah's cheeks are aching from smiling. She has not stopped since she meet Stella. Gathering her bags, she repeats herself, 'Thank you, thank you.'

'*Adio*.' Marina waves.

Sarah hadn't realized there was air conditioning in the shop until she steps back outside, nor how warm the evening is. It would be nice to wander for a little, see where some of the streets lead.

'Hello.' It is Helena. 'I've just come down for wine, too.'

'Oh hi, is Finn with you?' She looks up the side lane, but only an old lady in black follows.

'Sarah, this is my aunt Sofrona, Frona for short. Frona, this is Sarah.' She raises her voice for the second sentence. 'Finn's mother.' She keeps the pitch high.

'Ah!' The old woman's eyes light up and her arms extend, and she approaches Sarah on shaky legs. The embrace is gentle but heartfelt. 'A good boy,' she states in a Greek American accent, kissing Sarah first on one cheek, then the other.

‘Nice to meet you,’ Sarah replies. The aunt says no more, so Sarah turns back to Helena. ‘I thought you were going to bouzouki clubs?’

‘We are, but Finn is still asleep, and besides, it is early yet. But I am glad we have bumped into you. Tomorrow, you must come up to the house, meet everyone, have some lunch, spend some time, okay?’

‘Oh yes, okay.’ Sarah quite likes the idea. Helena seems more relaxed this evening; maybe the village is rubbing off on her, too.

‘Come about, oh I don’t know, eleven, twelve. We will eat around half two or three, if you want to stay at ours for a sleep at *mesimeri*, there are plenty of rooms.’

‘Thank you.’

Helena gives Sarah a little wave as she passes to go inside the shop, very relaxed, nice. The aunt smiles ‘A good boy,’ she says again and shuffles away.

It will be nice to actually spend some time with Finn. His life keeps him so busy, his visits have been so brief and he has so many friends to catch up with on the island that she sees little of him even when he is home. It was the same when they went to visit him in London to meet Helena for the first time, snatching pockets of time in between clients he had to see. But then, what he is doing is so new and cutting edge, apparently. He needs to keep on top of things. Sarah hardly understands his work anyway. He explained it to her of course—something like 'selling media space for shares in new companies that are cash poor.' But it didn't explain exactly what he does, how he finds these companies, what sort of media space, and how he knows about that. He has outgrown her by miles and lives in a world she can only look into from the outside. Well, good for him. At least he knows what he is doing with his life and has a passion for it.

Damianos, the man Stella tapped on the shoulder, nods as Sarah makes her return journey, as does Mitsos. The man serving has a halo of frizzy greying hair, and he also grins broadly at her and nods in recognition.

Her tread is lighter as she leaves the square. She takes the clip from her hair and lets it swing.

Sarah slows to admire the flowers in the garden up the lane that leads to Michelle's. The lady who was tending the garden is no longer there, but there is a smell of herbs from the house. Something is cooking.

Pushing her own gate open, Sarah swings the bags as she hops onto the porch. A Spanish omelette with salad and fresh bread drizzled with olive oil and oregano, perfect.

'Oh my God, where have you been?' Laurence strides around the end of the house, frowning.

'To get eggs.' Her smiles fades.

'Ah, there you are. We were so worried.' Neville comes out of the house. Sarah shifts her weight towards Laurence.

'I was only five minutes.'

'But we didn't know where you were,' Laurence accuses. She shifts back towards Neville.

'I'm fine. I'd better start or it will never be cooked.' She manoeuvres around Neville to find Liz in the kitchen pouring a large drink.

'I swear your leash gets tighter every time I see you.'

'Liz!' she whispers in warning and takes the glass offered.

'Can I make a toast, then? To longer leashes and loving husbands.' She raises her glass, finishes her drink, and pours herself a fresh one. 'Come on, we can cook together.' Liz's words slur ever so slightly.

'I saw Helena in the village. I am going up to her house tomorrow to meet everyone.'

'Oh that will be fun.' The emphasis lands on the word *will*.

'No, I think it will be fine.' But now Sarah is home, it doesn't feel as fine as it did when she was out. Trying to convince herself, she adds, 'She seemed more mellow somehow, as if the village has relaxed her.'

'You said yesterday she was as chatty as ever, so it can't be the village because didn't you say she had been a week here already?'

'Yes, I did, so I suppose not.'

'Well I am going to discover a beach tomorrow, so if you can get away, call me.'

'On your own?'

'Well I doubt Neville will want to come. Can you see him out of his suit, in swimming trunks, doing nothing on a beach? No, he has some plans to go and see some ancient pile of stones and a museum.'

'With Laurence?'

'No idea.'

Chapter 9

Sarah arrives hot from the walk. There was no persuading Laurence to come with her.

'Laurence, we cannot meet them for the first time at the wedding, and besides, they have invited us to their house. Not to go would just be plain rude,' Sarah argued.

'Finn is marrying Helena, and whether the rest of us get on or not is immaterial and I, for one, have no desire to spend my time pretending it is any other way.'

'But you socialise all the time with work.' Using his work as a levy was risky; he might turn on her.

'Exactly—work.' Laurence replied calmly.

'Then for Finn's sake come.'

'Finn's fine. He needs no display from me.'

And with a look, that had been the end of the conversation.

He had gone off with Neville first thing whilst Sarah lay in bed wondering if the day would be worth getting up for.

The dogs behind the solid metal gate bark furiously.

'*Nai*?' The intercom crackles.

'Oh. My name is Sarah and I ...'

'Oh Sarah. One minute; I bring the dogs in.'

The barking stops, replaced by the sound of claws clicking against tarmac as they scamper away. The gate buzzes and swings open to reveal a drive that sweeps up a shallow incline lined with rhododendron bushes. The hedges create shade, which makes the walking a little more pleasant, and around a bend, the drive opens onto a lawn that stretches in front and beyond a modern house which has clean, sharp lines which mostly appear to be windows. The dogs are nowhere to be seen. A large carport to one side houses six cars, and at the end of the drive, where one would expect perhaps a seating area in front of the house, there is a sunken swimming pool which extends under the glass front and inside. To the right of the pool, a door opens.

'Sarah, good morning! No Laurence?'

Sarah walks around the edge of the pool to be greeted with a kiss on either cheek from Helena.

'Come in. We are all here. Ignore them.' Helena indicates two children who are chasing each other and sliding across the marble floor from the staircase right up to the pool's edge. The section of window that separates inside from out above the pool appears to be able to raise and lower. At the moment, it is raised and there is a person energetically swimming lengths. 'My dad. You'll meet him when he gets out,' Helena says. There's a vague smell of chlorine. 'Stop that now or you will have an accident.' Her tone is sharp, but the children ignore her. One of the many doors off the hall opens and a man wanders out, newspaper in hand. 'Tom, one of my many cousins.' Helena says. He nods and winks at Sarah.

'Come, I am in the kitchen. I have done something crazy and you may have to help me out,' Helena continues. A woman in grey linen is ascending the sweeping stairs and Sarah's eyes are drawn upward. The hall is open, rising through three floors to a dome of glass at the top. Sarah tips her head to look up and up. The light and the height of the building reminds Sarah of museums in London but everywhere there is a modern edge. Helena is walking off, so Sarah breaks her gaze to follow.

'Jenny, where's Frona?' Helena asks a new face coming towards then. The teenager shrugs and scowls sulkily at Sarah. They enter a kitchen that seems to be teeming with women. A radio is on and someone sings along.

'Everyone,' Helena shouts above the din and the room settles and heads turn. Sarah links her fingers in front of her. 'This is Sarah, Finn's mama.' The womens' voices melt together and Sarah can pick out 'welcome,' 'wonderful,' 'hello,' and '*yia*.' Two of the women nearest come over, clapping flour from their hands to embrace Sarah and to place kisses on her cheeks before returning to their work.

Sarah is overwhelmed by the number of people in the house and she pictures, with just a tinge of regret, the coffee and book she left by the quiet of the pool before she came out.

The noise begins again: chatting, singing, everyone busy. 'Come, look what I have done.' Helena leads her to the counter against the wall where the lady in black that she met yesterday outside the shop stands. 'Frona, you're there. Look, here's Finn's mama, Sarah.' She shouts a little. Frona's eyes twinkle and she takes Sarah's hand and pats it between her own.

'Look.' Helena lifts foil from several shapes on the counter. 'I baked these this morning. I suddenly had this mad idea to make my own wedding cake, but now it is time to decorate it and I have lost my impetus.' She sounds both nervous and excited. Sarah has never seen Helena anything but composed, even when she is overflowing with energy.

'Mum!' Finn wraps his arms around Sarah's shoulders from behind and she feels every bone in her body melt. She breathes in the scent from his forearms and kisses the soft hairs, her son. It feels like she lost Joss years ago. When he became a man, he seemed to lose all softness and then, when he shifted his interest to work in finance, the whole meaning of his life seemed to become the endless and tireless chasing after money. He no longer felt like someone she knew. But Finn, Finn will always be her baby.

'Look what Helena's done.' Finn releases Sarah and throws his arms around Helena, who smiles and moulds into him. 'Mad or what, she could have just ordered it, end of worry, but oh no.' He is laughing and kissing Helena on the forehead.

'So shall we decorate it, Sarah? What do you think?' Helena says as Finn releases her. She bends and takes some packets from the cupboard below.

'Are you helping, Frona?' Finn addresses the old lady in black as he throws one arm around her shoulder. Sarah swallows and blinks as the idea of her son being engulfed by another family becomes real for her.

'Oh Finn, those things arrived.' Helena puts the packets she has retrieved on the work surface. 'Come and see.' She takes him by the hand. 'Won't be a moment, Sarah,' and off the two of them go, laughing and kissing. Helena seems much gentler than Sarah remembered, and Finn is clearly happy. But then, he was always a happy child, even as he struggled through adolescence. Half way through his A levels, Sarah can remember sitting with him in the kitchen, trying to work out where his interests lay. He wanted to go to university in theory but had no idea what to study. She asked him what it was in life that made it all make sense for him, hoping the answer to this would give him a clue as to what was dear to his heart, a suitable point from which to figure out what he wanted to do. But he had shrugged and smiled as if to say he didn't know what she meant but he was happy anyway. Even when he did decide what he wanted to study, it was clearly a means to an end, not a passion. But now, watching him with Helena, she can see he has his meaning by his side and he is hers. They are lucky.

'You know how to ice?' Frona addresses her in her American-Greek accent. Age has wrinkled and dried her olive skin and twisted her fingers but she has the same twinkle in her eyes as Helena, and Sarah presumes she is the grandmother.

'Well, I used to ice my cakes.' Another of the things she learnt during the endless days with the boys at school and Laurence on his long-haul flights, but it has been a while. Frona struggles with one of the packets. 'Here, let me,' Sarah offers.

Helena does not return immediately, but Sarah and Frona make short work of rolling out the ready-made icing and covering all the cakes. Frona proves easy to talk to and appears to have no inhibitions about what she feels comfortable sharing.

'Finn has been very good to me, you know. He's a boy to be proud of.' Frona lays a sheet of icing, using a rolling pin, over the last cake. 'The family know I have not been myself for some time and I wasn't going to come to the wedding, but Finn, he rings me up, from London, all the way to America, and he tells me he needs me there at his wedding to make everything complete. Such a nice boy. So I am here for him.' She pauses for breath. It seems Helena's way of talking is just something she has learnt. She doesn't mean to bombard with words. This old lady's way of speaking is the same, just smoother somehow, tempered by age, perhaps.

'Me not being myself, they, my family, called it depression,' Frona states. Sarah winces at the word, knowing that her own heavy darkness could be given such a label. But she would rather not know. Out of the kitchen window, she can see bright sunshine and a cloudless blue sky. The air conditioning in the kitchen is very efficient. 'How about we make roses. You can make roses, right? Stack the cakes and put them in a sweeping arch down from here to here?' Frona doesn't even take a breath to change the topic of the conversation back and forth. 'I said to my family, "Why does there always have to be a big fancy word for how we feel. We are human, right? Why can I not just be sad?" But they asked me again and again how I feel and I tell them. They say such pain cannot be just sadness, so they take me to the doctors and she put me on pills. Wet your fingers,' Frona tells Sarah as she smooths her first petal. Sarah feels she should make some response to the tale Frona is telling her but cannot think what to say. Her instinct is to keep the topic at arm's length.

'So I take the pills to shut them up and nothing changes and my boy, he comes to me and say would I like to go to hospital. "Hospital," I say, "for feeling sad?" But the family insist it is depression, so they take me to the hospital. Shall we colour some pink? No, better not; we'll stick to white.' This time, she takes a breath. 'And there, on the doorstep of this fancy hospital, is a doctor in his fancy white coat. "I hear you are depressed," he says, with no introduction and so now I am even more fed up with all these people telling me how I feel, so I face up to him.

'"Listen doctor," I say, "I have lived a long life. I grew up in the war in Greece. I saw some terrible things. I was reduced to fighting over tortoises for food. I have lived on a shoestring with my children and I have a full-blooded Greek husband."'

Sarah cannot tell if this last comment is full of pride, a joke, or a concern, but there's no stopping Frona now anyway.

'"I married him when I was fifteen, I had a child at sixteen. I know life."

'The doctor, he stands there quietly, so I continue, "Five years ago my husband, my companion through this life, dies. I miss him. I grieve. Yes, I grieve for five years, but what is five years compared to the all the years I was married and all we have been through? That is the trouble with you doctors," I say. "You take a human challenge, like grief or sadness, and you give it a fancy name and it becomes something worse, something so big, a person does not believe they can cope with it alone. You take something that is unwanted and you call it *abnormal* and you call this abnormal thing a mental disease. If it is a disease, how do we cope without you? You make yourself patients with your labels. We sink further with our labelled diseases until we come pleading for your drugs and expertise, convinced you must know so much more than us, as you gave our suffering a serious name. But give it a name like Natural Sadness or even call it A Human Challenge, and suddenly it is not a thing to be feared but an event to be overcome." So I say to this fancy doctor in his white coat, "Thank you, but I do not need your hospital or your pills. I need just what all humans need—good conversation, companionship, and somewhere I can give love."

'You know what he said?' Frona passes a rose of icing to be placed with the others to harden a little. "I have cured you!" That is what he said! At least, that is what I remember him saying; he might have worded it differently, but it was what he meant, honest to my God.' She crosses herself three times. 'I have cured you! Can you imagine the cheek?'

'He was probably joking,' Sarah ventures.

'Ha, don't you believe it! It would have shown some humility but no, he declared it was going to his hospital and standing on his doorstep that shocked me out of depression. So I told him.' She seals her lips and pulls off another piece of icing to be moulded between her crooked fingers. Sarah waits, but Frona seems to have forgotten that she was talking.

'So you told him?' Sarah prompts.

'Yes, I told him. I say "I have been standing here for ten minutes talking sense to you and in that time, my grieving has not decreased one jot. I still miss my husband, I still have a pain in my heart when I think of him, I still feel alone in my house in New Jersey, I still feel old, and these are the things that make me sad. So nothing has been cured. The only thing that has changed is your perception as you have become a little wiser."'

'Really, did you say that really?' Sarah giggles.

'And why not? The man was a fool, creating a career by turning emotions people don't want into mental *conditions* by calling them abnormal. Since when is it abnormal to feel loss over the death of your partner, loneliness because your children live far away, sadness because there are millions starving in the world, anger because the politicians are self-serving, and frustration—because it takes my legs half an hour just to get me to the bathroom?'

Sarah looks out of the window again. The sky is still blue, the sun is still shining, the dark weight inside her has shifted enough that she can feel the beauty—just.

'I tell you, unhappiness is a natural thing. Shouldn't living a life short of the years you had reckoned on make you feel unhappy? Should not having lived the life you wanted to live also make you so?' The old woman casts a sideways glance at Sarah, who is wondering if cleaning and tidying and cooking and being at Laurence's every beck and call is something she has a right to feel unhappy about, considering how she ended up married to him in the first place.

'Hey, how are you doing? Sorry I was so long but ... oh my God, that looks amazing!' Helena breezes back in. 'Here, let me put one on. Oh they are so delicate, oh no, arh, oh sorry, it just crumbled. Teach me to make one?'

Frona is grinning toothlessly. 'I was the same when I was her age, all energy and no delicacy,' she says to Sarah.

'Thanks, *Yiayia*.' Helena leans in and nudges her, shoulder to shoulder. 'Oh Sarah, Finn says can you go and help him. He is in the hall. Come on Frona, show me how.'

Sarah leaves the heat and smells of the kitchen. With so many staying in the house, no wonder it takes a team of them to prepare the food. She wonders, with the family being so well off, why don't they employ a chef? Although the atmosphere in the kitchen is so companionable, she can see it would be a great way to choose to spend part of the day. She treads lightly as she finds her way to the hall.

Finn is kneeling by a box by the pool. The sun streams through the ceiling dome, a beam of light just catching his feet. If he were in it centrally, it would make an amazing picture, sort of spiritual, religious even.

'Hi Mum,' he drawls, reading from a booklet.

'Frona's something else, isn't she?'

'They say to look at the mother of the bride to see how your wife is going to turn out. Well, I am looking at the granny and hoping.' He grins his mischievous, crooked smile.

'I haven't met her mum or her dad yet.' She sits beside him.

'Where is Dad anyway?' Finn asks.

'He went to Mycenae with Neville.'

'Oh,' says Finn. Sarah can hear so much unsaid in the one sound.

'Don't, Finn. He loves you and Helena. It's just he is not one to join in these types of preparations. You know how he is.'

'These types of preparations? How many youngest sons has he got to marry off to have "These types of preparations?"' he snaps.

'Don't get cross with me. I am here.' Sarah looks him directly in the eyes.

'Sorry Mum, but how personal can you get? It is my wedding!'

'Are you nervous?'

'No, yes, no, sort of. Look, can you figure these out?' He pushes the whole box towards her.

'What are they?'

'Floating silk lilies for the pool. I thought they came complete, but it looks like you need to attach the weights underneath.'

Sarah picks up a pink flower. 'Oh they are love ...' But her sentence hangs unfinished, interrupted by a scream that tears through the wall, echoing across the space.

'Is that Pru or Helena?' Finn is on his feet. Sarah is quick to follow. She had not realised Joss and Pru were here. They run down a corridor to a closed door behind which two people are having a most heated row. Finn flings open the door.

Helena is screaming at Pru at the top of her voice, arms and hair flying, tears streaming down her face. Pru is trying not to look smug. Joss appears from nowhere and pushes past Sarah and glares at Pru, gripping her by the elbow and pushing her towards the door.

'Do not treat me like a kid,' Pru snaps at Joss.

'Then don't behave like one. Walk out or I will carry you.' Sarah has never seen Joss so angry.

Chapter 10

Joss looks like Laurence when he is this angry. Sarah pushes herself back against the open door as the pair marches out. Joss does not even acknowledge that she is there although she strokes his arm to try and soothe him as he passes.

Helena is sobbing into Finn's shoulder. People are filling the room: the women from the kitchen and many others she does not recognise. A man who must be Helena's father pushes through and wraps himself around the other side of his daughter, opposite Finn.

'*Ti kanies paidi mou*?' His quiet words are still audible over the clamour in the room, along with Helena's sobbing.

'Prudence is a ...' Helena struggles for the words. '*Poutana,*' she spits, finally.

'Who is this Prudence?' her father asks. He speaks English fluently, an Australian accent with a twist of American. The relatives around Sarah quieten, their backs straighten, mouths shut. No one wants to answer.

'She is my brother's wife.' Finn's eyebrows arch in the middle, his 'asking forgiveness' look that

Sarah remembers well from when he was in endless trouble as a boy, from Joss pushing him into things he knew he really shouldn't be doing. Helena sniffs and takes a big breath to help straighten herself.

'Oh, you mean Pru,' the father clarifies.

Sarah watches, waiting for his reaction.

He nods, and the fatherly arm that was round Helena is now around Finn.

'Ach, I have a brother whose wife is so toxic, they have not been invited to the wedding.' He releases his hand from his shoulder hug and slaps Finn on his back. Sarah notices she is holding her breath. It seems that the people around her also relax.

Bloody Pru; whatever possessed Joss to marry her? But she knows the answer. His rush for financial glory, gaining status by the day, and Pru was his boss at the time. She made Joss believe that together, they could do anything. It was a natural coupling

The uncles and aunts, cousins and in-laws who held back when Helena's father came in the room now swarm over Helena and Finn, and the pair are lost from sight. Sarah wonders if Joss has left yet. She runs back to the hall only to see their car disappearing down the drive. She takes out her phone and texts.

'You OK? Do you need to talk? Love Mum xxx.'

The message can sit on his phone; he will see it when he has finished arguing with Pru. She just hopes he drives safely. Back in the room, the mass of people has not subsided and everyone is voicing an opinion or offering a suggestion. Finn is being attentive to Helena; someone suggests they go to their room and have some time together. Finn smiles weakly at Sarah as he leaves the room, his arm around his wife-to-be.

Sarah was having such a nice time in the kitchen with Frona before this. For the first time in, well she cannot even remember how long, she felt ... what had she felt? Connected, part of something, engaged in what she was doing. None of these descriptions is quite right, though. What she felt was a sense of belonging and acceptance, but not to Frona or the family—but rather (and she is aware how ridiculous this thought is), to the world. And Pru snuffed that moment out with her behaviour.

Do Frona's opinions on emotions seem suddenly appropriate?

How can Sarah not be sad about Pru and Helena arguing? The heaviness inside her shifts, a memory nudges at her, trying to be recalled. Sarah focuses, forcing it to take shape, but it will not. It is something to do with her sadness, the hint of a solution.

Feeling suddenly uncomfortable in the house with Finn and Helena retired to their room, she wanders out into the garden, where the sun's hot embrace catches her by surprise. Her limbs loosen and grow sluggish and her pace immediately slows. Looking back down the drive, the dogs are visible, locked in large cages tucked behind the garages. One lays panting, half-in, half-out of its kennel. She wonders if dogs become sad, too. They must, if they are caged too long.

Beyond the dogs' cage, there is a wall with an open wooden gate, both too tall to see over; besides, there is a single line of trees beyond. Sarah wanders over to it, rubbing the last of the icing from her hands. She hopes the dogs will not bark, and they ignore her. If Finn and Helena stay in their room, lunch could be quite awkward. She knows Frona, but she hasn't even been introduced to Helena's parents yet. Maybe today is not the day to meet them. Tomorrow, or even the next day, might be better. The truth is Finn and Helena will marry whether she meets them or not so really, in the scheme of things, it is not important. There is no rush. Maybe Laurence was right. One of the dogs lifts its head and sniffs before returning to its dreams.

The side gate in the high wall stands ajar, beckoning. Is there a formal garden on the other side, or a tennis court, maybe a vegetable plot? She could see what can grow here. There is no rush in her step as she pulls the gate open and steps beyond.

It is just rough ground, with hardy, low-lying bushes and tough grass and a single spreading tree growing centrally . A goat pops up, startled, from behind the nearest clump of gorse and gambols away. Such happy creatures. People would be better if they were more like goats.

Torin was a bit like a goat; jumping about, always eating, always happy. Everything life threw at him became an adventure. Something bad would happen and he would find a positive way to look at it, make it fun. Like when his money fell through a hole in his jeans pocket.

They had been up to the Cliffs of Moher, walking, the three of them. Torin had been discussing their plans, or rather his plan that they were following. They were to move to the fair city, get proper jobs, and raise the money to move to London, maybe via the Isle of Man, where the jobs paid better than in Dublin. His ideas seemed so big, so great at the time. London was a world away, a place of shiny lights and superstars. But on their return from the cliffs, he put his hand in his pocket to show the wages he had saved for the bus to Dublin and he found the money gone.

Sarah had felt like crying. She only had enough saved for her own ticket and she wasn't going without him, but he rebounded with energy.

'Great,' he said with joy, 'I'll hitch, and I reckon I'll be there before you.' But the way he said it sounded like such fun that she and Liz decided not to take the bus either, and the three of them said their secret goodbye to County Clare, standing with their thumbs out on the road to Dublin, praying that a stranger would stop to pick them up, rather than someone they knew—or worse, someone who knew their families.

Sarah lifts her hair from her neck to relieve the heat.

A figure appears at the top of the field and makes its way steadily toward her until they are close enough to speak.

'We meet again.' The shepherd is cheerful in his greeting.

'Hello.' Sarah is not sure if she should be surprised to see him or not.

'Are you happy or sad today?' His mouth stays firm but his eyes dance.

'Definitely sad just at the moment,' Sarah confirms. 'Sad, but not depressed.'

'Hm, you don't seem so sad.' He changes hands with his crook.

'Ah, sad, not sad, it's all part of life.' She tries the philosophical approach but it sounds ridiculous coming from her mouth and she starts to giggle.

'Yes, very sad today,' he teases, chuckling in return. Sarah notices his shirt is clean and ironed today, and he looks less like a farmer. His big black boots are polished too.

'You know I think the trouble with being sad—if you were sad, which you are not today,' he leans his head towards her, looking her in the eyes before straightening again, hands in pockets, crook tucked through his arm resting on the toe of his boot. 'I think the trouble is when we are low, we make bad decisions and you kind of know you have made a bad decision and so you stay up all night thinking about it, again and again, then the next day you are tired, irritable, and even more unhappy and you make even worse decisions. Someone says something harmless and you take it the wrong way and the bad decisions just pile on top of each other. Know what I mean?'

'It sounds like you are speaking from experience,' Sarah says.

The shepherd glances at her quickly but stays silent. Sarah can feel the sun burning her. She crosses her arms across her chest, her palms covering her shoulders. The single, large, central tree not far from where they are standing offers an umbrella of shade, and most of the animals are taking advantage of it. The shepherd follows her gaze, nods his head to one side, and they walk together into the shadow. By the tree trunk is a well-worn stone. Sarah wonders how many other shepherds come here and how often this stone has made someone a seat: for years, maybe centuries.

'You want to sit?' he asks, rubbing the stubble on his chin, his fingers teasing the new growth under his nose.

Sarah shakes her head. 'Are you growing it back?' He shakes his head, too.

'You think I should?'

They stand silently, looking out at the view across the tops of the village houses, to the mountains, pale in the distance.

Sarah ponders the dark weight she battles with inside, sometimes felt so acutely, sometimes shifting so she can feel hope, see beauty. What would life be like without it?

'Trouble is, sometimes we can get unhappy with someone else and because of our ties, we say we cannot leave.' She is not sure if she says the words aloud and a tear forms on the inner edge of her eye, threatening to fall. 'Sometimes, someone else's stress can become our own so although we are not truly unhappy, we are just unhappy with our circumstances.' Sarah surprises herself with her words. Heat rises up her neck and she is glad no one but the shepherd can hear her. She asks herself if what she is saying is true, but she doesn't know the answer and the meaning of the words drift, repelled by her internal walls, the ones built to keep her safe from challenging thoughts, keeping everything at a distance so nothing can make impact at all, disturb her numbness.

The shepherd sighs. 'That is the way of it,' he says slowly as if the conversation is about him. It gives Sarah courage to try and make her thoughts concrete, say more, explore a little.

'You know, I think so much is designed to gloss over our unhappiness; television, radio, dinners out, holidays.' She thinks of Joss and his chase after money blinding him to everything around him, and Laurence's and his golf. 'It's all just a way to take our focus away from what is really going on, that, for some reason, with everything around us removed, we are unhappy,' she concludes, wishing she could feel her words, but her walls are too thick.

'A big blanket of activity keeping all that sadness in,' the shepherd says. The goats have been eating their way towards them. He picks up a stone and throws it at the feet of the nearest one, with gnarled curling horns and a long beard. It skips away and the others follow.

'The thing is, all these distractions don't work. The unhappiness we ignore becomes the monster in the cupboard, grown more scary the longer we pretend it is not there. I wonder if I just face up to it, call it unhappiness and really look at it, if it would lose its power.' She tries hard to connect to her own words.

He rocks from one foot to the other. 'But,' he says loudly, letting out his breath and gaining some energy from his next words. 'Life is not all unhappy.'

'No, some of it is just ordinary, and even that can leave you feeling cheated.' These words feel easier to say as Sarah watches a bird hovering some distance away. Licking her lips, she recognises her thirst and then her stomach grumbles. It does not feel appropriate to return to Helena's for lunch. Better to head home. She will sit by the pool and read her book.

'But doesn't that give you freedom?' the shepherd asks.

'Pardon?' Sarah feels she has lost the thread of what they were saying.

'An ordinary, even a purposeless life. Does that not give us the freedom to go off and do anything we want?'

Sarah repeats his sentence in her head, but it makes no sense. What would she go off and do?

'Like what?' She gives a little laugh. Maybe it is obvious and she has missed something.

'What do you like to do?' He is drilling a hole in the dust with his crook, rolling it between his palms.

She is just about to answer, 'have a good time,' when she wonders what exactly she means by that. The last time she thought such a question, she must have been about seventeen. Torin asked her, 'what do you like doing most?' They had been walking and stopped at Nairbyl on the west coast. It was a misty day, and not once had they been able to see across to Ireland.

She struggled to answer the question then, and she struggles now. 'Nature' comes as the unspoken answer, but what to do with nature? It is a pretty broad category. Something to do with nature and nothing to do with money.

'I have no idea,' she answers, feeling a little deflated.

'Here's something that came to me the other day—we can choose.' He stops drilling and cups his hands over the top of his stick, letting his chin rest on top. 'Then we make the effort towards whatever it is we choose, then it becomes important, then it is what we like best.'

Sarah's stomach growls again.

'Right,' he says, his tone breezy. 'I am off for my lunch and a sleep. Nice to see you again.' And with a wave of his stick, he sets off up the hill the way he came, the sheep one by one lifting their heads and gambolling after him.

It is quiet once the animals have gone; no bleating, no chewing, no rustling.

'We can choose, make an effort, and then it becomes best.' Sarah repeats his words in a whisper, but it all feels just a little out of her reach.

A track leads down the hill and looks like it will join the road she took on the way to Helena's.

The shepherd could be right—look at Finn. He was floundering around, trying to find a foothold in London. Then Helena came along, he chose her, he made the effort, and now she is what he likes best. The rest of his life seemed to fall into place as a side product.

'But he is also wrong,' she says out loud. She chose Laurence, made an effort in their marriage, but she certainly doesn't feel her life is full of the things she likes best. Although it would be true to say that for a few years, he was what she had liked best, sort of. But then, how much effort had she really made back then? More to the point: where do they stand now?

She begins the walk home, kicking at a stone by the side of the path. The gorse thickens lower down the hill and the path snakes its way between the bushes. Bees hum on either side of her. The smell of the heat rising from the undergrowth is indescribably delicious.

'This, right here, right now,' she says out loud, and her senses fill even more with the bright colours, the lazy hum of the insects, and the smell of everything warmed by the sun. The high gorse on either side of the path hides her from the world and she stretches her arms into the air. Opening her fists, she closes her eyes and feels the sun on her face. Relaxing, she picks up a pebble from the track. She looks at its size and shape. She will keep it as a reminder of this moment, this feeling, this sense of everything being perfect in this instant.

Once down on the road, it all feels too civilised again until she rounds a bend and is met by another herd, this time of sheep. They are scared to pass her by. The herder whirs and clicks at them and a dog runs back and forth along the back of the pack until they break into a gallop past her, bleating, whinnying, and smelling of the sour droppings that are matted to their tails and underbellies.

'*Yia*.' The shepherd addresses her. He draws the beginning of the word out, letting it trail off to the end. Sarah feels a little thrill that she now knows what this word means.

'*Yia*.' She tries to mimic his pronunciation. He nods and walks by; his dog ignores her. He may even have thought she was Greek.

The village is quiet. No one is about. Sarah is not surprised—it seems hotter than yesterday. There is no dog, no neighbour in her blue hat watering her garden. Everything is still.

An electronic beep in her pocket demands attention. She wants to silence the intrusion and fishes hastily for her phone and sees there is a text from Joss.

'Helena way over reacted. Is Finn cross?' He would do better to talk to Finn directly, or even talk to her. This texting keeps everything so short, so at arm's length. She ponders how to answer and then decides not to respond at all, and then wonders if it is the first time she has ever wilfully cut him adrift.

Chapter 11

The gate to their holiday cottage is closed and there is nothing but a dusty patch where the rental car usually stands, so Laurence has not yet returned. Sarah exhales.

With yesterday's feta and a hunk of fresh bread on a tray, Sarah settles herself on the sun-bed in the shade of the fig tree with her book. She contemplates getting up again for a glass of wine but the will to move has left her. She is far too comfortable.

The feta is creamy and she can taste the olive oil in the bread. Some tiny creature rustles behind her in the dark recesses around the foot of the fig tree, and a dragonfly hovers over the pool. The neat lawn is trimmed to perfection but Sarah prefers the slightly rougher look to Juliet's garden, with its fruit trees and slightly wild look. There is also an overgrown pond and a wooden curved bench under a knotted olive tree. A rusting wire fence separates Juliet's garden from the orange orchards beyond where an automatic watering system hisses, keeping the roots moist.

More bread and feta would be welcome but that, too, would require movement. She wonders if

Finn and Helena have recovered, if they have even noticed she has gone yet. Perhaps she should have let someone know she was leaving. Maybe she could text them. She takes out her phone but decides that if Finn wants her, he will get in touch. She will read instead. But her book remains spine upwards, on the ground next to her as her eyes close. 'Just for a minute,' she tells herself.

The shadow blocking the sun wakes her.

'Oh hi. I didn't mean to wake you, but I guessed you were in the shade when you fell asleep. I was worried you would burn now.' There is a golden mist around the person's head as the sun behind them lights up their hair, the face barely visible in the bright sun.

Sarah cannot orient herself and it takes her a few moments to recall where she is and that it is Juliet from next door who is speaking.

'Oh, how are you finding this? I tried but I never got past the first chapter.' Juliet picks up the book. Sarah pushes herself up to sitting.

'Oh, it's alright. I'm not really gripped by it.' She yawns.

'I have lots of books. If you want another, just come and knock.' Juliet turns as if to leave.

'Can I ask you something?' Sarah asks.

'Sure.' Juliet's movements are languid, as if time does not apply to her.

'You, being here, are you living on your own? I mean, if you don't mind me asking? It's just that I was wondering what brought you out here? I'm just curious how you ended up living in such a beautiful place.' Sarah wonders if she is phrasing the question intelligibly. Sleep seems to be still misting her thoughts.

'I don't mind you asking at all.' Juliet leans against the back of the second sun-bed but when it shifts with her weight, she sits tentatively on its edge, as if to show she is not staying, not intruding. She sits with her knees together, elbows on top, wrists hanging crossed. 'I first came years ago when my boys were small.'

'Oh, you have children?'

'Well, not really children now. Two boys. They are nearly twenty-six now.'

'Mine are twenty-seven and twenty-eight,' Sarah says.

'Gosh, you must have been young when you had them.' Juliet scans Sarah's face and Sarah wonders if her mascara smudged under her eyes whilst she was asleep.

'I was twenty when Joss was born.'

'Young enough.'

'Yes, too young, I think now. So you first came here with them?' Sarah encourages.

'Oh no, it was a sort of mini-break. My mother-in-law stayed with them and I came here on holiday with Michelle.' Juliet nods in the direction of the cottage to indicate she means the same Michelle who owns the holiday home. 'Well, the long and the short of it is I fell in love with the country.' Juliet's voice becomes light, energised. 'So when I went home, I found a night class, studied the language and, years later, when the boys were grown and gone, I just upped and left.' She gives an easy laugh as if telling a tale from long ago that no longer has any impact on her, a different life.

'That sounds brave.'

'Hot-headed, more like. I had divorced back over there and it seemed everyone was eager to hand out advice about how I should live my life so it was a sort of reaction.'

'Do you get lonely?'

'Not at all. I talk to my boys on Skype. The people in the village are so friendly, and Michelle is here all winter. But more than that, settling here has shown me that the English way of living is only one way to be. There are so many other perspectives to try.'

'I suppose so,' Sarah says, her voice faint.

'Just learning the language showed me how whole other cultures can think in a different way. It comes through in the words they use, the way they form their sentences.'

'I wouldn't know. I only speak English.' Sarah's voice is still soft from sleep. Juliet seems so content with herself, so sure in a graceful sort of way.

A distant ringing takes Juliet's attention. 'Is that my phone?' She stands. 'Oh, yes it is. Excuse me.' And she trips across the lawn, crunches over the gravel of her drive, and is gone.

There is a confidence about Juliet that Sarah admires. Not the sort of confidence of someone born to easy circumstances, done well at school, been popular, and got a good job. It is more to do with her being clearly defined, almost as if she had a vision of who she wanted to be and then chose the actions necessary to become that person.

Sarah's thoughts make her quietly snort. People don't really do that sort of thing, do they? Choose who they want to be? Surely it just happens through events that come into your life? You can't just decide to be anyone. There are limitations. Her own limitations, for example, allow her to accept that she is not bright enough to be prime minister. Not that she would want to be anyway. Margaret Thatcher has cut a groove so deep, surely there is no woman who would wish to follow. But then, she considers, sticking to the concept, perhaps weighing up one's limitations makes it easier to see the possibilities.

No, she is thinking nonsense.

Juliet appears again with two glasses. 'You fancy one?' she asks.

'What is it?'

'Pimms.'

'Do you know of all the drinks out there, I don't think I've ever had a Pimms. Thank you.' The glass is cold; the ice cubes rattle.

'So what do you do to make living? Teach English?' Sarah asks.

'Oh no, I couldn't stand that! No, I translate papers for the British Council and I have some private clients.' This time, she sits more comfortably on the other sun lounger, looking back across the gardens. 'I don't often see the houses from this angle. It's pretty, isn't it?' She sips on her drink.

'Beautiful. Did you ever imagine you would live somewhere like this, or ...' Sarah hesitates. She has no idea where Juliet has come from or the life she is used to living.

'Never!' Juliet exclaims in such a sudden heartfelt way that they laugh in unison. 'No, really. I grew up in Bradford. I had never been abroad till my first trip here. Then, like I said, it was years till I came back. But you know what? The advice I got after I divorced Mick was all about where to live and what job I should do. Move there and do this job, move here and do that job. They all involved working in an office and living in a flat because that was all I had enough skills for and all I could afford.'

'Well, yes, but what else can anyone do?' Sarah says.

'That's what I thought, but then I realised the only limitations were those I believed in. I could only afford a flat if I lived in that area, but if you are willing to move elsewhere, there are no limitations as to what you can afford. A square meter in London could be a *strema* of land out here. Same with the work. If I wanted a guaranteed wage, then an office was my only choice, but if I was willing to accept a slightly less pre-determined lifestyle, then so much more opened up to me.'

'Very brave,' Sarah states.

'Or stupid.' Juliet raises her drink to Sarah and the glasses chink. '*Yia mas*.'

'*Yia mas*. Is that like cheers?' Sarah asks.

'It means "to our health."' Juliet smiles, her eyes lighting up. 'What do you do back in Blighty?' she asks with a bit of a giggle.

Sarah swallows, quickly. She hates this question. Over the years, she has come up with a slick response that does not leave her feeling too belittled. 'Well, I see Laurence and me as a two-man team. He goes out and flies planes and I am ground control. I keep everything on the ground under control. It's a fairly big house and the garden's rather extensive, so there is a fair amount to co-ordinate. And then there are the business dinners.'

'Do you entertain much?' Juliet asks.

'Every month or so.' Sarah's voice fades as she realizes how undemanding her life is. Juliet makes no comment.

A swallow dives over the swimming pool.

'I love watching them do that,' Juliet remarks.

'Are they catching flies?'

'No, skimming for a drink. A man came to stay earlier this year, and he had a camera that could slow down the action. It was quite amazing.'

A vision of gulls comes to Sarah, back in Ireland, lying on the top of the cliffs of Moher. The updraft from the sea allowing the gulls to spread their wings and just hover, moving neither up nor down, backwards nor forwards, just remaining at eye level as she and Torin lay there. She felt she could reach out and touch them, they were so close. To see a bird in flight at such close range, alongside them, was surreal.

Another swallow swoops.

'That one missed. It will circle round and come back,' Juliet says.

They watch its flight, its dive, and this time it drinks, trailing a wake across the pool.

'I wonder how they learn. Have any ever fallen in?' Sarah giggles. Her Pimms is gone.

'Never seen them miss. No, I imagine they err on the side of caution. But flying for them must be like walking for us. It won't be tricky.'

'No, I suppose not.'

There is the sound of a car coming up the lane and a green Saab pulls into the parking area in front of the cottage. It is not their hire car, so it can't be Laurence.

'You've got visitors,' Juliet says and stands, picking up Sarah's glass.

'Nice to talk to you,' Sarah replies, and she notices Juliet is barefoot again.

Neville's car isn't green. Perhaps someone is lost. She circumnavigates the pool, crosses the lawn, and steps onto the patio as the car door opens.

'Finn, what a lovely surprise,' she calls, her arms outstretched.

'Mum.' Finn looks terrible.

'Oh my goodness, what's wrong?' The face she knows so well is trying not to crumple. 'Come here, darling.' She tries to engulf his size in her arms; her little baby now so big. He sobs into her shoulder and she lets him cry without a word, just loving him, holding him close. When he gains some composure, she says, 'Let's go inside.' It feels more private in the sitting room. The air conditioning sighs into action.

'Bloody Pru,' he starts.

Sarah holds her tongue. She has been caught with this before; she knows from experience that the boys' enemies of today can be the best friends of tomorrow. Anything negative she says about them in the moment could be held against her later.

'You heard her, right?' he asks.

'I didn't hear the details of the argument, no,' Sarah sidesteps.

'Well best not really, oh but Mum.' He collapses on her shoulder again and shrinks, trying to become a child. Sarah rocks him, making hushing noises.

'I don't believe any argument with Pru has made you feel like this,' she says as softly as she can.

'No, it's Helena.' He is sniffing. Sarah gets up and nips to the kitchen for the paper towel roll.

'Here you go.' She sits next to him.

'She's called the wedding off.'

'No!' It comes out much louder than she intended. Her eyes prick with tears; she grits her teeth to keep composed. There's a sudden flash of the image of Torin's lifeless eyes, the damage irreparable, the loss of her soulmate.

'Helena has some weird logic saying I sided with Pru, which I didn't. I didn't even understand what they were arguing about. After we took some time out to be with each other, we began to disagree and her Dad came in and he saw Helena shouting at me, and he said I'd better go!'

The image is shaken from her head and Sarah restores her focus. No one has died here.

'He probably didn't mean from the house, Finn. Just from the room, maybe?' Sarah entreats.

'Yes, but Helena called after me, "Don't bother coming back. The wedding's off." Oh Mum.' His tears start afresh.

'Now, now, it all sounds like a big misunderstanding,' She holds him close. She hasn't held Joss like this since he was about eight, always the tough guy, but Finn, so sensitive. 'Let her calm down. Her family are around her, she is safe. Stay here tonight, and tomorrow we can go up together or I can call. Whatever you think is best.'

'No, it's over, Mum. It's all over.' Finn blows his nose but his eyes are still streaming.

'I'm sure it's not. It sounds like you both have a case of cold feet to me.'

She never had cold feet with Laurence, so she is guessing. With Laurence, she never really saw the situation as permanent, or even real for that matter. She was young—young enough to feel it didn't matter, the whole thing was a distraction, the agreement with Liz was a laugh and it did solve a lot of immediate problems. Besides, with Torin dead, nothing mattered. Marrying Laurence was a passing thing to be done whilst she decided what she would really do with her life. She felt a little guilty about making such a choice, but Laurence was so keen. The actual wedding just felt like a continuation of the surreal life she had been living.

After the wedding, she began to see how real it all really was. Then she fell pregnant.

'I'll call her,' Sarah says decisively.

'No, no, Mum. Don't.' His eyes focus on her, all watery but alarmed.

'Finn, Helena is the girl you are going to marry. She is feisty and funny and warm and pretty and she can talk your ears off.' Sarah pauses whilst Finn chuckles through his tears. 'You guys are right for each other, and no Pruella de Ville is going to spoil that.' Sarah winces. She says it out loud and cannot take it back.

'What? Pruella de Ville?' Finn is smiling and wiping his eyes, beginning to laugh. 'Mum, that is classic. Wait till I tell Helena.' Then he starts crying again as he realises Helena is not his to tell anything just at the moment.

'No, I didn't mean to say that. Don't you dare tell anyone.' But her arm is around him as more tears fall. 'I know, I'll have a talk to Frona, sort this all out so you two can get on with your wedding and forget about Ms De Ville.' The damage now done, she says it this time to make him smile, but it is a weak smile that doesn't light his eyes.

'But not today, Mum. Don't talk today. I just need some time without her family, on my own a bit.'

'Of course, love. This sofa is a double bed. The whole place is very spacious. Do you want a swim? I could find some of your father's shorts.'

But Finn just shakes his head.

'Talking of whom,' Sarah says as she hears tyres crunching on gravel. 'Do you want to have a lie down and I will fill him in?'

'No it's okay. Thanks, Mum.' He wipes his face clear of tears, straightens his posture, and plasters on a fake smile.

'Hi Dad.'

Chapter 12

Laurence has taken Finn to see some ancient ruins and then into Saros for a coffee. It will do Finn good. Laurence, if he is one on one with the boys, can make them believe that they can do anything. This sometimes got them into trouble at school, but on this occasion, it will be just what Finn needs.

The previous evening was like turning back the clock, with Finn home again and Laurence, as usual, not really joining in the conversation and going to bed early. True to the old days, she and Finn sat up late, but here in this warm country, they had the luxury of lingering by the pool to watch bats taking over from the swallows in the twilight as they swooped over the water for insects, and listening to scuttlings in the dried grass under the fig tree's tangle of trailing branches whilst talking about nothing in particular. It was quite magical and Sarah, feeling perfectly content in the moment, picked up a pebble from the edge of the stone flags surrounding the pool and put it in her pocket, a token of the peace she felt.

This morning, with both husband and son gone, Sarah decides she will go up to Helena's house and have a word with Frona, find out what the problem between Finn and Helena is all about.

Sarah puts on her sunglasses against the sun's glare. The village is busy; the man with his van full of household goods is in the small, sloping square with a brood of women, mostly in black, inspecting and chattering around him. The floppy dog is running around sniffing and avoiding people. Sarah wonders who feeds it. There is an open-backed truck out on the main street piled high with watermelons, with a robust-looking weighing scale hanging from a metal framework that has been welded to the tailgate which, in turn, is welded open with a couple of rusting metal struts. Motorbikes amble past, ridden slowly by ageing farmers. Mopeds spin by noisily, driven by their fearless grandsons. Sarah spots Stella crossing the square and waves and receives a cheerful wave in return.

'*Yia,*' a man says, walking past her.

'*Yia,*' Sarah replies, stretching the word, enjoying the sound. It is the man Stella tapped on the shoulder when they went to the corner shop, but she cannot recall his name.

Once on the road heading to Helena's, she tries to remember where the back way came out. She looks for the gap in the hedge as she passes the houses.

'Damianos.' She recalls the man's name, pleased with her memory and at the same time finds the opening and disappears into the bushes. Village hubbub and traffic noises are hushed by the dense thickets whose enclosure acts as a theatre for the hum of insects. It is another world: private, insular, romantic. The bees hover around the sun-loving flowers, pollen-laden legs dangling, a challenge to aviation. Smaller insects dart with greater intent, and a large black insect the size of her thumb threatens to collide with her as she hastily steps out of its way. Despite the scorching sun, the foliage is still green here. Sarah wonders if the track is a stream in the winter, keeping the ground moist year-round somehow. But it is just a guess. She really has no idea, and the ground is dusty and parched today.

The track opens out into the field of rough grazing land. On her far right, some flaky-painted square boxes are lined against the end of the gorse. She noticed them on returning from Helena's and today, she wants to know what they are. One with its lid ajar reveals neat rows of honeycombs on frames. They are beehives!

She hesitates before deciding to replace the lid. Of the others, one or two are lifeless, but the rest have bees crawling out of the narrow slit at the bottom of the box before spreading wing, hovering for a moment, and buzzing away. The boxes themselves look uncared for; the paint is peeling and some of the corners are coming away. The ground is littered with broken frames and honeycomb pieces and she is amazed any of the bees are still there. After inspecting the hives and the broken ones on the ground a little more, she recalls where she is going and sets a course for the side gate to Helena's house. Climbing the incline, she is aware she is partially keeping one eye open for the shepherd and sure enough, he is there, sitting on a rock under a tree.

'Good morning.' Sarah puffs a little; the gentle slope is still hard work in the sun. The shepherd levers himself off the rock and slides across onto the bare ground, offering Sarah the seat. She sits, feeling a little flushed, and smooths her skirt down several times. She cannot meet his eye immediately. In fact, for a moment, she cannot look at him at all until she takes a deep breath and composes herself. 'Thank you. By the way, what is your name?'

'Nicholas,' he says, but there is no joy in his voice.

'Nicholas? That doesn't sound very Greek-shepherd-like,' Sarah enthuses.

'Nicolaos in Greek.' His voice is flat, his emphasis on the first *o*.

'Hm, it sounds as if today is your day for being sad.'

'I got a letter from my wife.'

'Oh?' Sarah squirms. She doesn't want to know. It seems that everyone is struggling in their relationships. 'Where is she?'

'She was meant to come, but she is still in Australia.'

Sarah waits.

'It was no good. She can be a difficult woman. My family didn't like her.' He speaks as if to dismiss the subject but then adds, 'But we were married, so I stayed.' He picks up a pinch of stone and dust from by his feet and lets it tickle between his fingers back to the ground. 'She wore me away like a rough stone on a string and finally I snapped.' He looks down the field across the valley. 'So before I could do her any harm, I came here—to take a break.' They are the words of a man forcing himself to look at what he would rather ignore.

'How long have you been here?' Sarah gazes around at the goats. He doesn't look like someone on a break.

'Two years,' he replies.

'That's quite a break.' Sarah tries to keep the surprise from her voice. 'And you haven't seen her since?'

‘I won’t go there and she won’t come here. So first thing this morning, I sent her the divorce papers, asking her to sign.’

‘Ouch.’

‘There is no love lost, so I guess it’s for the best, but I feel like I have failed.’ He picks up a pebble and throws it at a goat that is munching too near to him. The herd scatters.

‘Well, it’s bound to hurt.’

‘Why? I do not love her.’

‘Well, maybe the realisation that you do not love her, that you have no love in your life hurts?’

‘Could be.’ He pulls at a grass to chew on. ‘But let us not dwell on this, how is your life today?’

‘Oh, you know, trying to focus on the moment.’ Her hand slips inside her pocket to feel her two pebbles.

‘Life is exactly what it is.’ He looks out at the distant hills. ‘War, peace, your tooth hurts, the ouzo bottle’s empty, you win the lottery. It is what it is at any given moment. Accept that and you are content.’

‘Exactly,’ Sarah agrees. His sadness seems to be receding and it is peaceful to be with him again.

'You know what I do now?' he says, suddenly bright. 'After I come here, back to my homeland, after I feel sorry for myself for a bit?'

Sarah smiles to encourage him to say more.

'I make a decision. Every morning, I decide—what is it that I will do today that will be important to me, that will make my life worthwhile, give it some meaning?'

'And your answer?' Sarah enquires.

He throws his hands in the air and slaps them down, one on each knee.

'Every day is different, and some days I decide that I will not do anything important at all—because that is my choice, too. But I have realised, sitting here, day after day with my furry friends,' he pauses to throw another pebble at the herd, 'that,' his words come slowly, 'if a person wastes even an hour of their time, they do not truly understand the value of life.'

Sarah, from their elevated position on the slope, looks down the field, over the rooftops, to the far-away mountains. She would like to put on some solid shoes and walk and walk and walk, across the plain, over the hills, and beyond to see what life would bring. Whatever came her way, it would be more than keeping house and preparing dinner. It would be something to make each hour worth living.

'So.' He yawns and stretches. 'Did you come to see me today or are you on your way somewhere?'

Sarah returns from the distant hills to the pain of Finn.

'Ah yes.' She scrabbles to her feet. 'Bit of an important mission this morning.'

'Well, I wish you luck then.' He stands.

'Thank you.' Sarah is surprised he does not ask what her mission is, but she is also pleased. She does not wish to go into any detail. It is all draining enough as it is. 'See you, then, Nicolaos the shepherd.'

'See you, er, you never told me your name?'

'Sarah,' she calls behind her.

'Beautiful,' he replies before sitting back on his rock and pulling a fresh grass stem.

The side gate to the gardens of the big house is open. It only occurs to Sarah as she reaches it that it might have been locked and she would have had to retrace her steps. She squeezes through and sees one of the dogs, thankfully in the cage, lying on its belly with one eye open. She hadn't thought of them, either.

One or two silk lilies float on the otherwise empty swimming pool, and the emotions of yesterday return. Her heart twists for the young lovers. She circumnavigates the shimmering water and rings the doorbell. The teenager, Jenny, that she saw briefly in passing yesterday opens it almost immediately.

'Oh hi,' she says and opens the door wide to let Sarah in with no further preamble.

'Can I speak to Frona?' Sarah asks.

'She'll be watching telly.' Jenny points vaguely at a door and then leaves through another door. The visitor has been let in. Her part is done.

It doesn't feel right to be opening doors into someone's private inner sanctum, so Sarah watches the lilies drift around on the pool for a while, hoping someone will come, but nobody does. Tapping and pushing open the door that was indicated, she finds herself in a white corridor with no windows, floor lighting, and modern art on the walls. The first door is ajar, and in the room is a large desk surrounded by chairs, the space too large for an office, too industrial for a dining room. The lights are off and it is empty. The next door is shut. Sarah puts her ear to the door; a television drones inside. She knocks and waits but remembers Frona is hard of hearing. She knocks again loudly and pushes the door open.

'Frona?' she asks before she is even in the darkened room.

Frona, patterned in coloured light, sitting on a hard-backed chair between two padded arm chairs, clicks the screen to black when she sees Sarah. 'Oh, Sarah,' she says. Shuffling forward and tipping her weight forward, she slides onto her feet.

'I didn't mean to interrupt you,' Sarah says.

'No my dear, no. It is just television. It has no feelings.' She takes Sarah's hand and pats it as she passes her to leave the room. 'Come,' she says as if she has been expecting her. They head further into the labyrinth, up some steps and through a door into a calm white room with a sofa and a high bed. Books line shelves that have semi-transparent white screens pulled down so the reading matter is visible but the colourful spines make no impact on the serenity of the space. Frona shuffles across the white carpet, adjusts a silver picture frame on top of a perspex table. The patio doors slide open to reveal an enclosed courtyard. An art piece of water pouring over a heap of stones, the water disappearing at the base, leaving the surrounding area dry, adds a central focus. The courtyard is shaded and reasonably cool. Seats of concrete are built into the walls, and these are heaped with cushions. Frona makes a sweep of her hand, inviting Sarah to sit down, and Sarah feels she has been granted an audience with the queen.

Frona takes up a position that the cushions have been indented to expect.

'So,' Frona says, 'how are you?'

'Fine,' Sarah replies. When asked such a question, she always replies 'fine.' No one really wants to know how she is and even she doesn't really want to know how she is, so she is fine. Sleepwalking through life. If someone pushes the point and really asks, 'How are you?' wanting a truthful reply, she says 'Excellent.' To say anything less would reflect badly on Laurence and the life he gives her.

'That's right, "fine,"' Frona answers as if she understands. 'And Finn?'

'They say men should not cry, but he cried like a baby.'

'Helena too.'

'What was it about?'

'No idea. All I know is Helena is stubborn. Early this morning, she makes several phone calls to her friends with astringent happiness in her voice and now she has gone to Athens for the day to shop with her mama at The Mall.'

'Oh.'

'It is all fake and bluffing,' Frona puffs.

'Has she cancelled anything? The church, her friends coming?'

'What would I know? I am Helana's favourite when it suits her. But I do not think she will call it off yet.'

'Yet?' Sarah can hear her heart beat in her ears.

'Yes, you know, she will flaunt her independence a little, sulk a little, and wait. Wait for Finn to come begging. When he does, she will refuse, he will have to prostrate himself, she will toy with him, he will be on the verge of giving up, and she will snatch him back and they will marry.'

'You make it sound like such a game.' Sarah experiments with a little laugh, her shoulders drop and her frown disappears.

'It is a game.'

'Not for Finn it's not.' Her frown returns.

'It is the game of courtship. They are a fine, energetic couple, they come from privileged backgrounds ...' Frona does not pause as Sarah cringes. 'And the drama of their courtship should be as splendid as their lives.'

'You make it sound so harmless, but Finn is heartbroken,' Sarah says.

'Let us give it a day, maybe two. You'll see.' Frona stands, as if indicating the audience is over. 'But you, you are the last person to worry about Finn and Helena.' One of her eyebrows raises and Sarah is not sure if she should read more into what was just said. 'Meanwhile, I don't think you have met Helena's baba yet, have you? Come on, let us track him down. He will be in the gym, no doubt.'

'Jim,' Frona commands over the music. The man running presses a button and the music stops, his treadmill slows. On seeing Sarah, he pulls the towel from around his neck and wipes his brow. 'This is Finn's mama, Sarah.' The man jumps from the machine. Wiping his hand, he shakes Sarah's heartily.

'Well hello, Mrs Quayle.'

'Please call me Sarah.'

'And call me Jim.' He walks over to a water fountain and fills a small paper cup.

'I understand Helena and your wife are in Athens.'

'Yes, shopping therapy and cooling off, I hope. So like her mother—feisty and stubborn. And like her *Yiayia*.' He winks at Frona, who hisses through her teeth and waves his dismissal. 'Finn's a great guy. Is he okay?"

'No. No really, he was so upset.'

'Yes well, he will get to know her and then it all won't seem so traumatic. Her mother did the same to me. I had my heart in my mouth for the first three years of our marriage. Calmed her down having kids. Shall we go upstairs? I'll have some coffee made.'

Whilst the coffee is brewing, Sarah is shown up, by a woman who does not look Greek and speaks no English, to a balcony that overlooks the whole area. Alone with such a view, she takes her time to orientate herself, picking out landmarks in the village, tracing roads out into the country. To her right, she easily spots the tree in the centre of the rough land. The ground is laced with tracks that the goats and sheep have eroded with their eager hooves. The trails converge near the top of the hill into a single ribbon that follow a winding track down the back of the slope.

A shiver runs down Sarah's spine as she spots a low-lying cottage deeply nestled into the hillside. So planted is it in the soil, little of the whitewashed walls are visible and the roof tiles are so mottled, so variegated that even they blend into the surrounding dried earth. Dots of colour suggest pots of flowers dotted here and there at its base. A rougher roof nearby could be the sheep's enclosure. She stiffens. A tiny shape emerges from under the roof tiles. Nicolaos! He carries something under his arm. Specks that Sarah has presumed were dried vegetation run to him and she realizes they are chickens. His free hand dips into whatever he is holding in his crooked arm and then draws an arch in front of him. The hens gather more and more as he sows their food. Sarah watches, feeling slightly guilty at her voyeurism but unable to look away. Finally, he takes the container from under his arm and, turning it upside down, bangs the bottom. She faintly hears the sound: dull, without resonance.

A sharper noise of feet on stairs behind her brings her to attention as Jim joins her, showered and changed. The coffee is brought up and Frona follows with a plate of cakes.

'I made these this morning.' She offers one to Jim, who accepts, takes a bite, and leaves it on his plate. Sarah tries to do the same, but it is too delicious and soon, it is all gone.

Jim talks about his life in Australia and America. Sarah wonders if the area has some connection with Australia, as Nicolaos the shepherd is from there too, but she does not mention it. As if reading her thoughts, Jim tells her there are more Greeks in Oz than in Greece itself and laughs. They pass a pleasant half hour before Sarah says she must get back and at this point, Jim asks where her husband is and why he did not come.

'He's taken Finn to some ancient monuments and for coffee, but I am sure you will meet him soon.'

'Well, I look forward to it,' Jim says. 'He's a pilot, isn't he?' Sarah nods. 'Best get him on our books then, get him flying one of our jets.' He chuckles.

Sarah winds her way down the drive, wondering what sort of family Finn has got himself involved in. It all seems too big somehow; the family, the house, the wealth, and Laurence is going to bristle and grow silent if Jim ever makes a joke like that to his face. She can see it now: his cheek muscle twitching, the scorn visible on his face at his career being reduced to being the possible employee of his soon-to-be in-laws. If it gets to that stage, she could even see Laurence warning Finn off the whole thing just to save his own ego.

Why could Finn not just find a quiet Manx girl and have the wedding in Ballasalla church and honeymoon in the Canaries?

But then, she really does not have room to talk. A rush of memories floods her senses.

Chapter 13

Shaking herself from her dark dreams, Sarah rolled so her legs fell off her single bed and she could lurch to standing. A step took her into the tiny sitting room. The sagging sofa remained empty. Torin's worn boots were not tucked neatly under the end; his sheets and thread-worn blankets lay folded on the chair as he had left them. The hollowness started in Sarah's stomach and rose to her throat, tasting of bile. The blood drained from her head, sending her hands flying, gripping the back of a chair to stop her overbalancing. Her legs gave way and, making no struggle to remain standing, she sank to the floor.

Vaguely, she felt bony knees in her back as Liz pushed past her to get out of their bedroom.

'Coffee?' Liz's tone was flat.

Sarah could see no point in answering.

Metal spoon tinkled against ceramic and water was poured.

'Here.' Liz sat on the floor next to her, putting a coffee down by her feet. Sarah stared at it blankly.

'I'm not going in today,' she said.

'Risky,' Liz answered, but with little interest.

'What's the point?' Sarah could feel the tears welling. Surely the crying had to stop sometime? She was drained and wrung dry by all the wailing. No more. She wanted no more. But still the tears came.

Liz got up, and Sarah knew she was going for toilet paper. It was a system they had developed; if one of them started crying first, the other went for tissue. Liz came back with a tea towel.

'We're out of loo roll until we get paid tomorrow.' That meant it had been a month. A month and still the pain tore at her insides like a twisting cramp. She looked up into Liz's blotchy red face, her eyes red-rimmed too, her chin wet. 'Come on, Sarah. Torin would not have given up, and he wouldn't want us to, either,' Liz soothed.

'I can't.' Sarah put her hand out for her coffee, to touch the warmth, but she did not pick it up. Liz stood, was away a few seconds, and sat down again heavily.

'Here.' Liz unscrewed the top from an unopened half bottle.

'Where did you get that? Aren't we out of money?' Sarah enquired with little interest.

'Don't ask,' Liz replied. Sarah knew Liz had resorted to shoplifting, but it was a petty detail in life; she didn't care.

The amber spirit was enough to encourage Sarah to drink; the promise of the intensity of her feelings being numbed enough to get cup to lip. They had drunk a lot of whiskey in the last month.

'Steady.' Liz's hand touched hers and Sarah slowed her drinking.

'I'm still not going in today.' She stated it flatly. Liz topped her mug up with more whiskey.

'Go in half-cut and you'll make it till lunch. We can go to Bar George for lunch. We'll get that lecherous old Jeremy bloke to buy us a liquid lunch, and then it's just a couple of hours till home.'

'Liz, I can't see the point.' Sarah let her voice wail.

'No toilet paper and no whiskey,' Liz stated. 'We lose these jobs and it's back to Country Clare. That wasn't Torin's plan.'

Sarah could hear Liz struggling to hold back her own tears.

The alcohol burnt a warm path down her throat and the tears turned into heaviness. 'We need someone like Jeremy to foot all our bills. Then we wouldn't need to go into that dead-end job.' Sarah took another gulp.

'He fancies you,' said Liz. 'I reckon someone like that would marry you with a little encouragement.' Liz's statement contorted Sarah's face into a grimace, her shoulders slumped forward, her chest sunk into itself and her head dropped forward. She looked at the thin ring on her finger, the tiny stone only just visible, remembering the feel of Torin's fingers as he put it there, that intimate moment. The thought of marrying someone old and lifeless like Jeremy in Torin's stead was ridiculous. A splutter of sad laughter escaped her, dripping coffee down Torin's t-shirt, which she had been sleeping in. The drips ran over the plasticised lettering that spelt *Iron Maiden* and soaked into the design below. She rubbed at them.

'You marry him.' Sarah threw the concept back at Liz.

'Come on. We need to get going.'

Dressing without being aware of her actions and brushing her hair without looking in the mirror, Sarah got ready. Liz made second mugs of coffee and laced them even stronger, and the two of them wobbled from the one-bed flat out into the sea air, leaving the smell of damp behind.

They made it till lunchtime although they did very little work. The paint-peeling back room felt more stifling than usual. The computers seemed slower, the number of envelopes piled high.

'I hate it when they put in several cheques for different accounts. There should be a rule—one envelope for each account they want to pay into,' someone said at one point when the supervisor left the room and the mood dropped to a level that was more in keeping with how Sarah and Liz felt. After that comment, workmates took more cigarette breaks than usual and others lingered around the coffee pot until Mr Kneale came back in and butt ends were hastily stubbed out and coffee mugs were abandoned, everyone settling at their stations, making a pretence at diligence. At the rate they were paid, very little else could be expected of them. The clock hands inched round to lunchtime and Sarah put her headset on the desk.

'Think of it as Monopoly. It's just the first shake of the dice,' Torin had promised. 'All we need to do is to save enough to make a bid for a spot to sell burgers on the TT race week and we are made.' His enthusiasm was infectious. He didn't work beside Liz and Sarah. The job he had was even worse paid, and hot. He fried up in a roadside burger van. But he had done the maths and he reckoned if he hired the van he worked in and was successful in bidding for a stand during race weeks, they would clear three or four grand profit. 'And with that, we go to London.' He had grinned as if London would be all red carpets and easy living.

But now he was gone.

'Come on. Bar George.' Liz pulled at Sarah's sleeve.

Bar George was busy as usual. Lawyers from the courts spilled over the trestle tables, the menu chalked up in big letters on the end wall, the floor-to-ceiling wine rack behind the counter constantly restocked so it never depleted.

'There's Jeremy.' Liz pushed through the crowds.

Sarah had no mood for the old man. The whiskey had worn off but luckily, things did not look quite so bleak as they had this morning when she was torn from her dreams. But she felt fragile and Jeremy, she did not need. Her stomach growled and she watched a bespectacled woman stabbing at potato wedges and dipping them in a small pot of house sauce.

'Ladies, ladies, ladies, what a pleasure. How are you this fine day?' Jeremy shook their hands, squeezing and feeling their upper arms with his left hand, inviting them to sit. They squashed onto the benches and people shifted up, apologising, making room. The trestle tables forced interactions with strangers, and it was how they had met Jeremy. There was never enough space.

'I was just about to eat. Have you lovely ladies eaten?' He leered at them. Sarah could not tolerate his fake jolliness and she stiffened her legs to stand and leave. Liz grabbed the bottom of her coat under the table, and Sarah found she could not rise.

'You know, we've had a hell of a morning. We need food and something a bit stronger, if you know what I mean.' Liz smiled across at him, looking so like Torin, Sarah's eyes stung.

'Well, be my guests, ladies.'

The next day, Liz shook Sarah awake.

'Come on. Money in the bank today,' she said.

'It's Saturday. Leave me to sleep.' Sarah turned her back on Liz, pulling over the duvet.

'Not only money in the bank but free lunch with the hunky Jeremy at his golf club.'

Sarah groaned.

'Look.' Liz sat on the bed. 'Do you really think Torin would lay down and hibernate if something had happened to one of us, or do you think it would have pushed him even harder to go out there and take the biggest bite out of life he could? Life can be over in a flash, Sarah, we know that. So let's live every day to the fullest.'

Sarah could not find any words. To be joyful would be like forgetting him. It was too soon.

'I woke in the night again,' Liz said, stroking Sarah's duvet-padded shoulder. 'I woke and it came all of a rush. Torin lived like he knew he was going to die young. He sucked the meat out of every day, he lived each hour to the fullest, he abhorred people who didn't. So it came to me that to honour Torin, we should live life like we will die tomorrow, squeeze everything we can from every opportunity, live like he did, and then if we die tomorrow, we can meet him in heaven with no shame.'

Sarah stayed silent.

'To stay weeping and hiding under the duvet is everything he hated.'

Sarah uncurled and turned her face to see Liz's and was taken aback at the tears on Liz's cheeks when the words had sounded so positive. 'We can still cry, Sarah, but that does not stop us taking every opportunity and using it to our advantage. Douglas and the Isle of Man were not the end of Torin's rainbow, you know, so they should not be the end of ours.'

The speech was enough to get Sarah up, suitably dressed and made up for lunch at the golf club. They had never been before. It was members only, expensive, an old boy's network where you had to be invited to join if you were a man. Women could join much more easily: a monthly payment was enough.

The taxi dropped them and the driver took a tenth of their weekly wage with a wink. Sarah pulled at the hem of her short tartan skirt.

'Still, if we get lunch for that, it's cheap,' Liz said to Sarah, referring to the money the driver stuffed in his leather pouch, turning the moment to the positive, just as Torin would have.

The foyer of the golf club was intimidating, with modern chandeliers, thick carpets and girls just a few years older than them in waistcoats offering with educated voices to take their jackets. Sarah and Liz opted to keep their coats on and were shown to a bar room to wait for Jeremy, who one girl seemed to know but had not seen yet that day. She checked back at reception and returned to say he was not on the green and could she get them a drink whilst they waited?

'Just water please,' Sarah said. The girl reminded her of the academic kids back in school, the sort of person with whom she had little in common.

'Why water?' Liz whispered.

'Because if Jeremy does not show up, we will be left with the bill, and my guess is the prices will be pretty steep.' She looked at the oil paintings on the wall and the tartan carpet that clashed with her skirt. The place was dark even though it was the middle of the day, with green-shaded brass table lamps glowing in various corners. The only other customers were two serious-looking men in sharp suits quietly chatting in tall-backed armed chairs by a blazing fireplace at the far end of the bar.

They waited forty minutes. Jeremy didn't turn up.

'Come on, let's have one drink and we'll go,' Liz said.

'We can't even afford a taxi back, so I suggest no drink and we get walking.' Sarah stood to leave.

'Excuse me, but may I buy you a drink?' One of the suited men from the high-back chairs appeared beside them. 'My cousin and I were just thinking about a spot of lunch but having tired of each other's company, we wondered if you ladies would rescue us by joining us? Add a little spice to the pot; what do you say?'

Liz need no further persuading, and four gin and tonics were assembled on a tray and taken to the table.

'Laurence this is ... I am sorry, my dear. I didn't catch your name?'

'Liz, Liz Donohue.'

'Liz Donohue,' the man repeated, 'and her friend, er sorry, my dear. Do tell me your name?'

'Sarah Kelly.'

'And Sarah Kelly. Ladies, this is Laurence and I am Neville.' Laurence stood politely and invited them to sit down.

The gin made a fast impact on an empty stomach and Sarah felt her world shift to a surreal plane.

'Just turned nineteen you say? Er Tom, another round please.'

After another gin, they moved to the dining room, Sarah and Liz on unsteady feet.

Neville was doing most of the talking and mostly addressing Sarah. He seemed slightly older than his cousin and his cuff links were gold whereas Laurence's were enamel. Liz mentioned this when the two of them went to the powder room for a quick debriefing before the food arrived.

'Oh look. Individual towels,' Liz squeaked and used two to dry her hands, dropping them in a wicker basket. A woman sat beside a table of perfumes. 'Are these testers?' Liz asked.

'Madam? They are for your use. Which is your scent?' The woman stood quickly to be of assistance.

'That one.' Liz pointed to a purple apple, and the lady handed her the bottle and turned to Sarah, who picked an elegant square bottle, which she regretted as it smelt like old women.

Back at the table, wine had been poured for them and a small plate of food sat at their places.

'We took the liberty of ordering for you,' Neville enthused.

And so the afternoon passed in polite, elegant surroundings with much alcohol. Dinner followed, at a Michelin-starred restaurant in Douglas, and from there they went on to one of the nightclubs that Liz and Sarah knew far better than Neville and Laurence, who looked out of place standing stiffly at the bar in their suits.

Liz and Sarah insisted on being dropped off on the seafront, reluctant to spoil the illusions of fine living by returning to the narrow back street door that led up to their damp apartment.

'Ladies, it has been a pleasure.' Neville's eyes were on Sarah and Liz's eyes were on his cuff links. Opening her coat and pulling her arms back, Liz told him the pleasure had been all hers and as his gaze left Sarah's face and fell on her cleavage he insisted that it had not. Laurence wished them both a good night, and just before he left, he asked Sarah if she could cook.

'Of course she can,' Liz answered, and they went their separate ways.

At home, Liz brought out a full bottle of whiskey from her coat pocket with a 'Ta ra!' and poured out generous measures into unwashed coffee cups. Sarah went to the toilet and looked in the mirror, trying but failing to regain some reality. She swilled her face and returned to the sitting room.

'I have it.' Liz was on her feet, dancing to no music with her mug in one hand and the bottle in the other. 'I have a plan and it is a very Torin-type plan.'

'What?' Sarah felt disinterested and tired, but the whiskey burned nicely.

'We join the golf club with the pretence of learning to play golf and bag ourselves some rich lawyer husbands. Brilliant or what?' She spun around, still in her coat, which flew out like a cape behind her.

'Lawyer husbands?' Sarah asked. The whiskey was doing the job like no other alcohol could.

'Yes! No more dead-end jobs, no more cheap clothes. No more empty whiskey bottles.' Liz waved the full bottle by its neck. Sarah looked down at her clothes, which had felt cheap and ugly at the golf club. 'Come on, what would you do with a regular, good income?' Liz asked. Sarah shrugged but Liz was excited and they—or rather, Liz—talked through the night. Several times, she pointed out to Sarah that she was unlikely to find another love like Torin so she may as well marry for stability and comfort, and what else was she planning to do with her life anyway? Each time Liz said it, an emptiness grew inside Sarah, replacing the pain and distancing her from reality.

Dawn broke, they left the flat and walked as far as the gate on the ferry spit to see the sunrise. They were both unintelligible in their drunkenness and they shrunk from the piercing light as the sun lifted from the sea.

‘So it’s a deal then?’ Liz slurred, her face turned away from the new day.

Sarah nodded.

‘So in memory of the life of Torin Donohue, we make a pact that we will join the golf club and bag ourselves rich husbands. Shake.’ Liz thrust her hand out to Sarah. ‘So every minute of our lives will be in Torin’s memory,’ Liz rephrased, and Sarah shook.

Chapter 14

Sarah surfaces from her thoughts. She is not sure why she is returning from Helena's house by the road rather than through the side gate and across the rough ground, but, seeing as she has forgotten to put on her watch, it is probably for the best if she goes straight back to prepare something for lunch. Finn and Laurence might return hungry. On the other hand, they might grab a bite whilst they are out. She should have brought her phone.

At the entrance to her lane, she pauses. The bread is nearly gone, the feta definitely is. What will she give them for lunch if they don't eat out? Laurence will not be having reciprocal thoughts. What must it be like not to have these thoughts about food two or three times a day? To be like him, to never think about food because someone else does? It must be so liberating.

Leaving the turning behind, she continues on, heading for the corner shop.

'Hello.' The *h* is guttural.

'*Yia Marina*.' Sarah tries to add a Greek accent and, thinking she has been successful, she wonders if a tourist would mistake her for a local.

'Ti theleis?' Marina says and Sarah loses all illusions and stammers.

'Bread.' She points to the corner of the shop where an area has been sectioned off and lined with shelves for the bread and eggs.

'Ah, psomi.' Marina picks up a big loaf and mimes cutting it in half, but Sarah shakes her head; if the boys are hungry, they will eat the lot. She goes outside to the fridges, hoping to find ideas about what to serve them. Terra cotta pots are stacked on the bottom shelf. The content is white and solidified. Taking one, she tries to read the label pasted on the cling film covering, but it makes no sense—some of the letters are not even characters that she knows.

'What's this?' she asks Marina back inside.

'Yiaourti,' is the reply. Marina mimes eating. 'Good, good,' she says.

It looks like yoghurt and the name sounds like yoghurt, so maybe it is yoghurt.

'Baaa, baaa,' Marina says and laughs and Sarah realises it must be sheep's yoghurt. Fresh bread, sheep's yoghurt, and olives. Sounds good. She adds a bottle of wine. Marina bags it all up take the note proffered and hands her the change and says *'Ade ya,'* as Sarah leaves. Sarah tries to memorise these words and as she crosses the road, she repeats them in her head. Passing the empty tables and chairs, she is only dimly aware of the chatter coming from inside of the kafenio.

'Deep in thought?' She recognises Nicolaos' voice and looks around. He is sitting on one of the benches at the edge of the square in the deepest shade of the palm tree.

'*Yia,*' she says smoothly.

'How did your mission go?'

It doesn't cross her mind to sit with him—it feels too exposed there in the square—but she steps into the shade and puts her bag down.

'Who knows?' is all she can think to reply. Nicolaos shrugs. For a moment, there are no words. Sarah transfers her weight to her other foot and looks at her bag, thinking to pick it up again and go home.

'Great men are forged in fire, and lesser men light the fire.'

'What does that mean?' Sarah looks from her bag to Nicolaos, who is grinning, his upper body bouncing with a silent laugh.

'No idea.' The merriment breaks from him in a one-sound explosion. 'Read it somewhere and thought it sounded good. Thought if I say it enough, it will fit somewhere, some time.'

'Oh.' She would like to add 'you prat,' in a teasing way but doesn't feel she really knows him well enough. 'At least you are merrier today.'

'I have accepted the reality of how things are with my wife, I guess, now the papers have gone.'

'Oh my, are you okay?' Sarah is not sure what to say. 'That must feel, well I am not sure. How does it feel?'

'Final, I guess.'

'Well, it is, isn't it?'

'Yup.' He rubs his hands down his thighs to his knees and back. 'So now the rest of my life begins, as they say.' The words sound convincing, but he does not maintain eye contact.

'And what will that hold?' She is not sure it is a good question to ask. What if he has no plans, no future, just a big gaping empty nothingness to look forward to?

'A boat.' He stands and re-arranges his rolled-up sleeves. Sarah picks up her bag and they walk.

'A boat?'

'Yes, I have always dreamed of building a boat. Ever since I was a boy, and all the time I was in Australia, my dream has been that one day I would build a boat. That is my dream.'

Sarah tries to think what her dreams are, but she knows she has none.

'How lovely to have such a dream.' All she can think is that she enjoys being in nature. Maybe that will take form one day and become something important.

'Dreams are vital,' he says with urgency. 'We need our dreams and a chance of them coming true to give us a reason to get up in the morning. Something to strive for.'

Torin gave her reason to get up in the morning, and then Liz and her pushing got her up until Laurence and the boys took over, but imagine getting up with energy for the day because you want to fulfil a dream, that must be exciting.

'When does fate take over our dreams do you think, and time corrupt our plans?' The words glide out. She is not sure she even meant to say them. 'Maybe it is too late for dreams,' she concludes.

'Why is it too late for dreams?' Nicolaos takes a string of beads from his pocket, holds some in the palm of his hand, and flips the rest back and forth over two fingers. 'Who says there is a time limit?'

Sarah looks across at him. He laughs as he says these things, but to her, what he says is no joke. The thought of there being no time limit, the thought that dreams are still possible is almost as scary as the thought that they are not. Her pace slows as they near the end of her lane.

'Some of the things you say really stir the pot, you know.' She laughs, but there is tension in her throat.

'For the solution to everything, you just have to ask yourself one question.'

'And what's that?' Sarah waits for the punchline.

'Ask yourself "What's real?"' He pockets his beads.

Sarah had prepared to smile at his answer and so she does, but the answer gives her no joy. She is not really sure what he means.

'Well, I have to prepare lunch, and that's very real so ...' She would rather take a walk with him, spend longer talking, let time drift. He makes her feel like all problems are solvable. But she has her duties and so, trying to impress him, she recalls the words she just learnt from Marina at the corner shop and says, '*Ade ya.*'

Her eyebrows lift and his eyes shine. '*Ade ya,*' he replies, and he moves away in a slow gait like he has not a care in the world.

'What's real.' She turns off the small sloping square to the dusty lane. 'The sun's real. The heat's real.' She looks at the sky. 'The blue skies are real. But then, in England it's grey, so that's not always true and at sunset here, it burns orange red, so it is definitely not true. So what is real?' Juliet's cat comes running down the track towards her. It bumps its head against her legs. 'You're real, aren't you, you little tiger?'

The car is not there, so they will almost definitely be grabbing a bite out. She could have gone for a walk with Nicolaos after all, but he will be gone by now and she would never dream of running after him. There are two missed calls on her phone; one from Laurence and one from Finn, no messages. Slipping into her bikini, she takes the shopping bag to the pool side and with guilt and pleasure and no plate, she tears off hunks of bread from the loaf and uses them to scoop up yoghurt.

'Not happy with my life.' She looks around her as she speaks. The words sound loud and hard. The darkness, the weight, the undefined sadness shifts inside her, making itself known, and she puts down the yoghurt and bread, her hunger lost. 'That's real,' she whispers.

Sitting on the lounger, she stares but sees nothing. The pool is a glass sheet of blue, the water seeping down the drainage grills in the flags around its edge. Her focus lands on an ant carrying a twig as it negotiates its way around the wet edge. It must be like a raging river to something so small and yet to her, it appears flat and still. The ant stops, puts down its twig, and remains motionless.

That's how she feels, like she is at the edge of a possible storm, a great raging river, but fear of the risks it might contain keeps her motionless on the edge, trapped in her unhappiness.

But what's on the other side anyway? Maybe she could cross it just to find more of the same, the same pointless existence, the same absence of dreams. The risk of uncertainty, the prison of who she is. But does it also hint at opportunity?

She takes a breath. What is her starting point, what is real right now? Her mother's house, that is real. The income it brings her, that is real. It's not much, but it is real and it's hers. What else? She reaches for the bread as she thinks. A noise from the lane tells her Laurence and Finn are back and she releases her grip on the bread. Putting everything back in the bag, she wraps a sarong around her and stands to take the food indoors to greet them.

'Mum, don't you think that Pru needs to apologise to Helena?'

'Hello Finn.'

'Hello, but don't you?' He kisses her cheek.

'Finn, you sound like a teenager. Hello Joss. I didn't know you were coming; is Pru here?'

'Hi, no.' There are no hugs or kisses from Joss.

'Have you had lunch?' Laurence asks. There is no hug or kiss from him either.

'Yes, you?' Sarah says and Laurence nods, goes inside, and reappears at the door with a jar of coffee.

'You want one?' he asks. She nods. 'Boys, you want coffee?' she asks. They both nod, almost in unison, and Sarah is reminded of when they were little boys being asked if they wanted squash. They sit with her at the table on the patio.

'Oh it is lovely to have you both here.' Sarah takes their hands, one in each of hers.

'Mum, I have tried to explain to Joss that Pru needs to apologise to Helena.' Finn retracts his hand. Joss looks old for his twenty-eight years, and rather bored. His boneless hand sits limply in her palm. She releases him.

'Oh Finn, I know you are upset by what has happened, but you are here now and I don't get to see you both at the same time very often, or even ever these days, so can we not let the argument just smooth over and enjoy being together just for now?'

'Mum, are you not aware of what is going on? Helena has called off the wedding.'

'Yes, yes, I know, but I don't think picking over an argument is going to smooth everything out. It will just start more arguments. Just let it be. I trust that you are not going to hold this as a grudge, either of you, because if you are, that is not the way I raised you.' Sarah puts her hand up as a visor; her chair sits in an area unshaded by vines.

'But Helena has called the wedding off. Someone needs to do something and seeing as it was started by Pru, then Pru should put it right,' Finn implores.

A part of Sarah cannot deny that she is just a little relieved that Finn can now see Pru the way she does, but she quickly recognises this as a petty response and pushes the thought away and focuses on the needs of the boys.

Laurence reappears and puts mugs of coffee in front of everyone before sitting, putting the newspaper on his seat onto his knee.

'Look Finn, I think Helena just has a case of cold feet. Just woo her a little, make her feel safe, and all this will blow over.' She would like to add,

'Besides there is no way Pru will ever apologise. It is just not in her nature,' but suppresses the urge as it will do no good.

'Yes, cold feet. You should have seen your Mother back in the day. She had such a serious case of cold feet, I thought she was going to call the whole thing off,' Laurence interrupts.

Sarah quickly shuts her mouth, which has fallen open. Did he really think she had cold feet? The heat rises up her neck with the memory. She struggled the week before their wedding; it felt so wrong, like she was pulling a confidence trick, taking Laurence for a sucker. It was not cold feet so much as guilt and her sense of right and wrong. Liz kept on at her, repeating the pledge they had made, telling her it was a promise. Her whole life seemed so unreal, as if she might wake up at any moment and be back in Country Clare in the pub with Torin, no longer living the life of champagne and weekend breaks to far-flung places that was their norm back then. The wedding day was so vivid, it could have been yesterday. She refused to put on the dress, the dress that would have cost more than six months' pay if she had bought it herself, the shoes slightly less. None of her family were invited. Liz hissed at her to seize the day until she finally made her reluctant walk down the aisle, lying to God and herself, condemning herself to a marriage in which she felt no love, not even much liking. Not from her side anyway.

No, it wasn't cold feet, it was not like Helena. Poor Finn; he sounds distraught.

'Look, Finn, let's be realistic. Helena is not going to change the course of her marriage and her future based on a comment by someone else. People just don't work that way.' She pauses. 'I think you boys must decide what is real. Helena loves you, and that is real, Finn. Joss is your brother, that, too, is real. Joss and you have all your lives ahead of you and it will be better to have a brother by your side than not. So any argument between Helena and Pru needs to be smoothed over so you can continue to be brothers and not be dictated to by ...' She nearly says 'by the women' but quickly corrects herself and finishes 'by anyone.'

She has the attention of them both, so she adds, 'Great men are forged in fire and lesser men light the fire.' She waits to see their reactions, and they both nod wisely. Laurence even looks up from the paper he was surreptitiously reading, folded on his knee.

Chapter 15

The pool brings a harmony of sorts to her sons, with Finn bombing Joss and Joss responding with his rarely seen childish side and splashing back. Laurence, who had stayed inside on his laptop, comes out, blinking in the sun.

'Who fancies an evening on a yacht?' he asks, his laptop balanced on one arm.

'You boys have not been sailing together since, since when?' Sarah pauses, her hand rubbing her head. 'Before Joss left home.'

'We were lucky living on the Isle of Man, sea all around us. The nearest bit of water now is the Thames estuary,' Finn says. 'You still a member of the yachting club, Dad? Come to that, I take it you still have the dinghy?'

'In the end garage. Haven't been out on it for years.' Laurence glances at Sarah. Sarah tried but never found her sea legs and although the idea appeals, the reality of being on something that is rocking and bobbing about does not suit her. The boys pull themselves from the pool and Sarah throws towels to them as if they are children.

'I don't suppose we will actually get to sail her. It is an evening trip along the coast from Saros to the next town, but at least we will be on the water, dine where we dock, and return late. What do you think?'

Sarah feels the dark weight in her stomach turn and tries to ignore it as she flings on her sarong. Why shouldn't the boys go out with Laurence, doing something they enjoy?

'Will you come, Mum, just this once?' Finn asks.

She shakes her head. 'I'll come to Saros with you, but then I think I'll look around the shops.'

'If you dine out, you could hang around to give me and Finn a lift back?' Laurence asks.

'I'll give you a lift back, Laurence,' Joss says. Sarah wishes he would call him Dad.

'Is it okay if I stay again tonight, Mum?' Finn asks, a sad edge returning to his voice.

'Of course; you don't need to ask. Don't worry, Joss, I'll hang around, find somewhere nice to have dinner and a café for a sweet. How many hours is the trip, Laurence?'

He peers at the computer, trying to put it in the shade of his body so the screen does not reflect.

'It's only three hours, one there, one back, and an hour to eat.'

'Yes, you should go.' Sarah finds her benevolent self. She can easily spend three hours just looking around the shops. There is also an old mosque that she might be able to visit, and there is the castle. The idea begins to appeal.

'I'll get dressed.'

She waves the boat off, pleased to see the three of them looking happy. There are five other people taking the trip as well and they move cautiously, as if they have never been on a boat before. A couple stand at the prow, lost in the romance of it all. The skipper is unhitching ropes and organising life jackets. The last mooring line is freed, and they motor away from the pier. Presently, the sail unfurls, flapping wilfully in the light breeze then pulling taut, filling with the wind and causing the craft to lean. Sarah knows that they are all happy and Finn will have a break from thinking about Helena and Joss about Pru. If he ever does think about Pru. She turns on her heel and decides to start with the shops in the main square. The establishments on the water's edge are all restaurants and bars. There is an open area, almost a square, facing the jetty. Here, the outside eateries sport linen tablecloths, candles, and waiters in well-fitting waistcoats and bow ties. The napkins are folded into fans and the place looks so civilised. It is much calmer than the bustle further down the harbour, where the cliental seem younger and the music louder.

'Hey Sarah.' Liz doesn't sound in the least bit surprised to see her. She is sitting at one of the tables, a waiter behind her ready to serve, two bottles of wine on the table and one glass.

'Liz? Where's Neville?'

'To hell with Neville,' she slurs, her Irish accent strong.

'Liz!' Sarah looks at the waiter, whose eyes are glazed with boredom.

'Come on. Come and sit down.' Liz pulls a chair and it leans over backwards. The waiter leaps into action to save the chair from falling. He rights it and offers the seat to Sarah.

'What's going on?' Sarah hisses, one eye on the dark green wine bottles, trying to work out how full or empty they are, how much Liz has drunk.

'He called her.'

'Who called who?' Sarah asks.

'He called his ex-wife.'

'Oh.' Sarah stops looking at the bottles and looks into Liz's eyes. The agreement that they do not talk about each other's husbands seems to have dissolved. Nevertheless, she is not sure she even wants to ask this next question but does anyway. 'To say what?' She puts her hand up to ask the waiter for a glass, but he has pre-empted her. A glass is brought and filled for her.

'She's to move in, take over his mother's rooms.'

'Oh Liz, I am so sorry. Is it really definite?'

'Neville said he could not do it to his children. "To leave her unattended is to leave her to die alone."' Liz mimics Neville's slow enunciation. '"What sort of man would that make me in my children's eyes?"' She completes her quote.

'What sort of man would expect his second wife to look after his first?' Sarah asks. 'What would he do if you threaten to leave him?'

'Huh?' Liz says and then hiccups and smiles at her own behaviour. 'I have not had your luck Sarah. I was left no house. I get no monthly rent. If I left him, how would I make a living now?'

'If you divorced him, you would get a settlement.' Sarah is aware the meagre rent she gets from her mum's house in Ireland would be nowhere near enough to pay the rent on a place on the Isle of Man or in the UK, let alone allow her to live to a civilised degree.

'He wanted to—you know—make me sign a pre-natural.' She makes hard work of the word. 'Pre-nuptial thingy. But I wouldn't. You remember that time we went to Egypt, went to the Valley of the Kings, that long drive to Luxor?'

'Yes, I remember.' Sarah recalls the air was so hot, the ceiling fan in the hotel made no difference at all. She lay on the bed looking up at it, unable to move with the heat.

'That was when he took out the pre-neptune thing.'

'What, on that holiday? He took it with him?'

'Um hum.' Liz nods. 'But I said if he loved me and trusted me, why would he need it? He said it was to show I loved him. But I said no, all or nothing. Do you know,' she raises a finger to emphasise her words but it sways around Sarah's face to such a degree, Sarah worries for her eyes and puts her own hand over it, pulling it down to their laps. 'That was why we didn't get married in the same year as you and Laurence, why he waited two more years. He thought I would give in and sign it, but I didn't.' She taps her nose.

What she is hearing does not altogether surprise Sarah. Neville is shrewd, always has been, a bit tight even, but what does amaze her is that Liz did not tell her this, that she kept the pain of it all to herself. How much else has she suffered in silence? She has never said much about nursing his mother; instead made it seem like it was a small but irritating job, but surely there was more to it than she let on. Sarah suddenly feels out of the loop of Liz's emotions.

'What are you going to do? Are you going to leave him?' Sarah's hand goes to her stomach, calming the knot, her other onto Liz's knee, stroking, reassuring.

'No.' It is almost a wail. The waiter breaks from his stare and takes a step forward to see if everything is okay. Sarah waves him back.

'Shh Liz, shh, it's okay. Look, we can sort this out.' But Sarah doesn't feel half as confident as she sounds.

Liz calms herself before she speaks again. 'You remember back at the golf club, the day after the night club?' Sarah nods. 'I didn't tell you this but halfway through lunch, when I got up to go to the loo, so did Laurence.' Sarah watches Liz's mouth as it moves. 'He stopped me on the way there, did he ever tell you? Stopped me to say that Neville really liked me and that although he liked me too, he would never get in Neville's way and that I should give him all my attention.' It sounds sad the way she tells it, as if she is trying to build up her own ego. Laurence has told Sarah this, but the version she heard was that he found Liz too strong, with her low-cut tops and her red hair. Laurence's version, told in bed one night before the honeymoon period waned, was that he didn't fancy Liz, so he steered her to Neville to 'clear the way' as he put it, to her. Now she is not sure which version is the truth.

Probably neither.

'Neville wanted me,' Liz concludes, far too loudly.

'Where is Neville?' Sarah asks. Liz would be best off home in bed with a coffee.

'I left him at home.'

'Has he called you?'

'I switched off my phone.'

The waiters are moving about around them. Liz's voice is carrying over the whole square.

'Can I have the bill please?' Sarah asks.

'What, are you going?' Liz murmurs.

'No, we are going.' Sarah stands and pulls Liz to her feet. Staggering a little, Liz upturns her bag onto the table and plucks out a handful of notes, which she thrusts at the waiter. He counts them out and lets a few drop back onto the pile of stuff Liz has released by her dramatic gesture. Sarah puts the mess back into Liz's bag before pulling Liz out from under the umbrella shades.

'Where are we going?' Liz asks.

'For a walk.' Sarah keeps hold of Liz's sleeve.

The sun is beginning to set. The sea reflects the orange and pinks in the sky; the hills on the other side of the bay have turned an inky blue.

Liz teeters near the harbour's edge. Sarah pulls her back and links arms with her, putting her on the inside for safety.

'When did you last eat?' Sarah asks.

'Neville made me some drop scones when I got up.'

'What time was that?'

'About three.'

Sarah does not want to know if that is the time she normally gets up, but she is getting the impression it is. How can she expect reasonable behaviour from Neville if she does not behave reasonably herself? Liz hiccups. But then, maybe Liz's behaviour is a response to Neville's misplaced concern, putting other people before his wife. However, with this stalemate before they got married over a prenuptial agreement, it seems the whole situation has been brewing for a very long time. Neville will not be quick to divorce her if it means he will lose half his wealth.

'I think a walk to the end of the harbour and back and then we go and eat something, okay?' It's not really a question. Her phone beeps. Sarah drops Liz's arm to retrieve it, but she is too late and it clicks off. She does not recognise the number. 'You okay if I return this call? I have no idea who it is.' Sarah asks. Liz nods and turns away to look over a makeshift table covered with a velvet cloth on which twisted silver wire jewellery is displayed. The girl minding the display eagerly watches as she plays with the ring through her lip with her tongue.

'Hello, I missed a call just now from this number.'

'Oh, hi Sarah, it's Helena. I must have sat on my phone by mistake.' Sarah breaks into a smile, delighted to be in contact even if it was a mistake.

'Hi Helena, are you okay?'

'Fine. A little surprised not to hear from Finn.'

'Oh, no, he is desperate to call you, but he didn't know if you would want to hear from him. He was so upset, and I have been trying to keep his mind off everything. He spent the day with Joss and tonight, he has gone sailing with Laurence.'

'Oh, he's not too upset then?'

'No, that's my point. He is so distraught I—we were trying to keep his mind from it all, give him a little breathing space, re-charge his batteries. How are you, Helena?' Sarah fumbles, she can suddenly see how it must seem from Helena's position. He has made no effort to fight for her at all.

'Do you like this?' Liz holds something up. Sarah puts her finger over her other ear and turns away.

'Helena, Finn is heartbroken, he believes you will not marry him and the whole thing has been called off. He is distraught. He believes there is nothing he can do to make it better.'

'He can try!' Helena almost snaps.

'Helena, he is a man. He has no idea what to try to do.'

'He should do what he feels is right. In this case, he feels going fishing is right, which says it all.'

'He's not fishing, he's ... never mind. Helena, he desperately wants you back. All he wants is for the wedding to go ahead. He is not happy about what happened with Pru, but he doesn't want that to alter your lives; your future together is more important than anything Pru could say.' Sarah is not sure what to say next, so she waits. When there is no answer, she adds 'Ever.'

'I've got to go now.' And the phone purrs.

'Who was it?' Liz asks, putting her hands behind her new earrings to show them off.

'Helena.' She pauses, wondering whether to ring Finn, or Laurence or Joss, or maybe it would be better to leave it until they are back on land.

'I'm getting hungry now. Shall we go and eat?' Liz says, turning back to the jewellery display.

'Hang on. I just need to text Finn.'

'Call Helena, use any excuse, just make sure you ring her tonight, love Mum xxx.' She presses send and then with an intake of breath types a second message. *'Use any excuse except that I told you to do it. Mum xxx'*

'Do you prefer these?' Liz asks, holding up a second pair in front of the pair already in her ears. Sarah tries to focus, but her thoughts are struggling with the mess everyone seems to be in—everyone including her. Something comes forward in her mind and she almost remembers it, something to do with Finn's wedding and relief from her unhappiness. It's so close to being words, to coming into focus, it just needs a nudge and her path to happiness would be hers for the taking, she feels sure. Just a nudge. It's nearly there, nearly, nearly ...

Liz staggers into Sarah slightly, pushing her off balance, and the memory is gone, like a snuffed candle, leaving a residue of smoke that bears no resemblance to the brightness of the thought that was nearly hers.

'What are you thinking?' Liz asks.

'No idea,' Sarah says. 'Come on, let's get some food.' Maybe the shepherd will be at the taverna, the one with the flower-giving chef.

Chapter 16

The restaurant is full, but the waiter encourages them to linger for five minutes and sure enough, a table becomes free. There is no sign of Nicolaos, inside or out.

Once Sarah and Liz are seated, a second waiter glides to their table. '*Ti thelete? Exoume ...*' The waiter recites what sounds like a Greek nursery rhyme; it has a rhythm and a flow that is hypnotic. At the end, he pauses for breath and Sarah interrupts.

'Er, in English?' Sarah requests.

'Wine?' Liz says.

He doesn't miss a beat, 'Red, white, or rosé? To eat, we have melitzana salad, Greek salad, green salad, beetroot with garlic, tzatsiki, courgette balls ...' The list goes on and Liz's shoulders round and she starts to slump. Sarah keeps one eye on her and tries to think what they had last time. In the end, the waiter makes a suggestion and it is settled, and as he walks away, Liz comes to life.

'You didn't order wine.'

'No. The idea is to sober you up.'

'Why?' Her cheeks rest on her hand, pushing creases of skin under her eye.

Sarah answers with just a look. Liz lifts her face from her hands. 'I can see no reason to stay sober.'

'You are going to have to talk to him. He's just not being reasonable.' Sarah shakes her head. Neville's thinking is beyond her comprehension.

'Anyway, if it all gets too much I have my secret,' Liz slurs.

'What do you mean?' Not knowing if Liz is joking or serious, Sarah flicks through a smile and back to serious.

Liz fishes in her bag to bring out a foundation-smeared makeup bag which she opens and from which she takes out a couple of small bottles of pills.

'What the ...' Sarah is speechless.

'You know. Just in case it is all too much.' Liz gives a drunken snigger and pulls out another two bottles, both with prescription labels.

'What are they? Where did you get them?' Sarah tries to keep the harshness from her voice, but she is shocked and scared.

'They are from Miriam's final days. Those are strong enough to kill a horse if you take too many, and these take all your worries away.' She drops the bottles that she has lifted just a fraction back onto the table and Sarah picks one of them up to inspect the label.

The food arrives and Sarah closes her hand around the bottle and scoops the others back into Liz's makeup bag, embarrassed that the waiter has seen. Liz sits up straight, animated by the sight of food, her fork in hand, ready to try all the dishes.

The waiter puts the last dish down and turns to talk to potential new customers who are looking at a menu.

'Is it really that bad?' Sarah asks Liz in hushed tones, to which Liz just shrugs and stabs at a meatball. 'I mean, would you, really?' Sarah persists.

'Oh I don't know. It just feels kind of comforting to think I could shock him that much.' Liz is beginning to sober up with the food, and Sarah feels a little relief that she recognises her old friend again, back from her drunken haven. But part of her wonders if she knows Liz at all anymore.

'Just to shock him?' Sarah picks up her fork but has not started eating yet. Liz shrugs and flashes a mischievous little grin.

'You are too much sometimes, Liz,' Sarah says and urges Liz to try the peppers stuffed with feta.

'They're amazing,' Liz says, speaking with her mouth full. The mood lifts and they chat about the heat, their accommodations, and other easy subjects. Halfway through the main course, Liz decides she had better text Neville, who immediately rings back. Sarah can hear his slow enunciation even with the phone pressed against Liz's ear.

'I am in Saros looking for you. Where's the car?'

'It's parked by the sea.' Liz looks down at her nearly empty plate.

'Well, do not drive it. Are you drunk? Where are you? I am coming to get you.'

'No, I am fine. I am with Sarah.'

To this, there is a moment's silence.

'You may be fine, but I have been worried sick. Where are you?'

Liz looks up and Sarah can see the trace of a smile on her lips, as if it is a game. Liz pulls her napkin from her knee and reads the taverna's name on it. 'The Ormofo Tavernaki.' Liz speaks slowly and quietly.

'Don't move.' The phone peeps; the line is dead.

Neville is there within ten minutes. He insists on paying the bill and asks Sarah if she wants a lift back.

'I am fine, Neville. I am waiting for Laurence who ...' But that is as much as he listens to.

'Right.' He takes Liz, with his hand around her waist, and propels her off towards the car-park by the sea. Liz is grinning.

Sarah surveys the remains of their food. A hasty, tense meal. Sarah had so been looking forward to her time alone, but there was no joy in it finally. Not that she holds anything against Liz, poor Liz. Poor Liz, poor Finn, poor Helena, poor Joss. 'And poor me,' she whispers to herself as she leaves a tip and walks away from the joyless dinner.

Everyone's concerns seem so big and so complex and so life-changing that Sarah struggles to keep it all in her head. After walking a couple of minutes toward the main square, she makes a conscious decision to not think about anything at all and she is amazed at how easily all thoughts and concerns drift away and she becomes lost in the warm air, the festoons of bougainvillaea that are slung from balcony to balcony, the red-tiled roofs, the urns of flowers on either side of deeply panelled doors, boys on mopeds, and women who pass by, leaving the scent of coconut oil and perfume.

By the time she enters the main square, she has the illusion that she has lived here all her life. It feels real. It feels alive. In a silly way, it feels like home.

She will go to a café and have a sweet. She selects the café under the plane tree which is lit from below, the lights turning the leaves silver green. From a distance, it could be a night painting by Van Gogh. A boy runs around her with a football, his friend chasing him. A couple saunter by, the man in a light suit, the woman in an evening dress and heels so high, Sarah fears for her ankles if she misses a step. The café under the tree is almost full. The waiter greets her in English and leads her to a table for two behind the tree's hollow trunk and leaves her to peruse the menu. Either side of her, lovers sit, holding hands, kissing, laughing, and Sarah's heart yearns, but she does not know for what. She has a husband who loves her, she has two successful boys, she has a beautiful home, she wants for nothing. Except her struggle for breath tells her there is something, something that would change her life from sleepwalking to living.

A dark-skinned man is approaching each table in turn, a cheap flat attaché case open, full of watches. His progress is slow even though no one shows any interest. It is her turn. He begins with a smile.

'Nice watch?' he asks in English and then something in Greek. Sarah glances. Rolexes, Cartiers, Breitlings. They look like the real thing.

'No thank you.' Sarah smiles.

'Pretty lady like you needs to know the time.' He eyes her wrist.

Sarah looks again. Amongst the watches are bracelets, silver snakes with enamel charm beads. 'Ah, the bracelets.' He hitches the case onto a raised knee and, balancing on one foot, tries to unhook the bracelet with the most charms. Sarah is about to say 'No thank you' but her eyes are still on the bracelet with no charms, plain, simple. His nimble fingers swiftly unhook the right one and, snapping the case shut and clamping it between his knees, he holds out the silver snake, offering to put it on Sarah's wrist. It would feel rude to say no and she allows him. It does look nice. As she looks down at it, she notices his shoes, the toe coming away from the sole on one foot, the other with no laces. Embarrassed, she looks up at him and smiles. Now she notices his fraying shirt collar and that he has a missing tooth. His eyes search her face, eager, hopeful.

'How much?' She is a little shocked by his display of poverty.

'To you, lady, it is cheap.' He shows her the price tag. Not even the price of a coffee at her favourite restaurant back home. It's obviously not really silver, but it is pretty. Without quibbling, she fishes in her pockets and pays. He takes the money with a broad grin. 'A watch for your husband?' he persists, at which point a waiter walks past, pausing to see if the man is being a nuisance. The man looks nervous and moves on.

Sarah admires her bracelet. She pinches the hook to keep it closed; the metal feels soft. Still, it is pretty.

Looking up, she sees Stella and her husband heading towards her. What was his name? She shrinks a little into her chair. She does not wish to be unfriendly, but she would just like this time on her own. It may be the only chance she gets to sit here in her own company out in the town. They get closer. Sarah picks up the menu, feigns interest, lifts it a little higher.

'Hello, you need help with the menu? They do have English ones you know.' Stella's voice is so full of life, it lifts away Sarah's reservation with these words.

'Hello Stella, hello ... ' Sarah turns to the man but she still cannot recall his name.

'Mitsos,' Stella bubbles and she takes his arm. The sleeve of his left arm is ironed flat and tucked into his trousers. 'Have you tried the, how you say, balls and honey? It's very good, but that is Greek. They have waffles, too.'

Mitsos speaks quietly in Stella's ear.

'He would like to offer you the balls and honey because it is Greek and you are in Greece,' she interprets.

'Oh how kind. Will you join me?' Sarah puts down the menu and Stella pulls out a chair to sit, pats the one next to her whilst making eye contact with Mitsos. He is clearly a good few years her senior, but they seem so happy.

'You are liking the Greece?' Stella asks.

'Well it has been a bit of an emotional roller coaster so far.'

'Rolla Kosta. What is this?' Thin skin crinkles above her nose, her eyes narrow, and she thinks.

'No. Roller coaster. It is a fairground ride, you get in a ...' She is about to say 'carriage' but thinks this might lead to another explanation, 'seat and it goes along a track like a train, only it goes up and down.' She uses her hands to explain, 'So quickly, sometimes your heart is in your mouth.' She wonders if Stella will understand.

'Ah, like the Crazy Mouse at Allou.' She nods her understanding. She sits up straight. 'Ah, I understand, the emotions you have been having are up and down like the Crazy Mouse ride.'

'Yes,' Sarah agrees and makes a mental note to Google the Crazy Mouse.

'Oh, so you no have fun?'

'Well, in between, I can see Greece is a very beautiful place.'

'Very beautiful.' Stella looks at Mitsos.

'Have you guys been married long?' Sarah asks on a hunch.

Stella turns to Mitsos and speaks in Greek. He smiles as Stella answers, 'Nearly two years now.'

'Ah newlyweds,' Sarah sighs.

'But we know each other for many, many years, only I was in a bad marriage.' The joy drops from Stella's eyes.

'Oh I am sorry.'

'Ha, ha.' Stella laughs. 'It was he who was sorry and Mitsos chased him off.' She wraps an arm around his.

'It seems everyone has a bad relationship somewhere in their lives.' Sarah sighs. Mitsos talks to the waiter.

'If you stay long enough, Greece will heal everything. You just have to be, *pos to lene*.' She talks in Greek, trying to remember a word. '*Ypomoni*. Ah yes, patience. We need patience. Nothing happens quickly but like the Crazy Mouse, the fun is in enjoying the ride.'

Sarah wonders if Nicolaos has enjoyed his ride. Greece did not heal his rift.

'Do you know Nicolaos the shepherd?' Sarah asks.

'The Australian.' Stella smiles.

'Yes, but he's Greek, isn't he?'

'But there is another Nicolaos who has sheep, so he is The Australian who has sheep.'

Sarah cannot fault the logic. A bird lands on the back of an empty chair at the table next to them. She watches it watching them, surveying the table for food. Their 'balls and honey' arrive and reveal themselves to be deep fried dough balls sprinkled with cinnamon and drenched in honey. They are light and crisp and delicious.

'*Loukoumades*,' Stella says, pointing to them with her fork. Three forks, one plate of dessert. Sarah cannot reply, as her mouth is full. She would like to know about Nicolaos but she feels it would be pressing the point to ask twice.

'You have met Nicolaos the Australian?' Stella asks, a laden fork by her mouth.

'Yes, a couple of times when I have been out walking.'

Stella cuts up a honey ball and, stabbing a piece with a fork, lays it, heel end, towards Mitsos to pick up. Sarah watches the bird, now perched on the next table. Stella and Mitsos make eye contact.

'Heart of gold that Nicolaos,' Stella says, breaking her stare and turning back to Sarah. 'He went out to Australia because his wife wanted it, came back from Australia because his wife wanted it. Now I hear she is not to follow, after all that work he has done.'

'Work?' Sarah asks, setting about another honey ball, cutting it with the edge of her fork and trying to scoop some walnut pieces up with it.

'Yes, he came back to get everything ready. The house was shut up for a decade, needed so much work, then he got the sheep together, planted the vegetables, but she did not come. She says she would come in the following year, but now it is the next year and she is not coming. Instead he has rented out the place and he lives in the old shepherd cottage.'

'So Greece did not heal his problems,' Sarah says, hoping she isn't showing too much interest.

'Ha ha. That is where people who know his wife would disagree with you.' She breaks into a gurgle of laughter and Mitsos says something in Greek, to which she replies. For a fleeting moment, a cloud crosses his face, but Stella's laughter continues and his face lightens until he, too, chuckles.

'Is she really that bad?'

'His family will have nothing to do with her. They say she's *dilitirio*, er, how you say, poison. But all these years he has been loyal to her and has not seen his family for her sake. So I hope now he will realise she is gone and be with his family once again. It would be a good thing.'

Sarah scrapes the last of the honey from the plate, hoping she does not appear too rude.

'Kala, den einai?' Mitsos says to her. She looks to Stella.

'He says they are good, aren't they?'

'How do I say yes?'

'*Nai*.'

Sarah turns to Mitsos, '*Nai*.' It falls way short of a conversation so to emphasise it she says it twice more. '*Nai, nai*.' The laughter is in his eyes as he nods in agreement.

'Nicolaos has grown wise with his problems,' Stella continues. 'One time, by the side of the road, he was smiling, looking at his sheep. So I say, "You are happy today," and he says, in Greek,' she pauses. 'Wait I think of it in English—ah yes, he says "The earth asks nothing of me so I ask what can I give to the earth and the earth replies 'Happiness. Be happy and make the world a happier place. So I try." That is what he said.'

Sarah can see Nicolaos sitting watching his sheep, saying this. She wishes him all the happiness in the world. Stella is taking to Mitsos, whose voice is like the hum of bees, warm and quiet. Sarah would love to speak the language, hear what he has to say, find out about his life. He has such kind eyes.

'Mitsos just told me that Nicolaos said something to him once. He ... ' She pats Mitsos's shoulder to show to whom she is referring. ' ...was talking through his thoughts with him as he was wondering whether to take me on a round-the-world cruise.' Sarah raises her eyebrows as Stella says this, but then reins in her preconceptions. Why should they not have enough money to do as they will? She cannot presume everyone is a poor farmer just because it suits her picture of the Greek village. Stella is concentrating as she listens to Mitsos and then translates, 'Nicolaos thought about the idea of a round-the-world trip for a minute and then replied, 'There are two types of dreams: one to realise, the other is to be there only to create hope, a direction, a reason.'

Sarah absorbs the words. How does someone decide which dreams you are meant to realise and which to hold as hope? More fundamentally, how does she create some dream in the first place?

'Ah that only applies if you have dreams.' Sarah tries to make light of her thoughts, but Stella's face becomes serious.

'You have to know what you want. How else can you live your life?' she says. Sarah's mouth tightens; she links her fingers on her lap.

Mitsos speaks to Stella, and Sarah looks away. She would like to be alone again now. She watches the children playing football, using the tourists as obstacles to improve their skills. Women saunter slowly in their fine dresses, a gypsy woman holds a hundred balloons, offering them to children, asking the parents to pay. It is hard to believe it is still warm so late. Looking up, the branches of the tree hang beneath a pink-tinged sky. It is a wonderful country. She is really lucky to be here, to see all this, to meet the people she has met. If she had not come, everything would have stayed the same. Nothing would have changed, and this shift she can sense is happening to her would never have been catalysed.

She looks back to Stella and Mitsos. Lovely people, she decides, and it must show on her face as they smile at her in unison.

But the question remains as to how to make the most of all this. She might feel like something is changing, but until something actually changes, everything is the same.

'Okay, we go now. We are meeting people.' Stella stands. Mitsos is paying the waiter.

'Oh okay. Thank you for the honey balls.' Now they are going, Sarah wants them to stay.

'*Lou-kou-mades*.' Stella breaks down the word.

'*Loo-koo-mar-thez.*' Sarah tries. 'Well, thank you again,' She catches Mitsos's eye. He says something directly to her.

'He says that he thinks Nicolaos was right, but he adds that some dreams are a blessing and a blessing ignored becomes a curse.'

Mitsos says something more. Stella looks horrified before she smiles, her open hand coming down on his chest in a gentle slap.

'He is teasing. He says that I am proof. I am a blessing to him but if he ignores me, I become a curse.' She laughs again and her hair swings and she takes her husband's arm and they wander off toward the seafront.

Sarah watches them go before wiping her mouth well with a serviette, wondering if that was a normal conversation for Greece. To her, it felt a bit bizarre but fascinating to know more about Nicolaos. Yawning, she checks the time. Laurence and the boys will be back soon. She feels too tired to face them—well, Laurence anyway. They will smell of the sea, their skins all fresh, rosy cheeked. Laurence will be puffed up if he has steered the boat or explained to anyone about the sails.

If she goes down to the harbour now, she will see them coming in from afar.

The water is like black glass, the sky now dark. The mountains on the other side of the bay are just visible, black against black, twinkling lights picking out helmets and villages.

A purring of an engine comes from around the headland. There are no sails; there is no wind. She hopes their evening has gone well and that Finn has phoned or at least texted Helena.

The boat pulls in stern first. Sarah catches the rope and loops it over a bollard. She grins at her boys but they are not smiling. The other passengers are, especially the couple and the captain. With a deep breath, Sarah wonders what's happened now.

Finn is first off.

Chapter 17

'Did you have a good time?'

No one answers. Laurence shakes the captain's hand.

They all walk to the car solemnly. Sarah grabs Laurence's wrist. He looks back at her, his eyebrows raised. She yanks at him to slow his pace.

'Now what?' she whispers, releasing him.

'Finn phoned Helena, tried to make it up with her. They seemed to be getting on well, they were even laughing, but then he said something about Pru, so now the boys have had a fight.'

'Oh for goodness sake, everyone is acting like they are kids.' She will corner Finn later, find out how things are with Helena

'The sailing was good, though. The captain was an interesting man, speaks several languages. Last year, apparently, he was held up by a pirate at gunpoint who wanted to sail to Morocco or somewhere. He has a commemorative plaque awarded by the police. A very interesting man.' There is admiration in Laurence's voice. She looks back to take another look at the sailor, who is round-bellied with thinning hair and sturdy legs. The captain looks up and smiles and the most notable feature is his eyes, as if the wisdom of the world lays behind them. She almost wishes she had gone along, too. Maybe he could have made some sense of her life.

'Come on.' Laurence is stepping into the car, impatient.

They drop Joss at his hotel. Finn does not say goodbye to him, and they drive home in silence. The term *dysfunctional family* comes into Sarah's head. She always thought that was reserved for families on low income, or unmarried mothers with hundreds of children, but there is no avoiding that her family is not functioning.

Finn goes to bed on the sofa with a grunt of a goodnight. Laurence is in bed and sleeping by the time Sarah has finished her shower. She looks out of the bedroom window, the fig tree silhouetted against a million stars. If she wasn't too tired, she would go for a walk beneath them, walk and walk until she found her dream.

The next morning, Finn goes out for a walk, taking his phone, and Sarah sits quietly as Laurence looks through his e-mails.

'So was the wind strong enough yesterday?' Sarah ventures. Maybe if she and Laurence functioned, it would be a start. But then, it is not as if they do <u>not</u> function, they just don't have much to say to each other. Sure, they talk about what she is going to prepare for dinner for the days he is home during the week, how the garden is coming on each year, his timetable and destinations for the month, and the boys.

'It was,' there is a long pause as he types, 'alright.'

'Did you have to tack?' Sarah tries to recall some of the sailing terms.

'What?' He glances at her before resuming his typing.

With a sigh, Sarah gets up.

If she walks down the lane, she might meet Finn coming back, find out if everything is alright with Helena. But really, she almost doesn't care any more. Everyone is so stuck in their own bubble. Maybe she will walk up to Liz's, take some wine, start the day as she would like it to carry on.

Down at the lane's end, the floppy dog runs past and back, avoiding being petted. One of the women in black, whom she has seen several times, mostly when the van is there selling its assortment of goods, is walking from one house to another. She waves and calls '*Yia*.'

'*Yia*,' Sarah replies, and some of the weight on her shoulders lifts. Finn turns the corner.

'Are you speaking Greek to the locals?' he asks, smiling.

'Of course, and you are smiling.'

'I am meeting her tomorrow in Saros for a coffee. Away from both families.'

'I am glad it's all blowing over. It'll be fine.' A little weight lifts from her shoulders.

'Well, if I play my cards right. Where are you going anyway?' He cannot stop grinning. It fills Sarah's heart with joy.

'I thought I would go and see Liz. Do you want to come, or shall we do something else?'

'No, you go. I am going to laze by the pool, get a tan for the wedding day.'

'Ah, so it's back on then.' She winks.

'Well she hasn't said as much, but I made her laugh.' All the smile lines around his eyes crease. 'See you later then.' And off he marches, energy in his steps, looking so much younger than he did yesterday.

There is a chance she will meet Nicolaos on the walk up through the olive grove to Liz's. He will probably be sitting there, camouflaged with the goats under the blue-green olive leaves. She wonders how old he is. Laurence is fifteen years older than her, but there is no way he is as old as Laurence. It reminds her Neville will be sixty-six soon; she must remember to get a card. The age difference between Liz and Neville and her and Laurence seemed almost insurmountable even for friendship when they first met, but as the years slipped by, the age gap seemed to get smaller, the difference acceptable. It is the young she increasingly struggles to understand these days. Having said that, there is an edge of comfort in Laurence's advancing years. If nothing else, it makes her feel young.

She turns into the olive grove where the cicadas are rasping loudly, but there is no sign of any goats or their shepherd. The disappointment she feels seems completely inappropriate and she reminds herself that she is married and that Nicolaos has shown only friendship. The rest is in her mind. Before she can ask herself what she means by *the rest*, she shakes her head and decides it is better not to know.

Concentrating on her immediate surroundings, she watches a thin lizard zig-zagging the track, then rustling off into the dried grass. She can smell the heat in the trees, the dryness coming up from the ground. It is an anti-climax that she reaches Liz's drive, leaving nature behind and returning to tarmac. Deflated, Sarah enters Liz's house through the patio.

'Hey Sarah, how nice. Liz is not up yet.' Neville jumps up from his chair in the shade, puts his newspaper on the seat, and opens his arms to greet her.

'You don't mind if I give her a nudge, do you?' Sarah sidesteps him and heads to the open staircase.

'No, sure. Make yourself at home. Have you had breakfast, or do you fancy an early lunch?' Neville sounds just slightly disappointed.

'No I'm fine. Thank you,' she calls down from the upstairs hall.

'Second door on the right,' Neville calls up. 'I'll pop down to the bakery for bread and milk.'

'Okay.' Sarah taps gently and pushes the door open. The curtains are pulled closed but they do not keep the light out, so she draws them and marvels at the views. Neville's hire car pulls out and meanders up the drive to crest the top of the hill before dipping down the other side and out of sight. Down the hill, more than half the village is mapped out before her. She follows the roads from the central kiosk along to the turning that opens into the small, sloping square where the van and his goods usually parks. He is there but only just visible behind a line of palm trees. Then, along from that, there is the roof of their holiday home, and that is Juliet next door, and behind, she can see the top of the fig tree, but the pool is hidden.

She traces the route back to the village square and along the road towards Helena's house. Along, along, and there! In the road, behind his sheep, is Nicolaos, his dogs ranging along the side of the herd.

'Who's that?' Liz mumbles.

'Morning. You want a cuppa? I'll get you a coffee. Neville's gone out for bread.'

The coffee is brewed. Liz stumbles down the stairs in a satin dressing gown, her hair unbrushed, last night's makeup now under her eyes.

'Here you go.' Sarah offers her a mug, which Liz takes to the counter and adds four spoonfuls of sugar.

'What you doing here so early?'

'Charming. Shall I go?'

Liz has only one eye open, which she closes tightly before she blinks them both open. 'I think I drank too much again.'

'It's the "again" that bothers me. What's going on with all this drinking?' Sitting on the balcony, Sarah rests her coffee on a low stool.

'He gets to me these days.' Liz takes her first sip and her face relaxes.

'Who, Neville?'

'Who else?' Liz sighs. 'It seems such a long time ago when we first met them, doesn't it? Then it was them that were so keen; now, the boot's on the other foot. Back then, it was all a bit of a laugh and a route to an easy life. No heartache involved, no jealousy. Well, not for me of him anyway.'

'What happened to our rule of never discussing each other's marriages or husbands?' If they discuss Neville, they may move onto her own marriage and Sarah is not sure she wants to look at that.

'That was before.'

'Before what?'

'Before Neville decided to move his ex-wife in with us.'

'Are you jealous of her?' Sarah's voice raises dramatically, disbelievingly at the end. 'For goodness sake Liz, the woman is the same age as Neville and she has cancer.'

'You think that will stop Neville?'

Sarah can feel the blood draining from her face. All these years when Neville had been manoeuvring for a reason to hug or kiss her, the long, lingering looks behind Liz's back, the accidental touches whenever he moved past her, she had thought it was her, and, due to the nature of their pact, she has never mentioned it to Liz. But as Liz never seemed to care for him much, she has even kidded herself it didn't matter.

'When did all this change?' Sarah puts down her coffee and sits next to Liz, taking her hands.

'Oh I don't know. We have been married nearly twenty-six years now. You grow to love a person; surely you have grown to love Laurence?' Liz is looking over Sarah's shoulder, staring into nothing, and Sarah does not reply. 'But I know he is a player, always has been in his own quiet, gentlemanly way. For a while, it was a game. I played around, he played around, nothing serious, just flirting. Seeing who could shock the other the most. Birds of a feather, me and him. But this with his ex-wife! I think after waiting on his mother hand

and foot all these years, and not having children because the "stress might be too much for her" ...' She mimics Neville. 'Years and years of promises and dreams of places we would go, things we would do when the old bat finally died. I think I deserve just a little bit of faithful.' Liz is shouting and crying.

'Has something happened? I mean, more than saying he is going to take in his ex-wife?' Sarah realises how ridiculous what she has said is, as if there need be any more.

Liz calms her crying and lets her head hang forward. 'No.' The word comes out breathily.

'So what's prompted this? I mean specifically, not that his ex-wife Agnes isn't enough ...'

'Oh it's just the way he looks at the Greek girls, the flirting over paying the bills, the "I'm just a harmless old man" act that allows him to hold their hands longer than is reasonable. But I know what he's really doing, his little cheap thrills. Which makes me what?' The pitch of her voice has risen again. 'It makes me worth less than a cheap little thrill to him.'

Back when they all first got together, Liz had all the power in the relationship. She knew it, and Neville doted on her. They took back-to-back holidays those first two, nearly three years before they got married. Liz jetted around the world whilst Sarah was having Joss and then Finn. Sarah hoped her own travels might come later, when the boys had grown a bit perhaps, but it never happened. Then Neville and Liz's jet-set lifestyle ended abruptly. Four months after they got married, Neville's mother moved in with them and Liz became her full-time carer.

Those holidays gave Liz such surety that she wanted to marry him, perhaps assuming the rest of their lives would be a continuation of the travel.

Sarah puts her arm around Liz.

She can remember deciding to finish her own affair with Laurence when Liz and Neville packed bags for Australia and Laurence's excuse as to why they were not going, too was work, again. Besides, he calmly put his point, he just done two trips to America; he needed a rest from flying. It began a whole host of questions that Sarah put to herself about Laurence all that week when he worked and she sat alone in the bedsit. With no Liz around to persuade her otherwise, she decided to tell Laurence it was over the next time they met. He offered to take her out for her nineteenth birthday, and it seemed an appropriate day to cast him off and get on with her life. She put on the dress he had bought for her the previous week, wanting to look nice for him, which her young mind reasoned might soften the blow. She practiced her speech in the mirror, watered down certain phrases to cause least offence, and felt she was ready. They were to meet at a restaurant, which, as it turned out, was pretty full. Sarah was glad of the background chatter. It would stop her voice from echoing out into an empty space.

The two glasses of wine before they were seated also helped. To tell him over the entrée seemed a bit rushed, so she decided to broach the subject over the dessert. But when the profiteroles came, her words became tangled in her mind and it was natural to decide that the after-dinner brandy would loosen her tongue.

The brandies came and so did the box, long and gilded. Laurence slid it across to her with a card that said *Happy Nineteenth Birthday*. It was not so much the pearls that stopped her words, but rather the effort Laurence had put into the evening. It would have been so callous to fling the box back and say something like, 'Actually this is not working for me.' So she went along with the play and agreed to meet him the next day, resolving to give him back the gift and break it off cleanly.

'You are in love with Neville?' Sarah asks, returning to the present.

'Like a crazy teenager,' Liz sniffs through her tears. 'There's karma for you.' She attempts a laugh.

'But don't you love Laurence after all these years? I mean, just a bit?'

'To be honest, Liz I am not sure what I feel for him. I never think about it, we never talk about *us*. I just live.'

'Well he's not Neville. Does he still buy all your clothes for you?' Liz's giggle is soft, sympathetic. Sarah finds no reply.

The following day Laurence asked her to meet him after work, in the airport foyer. When she arrived, an air hostess said he was running late and she took Sarah through to the staff room. As she walked into the crowded room, the chatter stopped and all eyes turned on her. The sudden attention was too much and she spun on her heels to leave, only to encounter Laurence in the doorway. Before she had time to say a word, he dropped to one knee and held out a small, square box containing the biggest diamond ring she had ever seen. What could she say in front of all those people with all those champagne bottles popping?

She twists the ring on her finger as she breaks her stare, thinking of all decisions Laurence has made from that day till the present. 'You know, I am not sure I have made any decisions since,' Sarah wants to say 'since Torin died,' but she cannot hang her whole life from that point, she has to take responsibility somewhere. She starts her sentence again. 'Actually, I am not sure I have really had the courage to make my own decisions—ever.' It felt overly dramatic, but just in that moment, all she could see was her mum making all her decisions for her till she ran away with Torin. Then Torin made them, then Liz, and now Laurence. Even her boys make all the decisions that affect her. She just goes along to keep the peace.

'I just go along with everyone and keep the peace,' she summarises her thoughts.

'It's why we all love you, Sarah.' Liz sips her coffee.

'It's sleepwalking through life,' Sarah says.

Chapter 18

Neville returns with fresh bread for Liz's breakfast.

'I'd better go.' Sarah stands; it might be a good time to leave Liz to confront Neville. 'Laurence will be wanting his lunch soon.' She makes her excuses.

'See you,' Liz says, lacing her second coffee with *Metaxa*.

Sarah avoids Neville's demonstrative goodbyes and hurries off down the drive and into the shade of the olive trees. Dry twigs snap underfoot; branches catch at her hair.

'Poor Liz.' Her words are a sigh. 'No kids, no holidays, no nothing, and now a breaking heart.'

'Who has a breaking heart?'

Coming to an abrupt halt, she looks around for the source of the voice. 'Oh, you made me jump,' Sarah says. The camouflaged goats rustle in the surrounding bushes and Nicolaos is leaning against a tree. 'How do you decide when to be in this field and when to be in the one over there?' She points in the vague direction of Helena's house.

'I wake up and toss a coin.'

'Do you? Do you really?'

'No.' He pushes off from the tree with his shoulder to lean on his crook instead. 'I just see which I fancy on the day.' He chuckles. 'So who is broken-hearted?'

'Oh, just an unexpected turn of events for someone I know.' Sarah keeps it vague.

'Not you, then?'

'No, I have a loving husband and two boys I adore. I have more than I deserve.' As she speaks, Sarah cannot meet his eye.

'Don't say that. Life might hear you and give you less.' Nicolaos's voice has a serious edge even though he is smiling.

'I don't think life hears anyone.' Now she looks at him.

'Don't you? It seems to me that it listens carefully.' He takes a breath. 'Back in Oz, I had two friends, each running day-fishing businesses. One sat back in his cockpit of his boat and looked up at the blue sky, drank his martini, and said 'I have more than I deserve.' The other friend said, "Wow, look what I've got," took photos of his boat, shared it online, printed fliers, and pinned them around town.

At the end of the year, the guy who thought he had more than he deserved had a big notice on his boat saying it was for sale. Not enough clients to keep him going.'

'Right, and the other guy was doing such a booming trade, he bought his friend's boat and had twice the trade the following year,' Sarah finishes the obvious ending to his story for him.

'Ah so you know them, then?' Nicolaos says dryly and puts one hand in his pocket. Sarah hears the clicking of beads.

'But that is not "life listening." That is the result of one person making an effort and the other not.' Sarah starts to walk again, a pause between each step. The shepherd falls in by her side.

'Really? Is it? I have a friend, and this one is for real, who is a psychotherapist. She said, when she felt the number of clients she had was dropping, that she would begin to take action. The first few times she had to go as far as advertising in two different places to gain more clients but, she said, as time passed, she had to do less and less when the numbers dropped off until finally, all she had to do was think the thoughts, have the intention of doing something, and her phone would start ringing.'

'But surely that is just the experience of becoming established?' Sarah asks.

'Oh is it? You know what we call a "thought" is a connection that goes between a synapse and a neurone. A transfer of energy.' He stops to pull a grass and chews the end a little before continuing. 'Everything is energy, isn't it?' It sounds like a genuine question, but he does not wait for a reply. 'That's what they say. Everything we can see, hear, touch, taste, and smell. Each is made of different wavelengths of energy vibrating at different frequencies. They say our brain picks up these frequencies and interprets them into what we perceive to be our physical reality.' He stops to look around himself, as if putting into practice the words he is speaking. 'Same for the goats, I guess. Their brains interpret a set of vibrations and call it a leaf, a thing to taste and chew. We perceive the things around us as physical or solid, but if we break them down to their smallest particles, they're all just energy.' The track has narrowed and he walks in front, his crook across his shoulders, his arms hung over either end.

'So I reckon every time we think a thought, we send out that thought's specific vibration. If a thought makes us feel good, if it's a positive thought, it is vibrating at a particular frequency. If a thought makes us feel bad, a negative thought, it's vibrating at a different frequency. My guess is positive will attract positive.' He turns to face her, letting go of his crook with one hand so it rests only on one shoulder.

'Like happy, carefree, confident people attract positive things.' He turns to look at the view, chooses a spot, and sits down.

Sarah thinks of Juliet and Stella as she lowers herself carefully onto a flat stone a small distance away from him. She watches a beetle navigating its way across the twig-strewn path, avoiding her feet. She says nothing,waits for him to continue.

'I think,' Nicolaos says after a pause, 'the more focus you give to a thought, the more thoughts of the same wavelength or vibration, whichever you want to call it, will join it and it grows, it becomes stronger, more stable, more able to attract other, equal frequencies. That's why my psychotherapist friend needed to advertise the first time but after a while needed only to think.' He throws a pebble at the feet of a nearby goat. It jumps and frolics away.

'Perhaps the more attention we pay to a subject, the easier it becomes to think about it, and then, of course, we see more evidence in our worlds supporting our thoughts about it. Like if we think the world is a terrible place, we spend a lot of time watching the disasters on the news and reading negative, thrill-seeking papers and spend hours talking to the friends we have chosen because they also think the world is a cesspit, then more stories that support this view will literally find us. If someone is like this, then when they meet someone who thinks the world is a wonderful place, I am sure they will have a choice set of words to describe this annoyingly positive person. Dreamer, delusional, unrealistic optimist. Negative words, because this person will grate on them.'

He stops talking and becomes very still.

Sarah has read versions of what he is saying before, heard lunchtime gurus on daytime television spouting this sort of stuff, but it feels different out here in this sleepy, warm country under the dappled shade of the olive trees. When she is happy back on the Isle of Man, it's true, she attracts positive people. But sometimes her thoughts, of their own accord, become so dark, she ventures nowhere and meets no one. It's not like she has a choice.

'It is a very hopeful doctrine,' she finally says.

'Hope is the life force.' Without looking at his face, she hears his smile as she continues to gaze at the view. 'Without hope, we would be dead.'

'Very dramatic,' Sarah scoffs.

The goats munch. A car in the distance grates its gears.

'When I still lived with my wife, she had her room and I had mine.' Nicolaos speaks quietly, as if not wanting to break the peace that has settled over them. Sarah looks up at the sky through the olive branches: endless blue. How lovely to be able to feel assured that every day will be endless blue. Nicolaos clears his throat. 'I would hear laughter through the walls as she spoke on the phone to her friends. It grew lonely, so I started watching a lot of television with headphones on. Have you ever done that?'

Sarah shakes her head, she is not that keen on television.

'With the sound going straight into your head, you are sucked into the unreal world completely.' He looks at his feet and pushes a stone with his heel so he can stretch his leg out. 'I watched cops and robbers, gangsters, thrill-seeking stuff. Grim stuff because my thoughts were grim, I thought I would never be happy again. But I would get cross at the characters getting into the cars with a gun against their heads or not fighting to stop themselves going into a room where they know the person who wants to kill them sits or walking calmly in front of the firing squad, you know the sort of thing. At that point in these films, I would call it unrealistic and change channels. But then it came to me—as long as the trigger of the gun against his head was not being pulled, there was hope; as long as they were walking into the room and not being carried in as a corpse, there was hope. As long as the soldiers had the butts of their rifles on the floor and not with the barrels pointed at their heads, the people in the firing line had hope. Hope that they would be rescued, hope that their adversaries would change their minds, hope that they had misinterpreted the situation and that their lives were not threatened at all. It all boils down to hope. People continue on, even doing what their enemy asks of them, as long as they have hope. So that is why I say without hope we are dead.'

'Did it help?' Sarah says. 'At the time, with your wife, I mean?'

His chuckle is dry and short. 'I invited her to sit and talk with me the day after I had these thoughts, but she refused as usual, saying we had been over and over everything and nothing was going to change, that it would just end in an argument. But eventually, I got her to agree and instead of picking over the bones of the past and inviting a conference on what was whose fault, I started with hope.'

Sarah listens intently. As the goats close in on them, she picks up a pebble and throws it at the big one's feet. It starts and all the herd run a few paces away. The munching grows quieter.

'I asked her what would make her happy. She said moving back to Greece. Obviously, we both had jobs in Oz, and we had no income in Greece, so it looked impossible. So I said, 'I will go first, clean up the house, create an income, and you can follow when you are ready. I can still see her face as she turned to look at me. For the first time in years, she looked me right in the eyes.' Sarah finds she, too, is looking in his eyes. They are a deep brown, soft.

As he meets her gaze, his eyes speak of kindness and humour. 'And in her eyes, I could see hope, not just for her to come to Greece but for us as well, as man and wife. So I came back to Greece with hope in my heart. I came alive.'

Sarah does not take her eyes from his. 'So you sending her the divorce papers the other day was the end of hope?'

'Only briefly.' He breaks their stare and slaps his knees before rubbing his palm on his trousers. 'For life to make sense, it must have meaning. We talked about this the other day, yes?' He stops rubbing and looks out across the plain. 'Well, for many years, I tried to make my wife my meaning, but she was a difficult, hard woman. When I was young, when she was young, that was exciting, but as the years went by, it became a source of misery. It is hard to make a source of misery your meaning. So when I moved here, so far away from her, I had to find another meaning.'

'I thought you said you woke up each morning and decided what sort of meaning you were going to give the day?' Sarah gently teases.

'I did and I do, but I have big and small meanings now. My big meaning is to make the world a better place. My middle-sized meaning is to produce a better herd each year so I can make the world's best goat cheese, and my small meaning is to do something each day to make myself happy.'

'And that's enough?' Sarah asks.

'Live your life's choices to extremes, do everything to the best of your ability, and take pride in what you achieve and then, whatever you choose is enough.' It sounds like an often-spoken mantra.

Sarah turns his words over in her mind. Laurence achieves. He just changed who he flies for with a massive increase in pay and everyday, he successfully achieves the transporting of hundreds of people to their destination. The boys both achieve, daily. Even Liz achieved something, keeping Neville's mum comfortable all these years. Apart from cooking, what does she achieve on a daily level? What has she achieved this year, or last year, or even the last five years? She has achieved nothing since the boys left home.

The weight in her chest has returned. She squints her eyes against the sunlight. If she is honest, her perfect little life, in her perfect house highlighted with ritual dinners with Laurence at quality restaurants every Saturday he is home, is not enough.

She gasps at the ingratitude of her thought, the guilt. If she looks at her life, her life with Laurence, her life with the boys, her life since Torin, all of it, there is only one person who is responsible. She pulls in and bites on her bottom lip. There is a rushing sound in her ears and watery film covers her eyes. It is easier to sleepwalk through life.

'You okay?' Nicolaos asks.

Chapter 19

'I am a sleepwalker,' she says.

Nicolaos's mouth curls to laugh but he looks at her and his face straightens.

'It's true. I might as well not be alive.'

'Careful, life might be listening.' Lifting his weight, he takes a couple of crouched steps and sits next to her. Even though he's on the ground with no rock for a seat, he is the same height as Sarah and she dully realises how tall he is. Taking out his beads, he grasps hold of her wrist to put them in her hand.

'Flick them over your top finger one by one. When you reach the end, swing them all back into your palm again.'

She has little interest, and with the first efforts, her rings get in the way, but after a couple of tries, the beads satisfactorily click together.

'You see, everything starts with a thought. You think to push over a bead and then you push over a bead.'

The last bead goes over and Sarah performs a very unstylish flick. The beads land back in her palm and she begins again.

'Thoughts are the whole problem,' she says. 'Most of the time, I just get on with life but then, from nowhere, an ugly dark thought comes and sits heavily in my stomach and blackens my day, or my week, or longer. I think I did a very wrong thing a long time ago and it haunts me this way.'

'But.' He draws the word out slowly, gently. 'Thoughts are not the truth. They are just thoughts. They do not arrive from God. Do not give them this power.'

Sarah stops clicking beads to look at him. The stubble on his upper lip shines with perspiration. The heat is relentless.

'If a thought serves you well or makes you feel positive, then keep it. If it does not, then let it go, reject it. This is one of the secrets to happiness, I think, and if you do it often enough, it becomes easy.' Sarah stares at him intently. 'But no one can do this for you. This one, you have to do for yourself.'

Her face must show scepticism because he adds reinforcement. 'You are not obliged to think your thoughts, you know.'

Having never considered her own thoughts in these terms before, Sarah says nothing as she plays with the idea that she is not obliged to think her thoughts, that it might be that they are not the truth.

But she knows what she has done, she knows what the truth is.

'Are all your thoughts right?' He looks directly at her, scanning from one of her eyes to the other. 'It is very grandiose to believe that they are. Thoughts must be examined, questioned.'

'But we know really, don't we?'

'Do we?' It is not a question. 'When my wife used to stay with her sister in Perth, I would say to her, "call me." It came about that she would call every day at five o'clock. One day, she did not ring, and I had three thoughts: that she was not with her sister and she had lied to me, that she had had a car crash and was badly hurt, or, and this was the worst, that she simply did not love me enough to call me anymore. The first thought, that she had lied to me, made me angry; the second, that she had had an accident, made me anxious; and the thought that she no longer loved me made me feel rejected. I knew it was one of the three, so I was deeply unhappy.'

'And which was it?'

'Someone had felled a tree which had brought down the line to my sister-in-law's phone.'

Sarah gives a little laugh.

'But you see, I thought I knew. In my mind I was saying, "She hasn't phoned," but the truth was she couldn't phone. But I thought I knew and allowed my thoughts to run wild, and it brought only misery.'

'But I know I did this bad thing.'

'You know you did it or you know it was a bad thing?'

'Both.'

'You want to tell me?'

Sarah stops clicking over the beads and looks closely at them. They are a deep orange, and inside one is a fly.

'Amber.' Nicolaos points at the beads. 'I bought them for myself the day I posted the divorce papers because they are beautiful and looking at them and feeling them makes me happy.' He puts his hand in his pocket and pulls out another set. 'There are my old ones.' They are slightly smaller, the colour of the sky.

'I married for the wrong reason,' Sarah says.

'This is the bad thing that you know you did?' Nicolaos runs the blue beads along the string from one hand to the other, an action so familiar, he does not appear aware that he is doing it. Sarah nods.

'Well, some cultures would say love is not a good reason for a marriage anyway.'

'I married because he had a good job, because he had money, because he would offer security, and because Torin was dead.' Sarah recites the list.

'Torin?'

'Torin. The love of my life, my childhood sweetheart, the man who made living fun and exciting and worthwhile.'

'And he died and took the excitement with him?'

'He took me with him.' The trees begin to swim behind tears.

'And you chose to die with him?'

The tears stop and her lips tighten into a line. 'Are you making fun of me?'

His beads keep clicking.

'No, just observing.'

It is not the reaction she expected, and he clearly does not understand how wicked what she did was.

'I married Laurence because he asked me. I married him because I didn't feel I could say no. I married him because I made a pact with Liz to marry a rich man. I married him because I was doing nothing else with my life.'

'Ah, there is your sin!' He stops clicking beads. 'You were doing nothing else with your life.'

'It was greed.' The rushing stops in Sarah's ears but her mouth is dry.

'It was laziness.'

Her eyes flash. 'I was grieving.'

'Then you should have bought some amber beads. It was laziness.'

Sarah stands, opens her mouth to speak, shuts it, and sits down again.

'Laziness,' Nicolaos repeats.

Her chest feels like it is imploding. 'Marrying out of laziness. That has to be as bad as it gets.' Her voice is flat.

'Has it?'

'Oh don't. It must be the worst reason in the world to marry.'

'For whom? Your husband is not divorcing you, so perhaps it is not so bad for him. You have children?'

Sarah nods.

'So your marriage was good for them.'

'Yes, but to lead Laurence on like that, to marry him letting him think that I loved him, how deceitful is that? I have robbed him of all these years when he could have found someone who did love him, have a real marriage with him.' There is a tightening in her throat. 'He could have had what Torin and I had even if I couldn't.'

'Maybe he did. Maybe you were it.' Nicolaos picks up a pebble to throw at the lead goat. 'How old were you when Torin died?'

'Just turned eighteen. He was twenty.'

'What happened?'

After a deep breath, Sarah looks over the plain and tracks a dot that is a car tracing a tarmac curl of grey between the regimented orange groves.

'We moved to the Isle of Man, him, me and Liz, his sister. I don't know if you know this, but the island is famous for the TT races, motorbike racing on the roads.'

'He was a motorcycle racer?'

'No, he was selling burgers. We—Liz and I—hung around his van, which didn't harm trade.' She gives a little laugh, pauses as her glory day memories flood through her mind. 'Anyway, one biker came for breakfast lunch and tea and we got to know him. Bernard, he was called. We even went for a drink with him. The last day of the races came and went, and he won some medal for something. The whole island was winding down, people leaving by the boatload. Torin's lease on the burger van was up.'

The sigh is so heavy, the weight of the world seems to hang in it.

Sarah once again smells the warm heather at Creg-ny-Baa. Torin chose this sharp, notorious corner on the mountain course because here, spectators filled the car park of the double-fronted hotel that had stood back from the ninety-degree bend for decades. Wooden stands had been erected in the fields on either side for spectators to cheer and watch in fear and awe.

'Here.' Torin pulled the van into a siding just beyond the pub. He had chosen well. The stands were overflowing with hungry spectators, and Torin sent the girls searching for more frozen burgers as the regular customers came for breakfast, dinner, and tea as well as for snacks in between. They got to know some of them by name.

But now, the races were all done and only one or two motorbikes passed, taking advantage of the roads that were still closed to traffic. The speed of these unofficial, straggling wannabes was sedate compared to the professionals of the previous days, and they were given little notice by anyone left by the course. With the fields now empty, Liz lay on her back watching the high white clouds. The heat wave continued.

'I wonder how much he has made altogether,' Liz mused. 'It must be enough for our next move—to London.'

She rolled on her stomach. 'Oh look, Bernard's back.' The day before, Bernard had celebrated his success with bottles of beer all round, and he proudly displayed his medal to anyone who would take notice. Behind him today was a car, the driver's window down. Bernard waved his burger at the girls and got into the car, which drove off.

'I wonder why he is not on his bike. He's staying here, isn't he?' She rolled over to look up at the Creg-ny-Baa hotel, where many bikes were still parked, and she could not tell if Bernard's red Suzuki was amongst them or not.

'Hey, look what Bernard forgot.' Torin came out of the side door of the burger van jangling some keys.

Neither Sarah nor Liz found this very interesting and neither responded. Sarah lay on her back, staring up at the blue.

'Hey, look.' Torin jangled the keys again.

'So what?' Liz said.

'So, shall I?'

Sarah turned, deciphered the look on Torin's face, and scrambled to her feet. 'Can I ride on the back?'

'Oh guys, that's not right.' Liz sat up as she caught on.

'Yeah, okay.' Torin swung the keys round his finger, marching off. Liz scrabbled to her feet.

'Did he say you could?' she called after them.

'Jump on, Sarah.' Torin effortlessly straddled the bike with Sarah pulling on his jacket to clamber up behind him. With a turn of the key, there was a brief, high-pitched whine before the engine throbbed. Torin twisted the grip and a bass note vibrated up through her. She felt a thrill as if suddenly drunk. She wanted Torin, and her hands explored their grip around his waist.

'Hold on,' he shouted.

'Don't be a prat,' Liz called, only just audible, as they were gone with speed flowing through Sarah's hair, and the world was a wonderful place.

They only went down the hill and back.

'Right, off,' Torin commanded as the bike ground to a halt next to Liz.

'Oh why?' Sarah wined.

'I want a proper go.' That was all he said. It was then that Sarah noticed he still had his short wrap-around apron on, smeared with grease and ketchup over a faded Megadeth t-shirt. 'I'm going to go up to the A14 and then I'll go down as far as the first houses in Douglas. Cheer me on when I come round this corner.' They didn't have time to answer as he twisted the grip and the bike shot off, one of Torin's legs not yet on the foot rest.

They waited ages. Liz lay down again and still, he did not come.

'There is no way he could take this long to get there and back,' Sarah said. Liz had her eyes closed. 'Hang on. Liz wake up; here he comes.' Liz was awake in a second, and they ran to the edge of the road with their hands in the air, cheering him on. As he came to the corner, Sarah mouthed 'I love you' and she saw his eyes leave the road for that moment. The back wheel of the bike juddered, left then right. His foot lifted from the rest for balance. For a moment, control was lost. Sarah exhaled as the bike stabilised.

A car appeared from nowhere, driving with speed. Torin leaned right to corner the notorious

Crag-ny-Baa. The car was coming fast, and its wheels skidded the corner. It was in Torin's path.

The back wheel of the bike slid. Torin leaned left and then right. He zig-zagged out of the car's path. Sarah heard Liz exhale. The car passed him safely. The driver's head was turned away from them, looking over his shoulder, back at Torin.

The bike was screeching, unable to regain balance. The tyres descended the hill in parallel. Rubber smoke rose until the back wheel split from under him. The bike went one way and Torin the other.

With a sickening metallic shriek, the bike slid off across the tarmac and over the bracken. Torin skidded on his back over the gravel edge of the road, up the grass incline. Speed took him into the air. He sailed clear over the barbed wire fence and behind a hillock. For that second, Sarah thought he had come to a stop there. But he bounced and, like a rag doll, arms and legs at every angle, he sailed over the stone wall beyond and was hidden from view. The green car that had stopped on the bend now accelerated away.

'He's fine,' Sarah shouted to Liz as she started to run. He had missed both the barbed wire fence and the wall; he had been lucky. An unsolicited chuckle rose to her throat at how funny he had looked as he sailed through the air. The brief chuckle smothered her gasp for air and released sprung steel muscles around her chest. Liz did not respond. Her eyes locked, her jaw hung open, and she stood unmoving.

Sarah thrust her way through the barbed wire fence as it tore at her jeans, gouged lines in her arms, and ripped hair from her head. 'Torin,' she called towards her unseen hero, 'that was spectacular, but I think you're going to have some bruises in the morning.' Her laugh was loud and hollow and shrill.

Rounding the wall end, there he was, in his ketchup-covered apron, leant up against a hillock, pretending to be dead.

'Ha ha, very funny.' She looked away from him, searching for the bike, an intense buzzing inside her ears. 'Come on, what are we going to do about Bernard's bike?' And then she looked back at him and she felt cold, ice cold, and her limbs became rigid as her denial no longer fitted the scene before her. Torin's left leg was bent back under him, his right arm at an odd angle behind his head, touching his opposite shoulder, and his eyes stared at nothing.

He blinked.

Sarah fell on all fours and crawled to be face to face with him.

'Torin?' she whispered. He blinked again. 'You've torn your favourite t-shirt.' She glanced briefly at the neckline. There was red moss on the fence post that came through his shoulder. Her trembling hand came up to touch his cheek. His hair was matted to his head with fresh but darkening ketchup. 'Torin,' she said as softly as she could; she did not want to chase him away. He gasped and his in-breath rattled. 'My love,' she whispered. He mouthed the words in reply. The whites of his eyes widened, his pupils dilated.

Sarah moved her head so he would look in her eyes. He struggled for another breath, but there was no strength in his fight. He blinked once more, and the light changed.

'Don't go,' she whispered. 'No, please, please don't go.' But she knew no one could hear her words and a darkness swept over her, pinning her to the ground, making her unable to move even when two ambulance men tried to lift her. They prised her hands loose of Torin's t-shirt and lifted her rigidly into an ambulance, where someone tried to make her drink tea. But the world no longer rotated, and her heart beat only because that was what it was programmed to do so she could continue to walk through life even though she would never wake.

Chapter 20

Nicolaos sits silently after she stops talking, his beads dropping one onto another. The goats close in around them, but neither of them throw pebbles to move them away.

'So you married Laurence not because you were lazy but because you had given up.' The shepherd's words come slowly, reflectively.

'I know,' Sarah says. There are no tears.

'Have given up.' He corrects his tense. 'So inside your head, you say your life was over when he died, so inside your head, you say there is no more happiness or love for you, so inside your head, you make no decisions or choices because you want to play no part.'

Sarah nods. The amber beads hang from her fingers, swinging with her breathing.

'Because if you live this way, you are never responsible ever again.' Nicolaos swings and palms his beads.

Sarah's amber rosary stops moving.

'That's it, isn't it?' Nicolaos turns his head to face her. 'You have opted out of making decisions so you will never again be responsible for the consequences.'

Sarah's hand, the beads visible between her fingers, cover her stomach. Her face contorts.

'Didn't you say you never actually made the decision to marry Laurence or something?' he asks, but Sarah looks away. 'Who decided to have the children?' His words bear no mercy. Joss was an accident that she did nothing about, but does that make her so guilty? Even if it was Laurence who suggested they give their son a sibling, had she really resolved to be such a puppet in her life? The dark weight inside twists its sickening knot, pulling at her heart, jerking her forward until she knows, oh God yes, she knows, that she has avoided every decision since the one she made to mouth 'I love you,' which killed Torin.

'It was my fault.' Her utterance is high-pitched and inhuman. The tightness in her stomach grows and strangles her from the inside. One of Nicolaos's arms wraps around her shoulders, encompassing, strong. He pulls her into his chest and wraps his other arm around her, too. She can hardly breathe, her cheeks are burning, her nose is running, her shoulders shudder as the emotion forces its release, emotions that feel like they are going to engulf her, and she sinks sobbing into Nicolaos' chest.

His grip remains firm as her guilt suffocates her and her sobs release the years of suppressed emotion. She had forgotten about the car. For years, the memory had been just her mouthing 'I love you' and Torin dead.

As she continues to sob slowly, the intensity of the guilt she has harboured for years begins to ease. The sadness is still there, but the intense emotions she felt as a teenager begin to fade and they are slowly replaced by emotions that are more appropriate. His death seems real and tragic and sad, but no longer insurmountable. She continues to weep, mourning her loss as these more manageable feelings seep through her. Nicolaos's arms stay strongly around her until she feels driven to find fresh air and as her head surfaces, his grip releases, his arms fall away.

'Can you imagine Torin growing old, his joints creaking and groaning, his mind fading?' There is compassion in Nicolaos's voice.

Sarah snorts and then sniffs. 'No, Torin could not have put up with growing old. He would have walked off into the sunset.' She is thinking of the car, how it stopped but then drove off.

'Which is what he did.' Nicolaos rubs the flank of a goat that is almost on his knee. He pats its rump and it moves off, but not very far.

'He was only twenty.'

'And he chose to go on a bike and he chose to go very fast, and so he chose the consequence.'

'But if I hadn't mouthed *I love you*?' Sarah searches her pockets for a tissue but finds none and wipes her nose on the back of her hand instead.

'He might have looked at you anyway, or looked at Liz, or gone even faster, or slowed down, or not seen the car.'

'If we had listened to Liz? If I had not encouraged him by riding pillion?'

'He would have gone anyway.' Nicolaos' voice is strong, reassuring in its certainty. 'But you have decided that it was your fault, so you sacrificed yourself to a loveless marriage because even love is deadly. As long as you blame yourself and fail to forgive yourself, you will never move on.' His beads click but his concentration is on Sarah. 'I hope you don't think I am being presumptuous, although, I suspect, you are ready to move on but the weight of the guilt is pulling you to ... well. I don't know. You tell me where it is pulling you.'

Sarah is struggling for breath. Her chest is so tight, her eyes are wide open in fear that she may never breathe again.

'Breathe,' Nicolaos commands as he takes her hand. She spasms and sucks in air. No words can escape her.

'Here's the thing.' Nicolaos' tone takes on a jolly edge. 'And I know this after my years of struggling in marriage! As we talked about before, it is important to listen to your thoughts, dispute them when they are out of line, and replace them if they are not positive, because our thinking affects our behaviour and our behaviour dictates the feedback the world gives us.'

With a pause in his talking, the cicadas seem louder than ever. A car changes gear on the road.

His large hand with the blue beads threaded through his fingers sits on top of hers, which loosely holds the amber set. Blue beads, hand, red beads, hand. But she is still out of control, fighting to stop the tears, gasping for breath. She is glad when Nicolaos continues to talk.

'My self-talk was so destructive, I would sit in my room with my silent television, saying to myself "my life sucks," and that there is no way out and "I am unlovable" and all these statements that are the end of any conversation I could have had with myself. What else but unhappiness could possibly follow?' He tuts as if he is in wonderment that he survived at all. 'I realised that if I sunk any lower, I would no longer be able to function. My work would suffer.' He shakes his head as he says this, as if the idea were incomprehensible. 'The sadness we like to label as *depression,* it is a luxury, you know. Poor people cannot afford it. I could not afford it.' He faces her as he talks, as if he has got to the important part. 'So when I started to consciously listen to my self-talk, I saw how destructive it was and so I weeded out the negative things that I was saying that were of no possible use to me. I replaced them with positive thinking, sort of repeated mantras that put me in a better place.' He looks back at the sheep edging closer. 'The result was that the people around me, the people I worked with, began to respond to me in a different way.' He chuckles briefly. 'I even began to have a social life, as colleagues asked me out for drinks and to barbeques until my television became nothing more than an object that collected dust in the corner.'

Sarah feels weak and exhausted. But the tears are subsiding as Nicolaos' voice rolls over her like comforting balm.

'I am so sorry.' She flicks her hair back, making a huge effort to compose herself. Pulling her hand from underneath his, she straightens her t-shirt and sits up straight. Nicolaos retracts his arm and runs his beads from hand to hand as she holds her chin high.

'Ach, it is life,' is all he says.

'Yes, but I have no right to burden you with my life. You have your own.' Sarah clears her throat.

'Funny, I thought I was talking about my own.'

Sarah looks through the network of branches above her head, squeezing her eyes almost shut against the sun. 'I'd better get back and make lunch.'

They stand and fall in step and walk without words until the olive trees thin out and Sarah is on the track that leads to the road into the village.

'You okay?'

Sarah nods.

'Any idea what you might do now you have woken up?'

Sarah shakes her head.

Nicolaos picks up a small stone and throws it at her feet as if she is a goat getting too close. She sidesteps away so it does not hit her. He is grinning. Sarah scoops up the pebble and puts it in her pocket with the other two. There is a strange lightness to her limbs that fills her with hope, but she does not know what it is hope for, nor why. It seems odd that after recalling such sad memories, she feels a sense of joy.

'Laurence?' She calls inside the house, but there is no answer. She pours herself a glass of water and takes it outside. 'Oh, there you are.' Laurence is sitting by the pool, reading a paper. 'Where's Finn?'

'Joss came by, took him into Saros for a coffee. Pru wanted to talk to him apparently.' His tone is clipped, off-hand.

'Oh God, that could be trouble.' She sits on the other lounger. It would be nice to tell Laurence what happened with the shepherd.

'You could've told me.' He bites the words.

Sarah blinks and shakes her head. 'Sorry?'

'The only way I knew you had gone to Liz's was because Finn told me.'

'Oh.'

'Yes, exactly. I would have been sitting here with no idea where you were, worrying. It really is irresponsible of you, Sarah.'

'Well, he did tell you and I am back now, so no harm done.'

'It's not good enough, Sarah. We have talked about this before.'

Here it comes. This is usually about the time that the darkness inside becomes heavier. But this time, the heaviness does not come. Instead, there is a tension in her chest that rises to her throat and, uninvited, bursts out of her mouth.

'Well, if you didn't suffocate me, maybe I would not be so keen to have these moments where you don't know where I am.' Sarah slaps her hand over her mouth. She had not expected that.

'Pardon?' Laurence puts down his newspaper.

'I was just conjecturing.' She stumbles now. 'That perhaps, if you weren't so keen to know, well if I took more time alone ...' Sarah cannot find the words. She spends hours, days alone when he is on a long-haul flight, she cannot defend herself. Laurence's mouth shuts into a tight line, his eyebrows lower. *His anger comes from pain. You cause this pain. Look what you did to his life.* The thought flies rapidly through her mind

'Why do you even want me, Laurence?' She puts her glass on the teak poolside table and her arms drop, her hands hanging heavily. Laurence has a red face and neck; there is a lobster tan line were his shirt cuts a *V* onto his chest. *Loose-skinned neck, like a plucked chicken.* She cautions herself over such gratuitous thoughts but is thankful for them, as they do stop him from appearing scary.

'What?' His eyes dart left and right, his cheeks push up to his eyes as he grimaces, trying to understand.

'I am serious. Why do you want me to be in your home when you come back from your extended trips?' There is no anger in her voice, just exhaustion. He shuffles to a more upright sitting pose, his hands crossed over his swimming trunks.

'First, you are my wife, so where else would you be? And secondly, it is our home, not my home, and thirdly, I work hard to bring in enough money to give us the lifestyle we enjoy and none of my "trips," as you belittlingly call them, are extended.'

'Laurence, we don't talk, we don't have joint activities we do together, and we haven't made love for, oh I don't know how long.'

He stands. He is less imposing in just a pair of bathing trunks than his usual suit.

'We do talk. We go for a meal every Saturday if I am not working. Look, I don't know what you have been discussing with Liz, but it does not become you to behave in this way.' He takes a step towards her. 'Neville tells me Liz is unhappy about some decision he has made with regards to his family. Well, that may be so, but that is Liz's problem. I don't want her life reflecting on ours, am I clear? Do we not have a good life, dinner parties, expensive hotels on our holidays, Michelin star Sunday lunches? We have our sons. We are a family.'

'But why me, Laurence?'

'What do you mean why you? You are my wife, you support me, you stand by me. I come home and you are there to greet me. I don't know what you mean by "why you."'

'I mean as opposed to someone else. Someone who really adores you.' Her heart bangs against her ribcage; she seems to be having trouble swallowing. Someone brave seems to have taken over what is coming out of her mouth, someone who is not scared of the consequences, and it is terrifying.

His face whitens and his eyes squint against the sun. Poor Laurence. He has never, not once, stopped to ask her how she feels about their lives, about him. All this will be coming out of the blue for him. He deserves better.

'I feel I have only been half a wife to you, a fake. I feel so much guilt, I spend all my time trying to please you. I am so, so sorry.' She looks at him, feeling such pity.

He gains some colour and his cheek muscles begin to twitch.

'You are sorry? You are sorry for me? You are so conceited, Sarah.' His fists clench. 'How arrogant of you! Did you not think that Neville and I knew your little game when we first met you? Did you really think we were so stupid? Please, how insulting. You were two poor Irish girls on the make and you obviously had planned to bag yourselves some rich husbands. Well, I may not be rich by world standards, but I was richer than anything you had ever seen. It was like sitting ducks.'

Sarah blinks rapidly. 'What do you mean "like sitting ducks?"' Her words come out stammering in response. Everything has shifted. She is suddenly in a dream remembered, a certainty mixed with surrealism.

'You think you were the only ones with a plan!' Laurence scoffs.

Sarah can feel her knees trembling. She staggers towards him, but only so she can sit on the lounger. He moves out of her way.

'I don't suppose you remember the one question I asked on our first night out.'

Sarah's mouth opens and closes, miming the words 'can you cook.'

'So you do remember, eh? Well, if you had been any smarter you would probably have figured it out. I'm amazed Liz didn't. Neville had no intension of marrying her at all until his mother fell ill. Liz was the perfect solution to that problem. How could she not know his mother had been declining for six months and needed daily care before the wedding unless she was completely and utterly self-obsessed?'

It is like hearing that the world is round after believing for years it was flat. Suddenly everything falls into place, suddenly making sense.

'But me, us? You had no sick mother.' Sarah's voice has lost all confidence.

'I wanted sons and I didn't want to return to an empty house. Nor did I want complications. You were opinion-less, undemanding, and easy on the eye.' It is the ultimate dismissal.

An empty cavity opens inside Sarah's chest. She wraps her arms around herself, trying to hold everything in.

'The extended trips, the weekends of golf?' She squeezes herself tight, preparing for the truth.

'Oh come on, Sarah, what do you think? I am a man and there was no zest of that kind between us.'

'So.' She hesitates. If she says the next words and the answer is what she thinks it will be, there is no going back. She stands again before she speaks. 'Have you never felt any love for me?'

'Do you feel love for me?' Even though the words come out cold, emotionless, she cannot believe he could be so harsh, so unfeeling.

'You mean all these years when I have gone through the motions, trying to behave so as not to hurt you, all this while you have felt nothing?'

'I am not sure what you are expecting me to say. It works, Sarah. We have two great boys who I am immensely proud of. I have a well-maintained home that I come back to, meals on the table, pleasant company, and you have what you wanted: a good income, a beautiful home, and all the clothes and makeup you could desire without having to lift a finger to earn them.'

Sarah can find nothing to say.

'It works, Sarah, and you *will* be there when I get back from my trips because I am sure you don't want to go back to County Clare. And besides,' he loses his edge; his voice softens and becomes more familiar, 'it will probably work even better now we are both on the same page.'

Pushing past him, she heads for the house, the way blurred. She blinks away the tears. The house is too much of a dead end, she must move, keep moving. The gate is left to swing behind her as she runs.

Chapter 21

She cannot run to Liz; Liz is in a bad enough state as it is. Nicolaos? A shepherd she met on a hill? No, that's crazy. She can't worry Finn, and Joss is too like his father. Besides, he might tell Pru and she would probably delight in her suffering. Who does that leave? No one. She knows no one here.

The tears in her eyes blur everything into sunlit prisms. It comes as a shock to know that all these years that she has been clinging to the idea that Laurence cared for her and that made her feel, well, loved, needed, safe. But all this time, Laurence had never deluded himself with the same belief. They played the same dirty trick on each other, but it is she who has just had the illusion ripped apart, it is she who is in shock. He faked it for how long? Twenty-six years this year. Twenty-six years, he said nothing. Twenty-six years, she said nothing. Twenty-six years of her life wasted.

She pulls the thought back. It was not wasted; she has Joss and Finn. She takes a side road. She cannot face the square. She is not really sure where she is or which way to go, just moving, running from Laurence's cold, matter-of-fact stance. She feels so used, humiliated by him. But he has only done to her exactly what she did to him. Her eyes fill again, disgusted with herself. The lane she has mindlessly taken begins to climb a hill. There are trees on the top that beckon her. The heat and the incline slow her to a march but her arms pump and her legs stride as fast as they can. Sweat pours from her brow.

She knew what she doing to Laurence was wrong, unfair, but she never really thought how cold and hard his life must be without love. How had she kidded herself he loved her all these years? Now that he has told her that he never felt love for her, it has been obvious in all his behaviour. All these years she has excused him, been kind to him, believing he just found it hard to express himself. What about the dinners on Saturday night, the flowers he would arrange on the hall table when he came home from a long turn around, buying her clothes? Was that not him finding a way to let her know the depth of his feelings? Were they just his pleasures and amusements? If so, that makes her what? A pawn, a doll? She deserves to feel ridiculed. But what hurts more is the bleak reality of abandonment that has engulfed her now she knows she has been living all this time without love. The knowledge that she is unloved bites the hardest. Her sight blurs again as she crests the hill. The trees are to her right. She has bypassed them in her determination to keep going, keep moving, onward, upward.

Reprocessing snippets of Laurence's behaviour that jostle to be recalled, she cannot believe how clinical he has been, dispassionate, uninterested.

She suddenly recognises the landscape around her. She has come over the hill and has joined the road that becomes Liz's drive and the house is now just down the other side before her.

Her friend being so close draws her. She will talk to Liz; she must talk to someone. Sarah clutches at her chest as a pain shoots across. She is out of breath from the climb. She stops for a moment and the heartburn spasms again. She doesn't wish for more pain, but a heart attack would solve everything: no more struggle, no more awareness of her misery, just a blank end to it all.

Gripping her ribcage, she looks forward. The house looks still.

If Neville is there, she doesn't want to talk to him, but nor will she care if she is rude. She wants to talk to Liz alone. The pain pinches again and she winces.

'Liz,' she calls as she reaches the patio. The doors are shut but she tries them. They are not locked. The house feels chilled after the sun, and dark. It takes a moment for her eyes to adjust until she can make out the stairs to Liz's room. The nearness of her friend brings a release, and the tears come faster as her legs wobble. 'Liz,' she calls again in an unsteady voice before she can see no point in making any further effort and her boneless body half-sits, half-falls onto the sofa. She lays there sobbing deeply, alone. Liz does not come. The house is silent.

Sarah has no idea how long she lays there, but as her wailing subsides, the pain in her chest demands some action. She makes an effort to sit up. Liz's makeup bag is on the coffee table, the contents spilling out. Bottles of pills amongst eye shadows and mascara-blackened cotton buds. Liz always keeps her hangover pills in with her makeup. Maybe there will be some indigestion tablets. Sarah tips the rest of the bag out and several brown plastic bottles with white labels are amongst the cosmetics. Bottles like the ones Liz had made tasteless jokes about in the restaurant. Picking the nearest up, she finds Neville's mother's name typed above the directions for dosage. Prescription drugs. Extreme pain killers that she took near the end.

They offer a direction.

The easiest way out of all.

The tears dry up within seconds of making the decision. The heartburn is immaterial; soon, nothing will hurt. She picks up all the bottles and takes them to the kitchen counter. Lifting a glass from beside the sink, Sarah fills it with water and, settling stiffly onto the kitchen stool, she begins to systematically undo the bottles and pour out the pills, making neat lines with the contents next to each uncapped bottle.

There is easily enough.

She takes one last long look out of the window, the sun brightening the colour of everything it touches, the world a beautiful place but with no place for Sarah. A butterfly fights the windowpane, its wings brushing at the glass, a futile dance until death.

'I know how you feel,' Sarah tells it and hears her own words keenly, knowing they will be her last. Tomorrow, the sun will still shine, the butterfly will probably still be fighting for its freedom, everything will carry on as normal, only she will feel no more pain.

The butterfly, spent, takes rest on the sill. Sarah's last act will be a kind one. She slides from the stool and, moving slowly so as not to scare the insect, she opens the window and watches as its antennae twitch, its wings open, and it takes flight into the sunshine, red wings brilliant against the blue sky. It flies higher and higher and further and further away until Sarah is not sure if she can see it at all.

With a sigh, she returns to the lines of pills, sliding back onto the stool. She takes a drink of the water to wet her throat and picks up one pill after another. She can probably manage to swallow five at a time.

Pills in hand, she tips her head back and opens her mouth, adjusting the pills in her hand so they will pour from her palm more easily.

The back door smacks the wall, ringing like gunfire as it suddenly and forcibly opens. Sarah jumps and drops several of the pills. Nicolaos falls through the open door, shoulder first. He holds a wood plane and a chisel.

'I have come to fix the door,' he says before looking up. Steadying his balance from his charge, he raises his head, at first surprised to see Sarah and then a frown follows as he takes in the counter top, her position in front of the lines of pills, and the absence of anyone else in the room.

Sarah's back stiffens. She still holds the glass of water near her lips; in her fingers, the few pills that remain in her grasp. In one bound, Nicolaos is upon her, squeezing her cheeks to open her mouth, knocking both pills and water from her hands. The glass smashes. Sarah struggles. Nicolaos grips her harder, her mouth open.

'How many have you taken?' he demands without loosening his grip. It is impossible for Sarah to reply; his fingers are locking her jaw open. She scrabbles at his arms, his immovable arms.

'How many?' he shouts in her face, releasing his grip and pushing her backwards. Grabbing the counter to regain her balance, she is on her feet.

Who the hell is he to be so angry?

In that moment, he is the source of all her problems, all her pains. He is the unfairness of life, the loss of Torin, the cold of Laurence and her self-hatred, her disgust at who she has become.

'None!' she shouts. The word comes out like a curse, venom of spite, and Nicolaos rocks back on his heels with the force of her hatred.

Again she runs, across the room, out through the patio, down the drive, over the wall, and into the olive trees. The branches ripping at her hair, she stumbles and falls, but she is on her feet again and running. She hears material tearing as her arm is pulled back by a wooden post but she is heedless, her pace hardly faltering. As she leaves the olive grove, tufts of hair remain clinging to branches and her left knee has the imprint of the stone where she fell. But still, she keeps going. The downwards slope of the hill hastens her steps on the track and she does not stop until she is on the main road, where she turns away from the village. Gasping for air, holding her sides and bending over so she can breathe, still she keeps going. Slowed to a march but still brisk and purposeful, she keeps walking with no idea of her destination or when she will stop, or if indeed she will ever stop.

Chapter 22

Her thoughts are tumbling in chaos, the image of Nicolaos's fear and anger condemning her. Tears dry on her skin as she marches, the pumping of her arms releasing her anger, her frustration. Overpowered by too many emotions jostling for dominance, her mind goes blank, a numbness sweeps over her, her legs keep striding, and she becomes the movement. The road passes unseen beneath her, the unnoticed landscape around her nothing but fields and fields of fruit trees as she heads deep into the country.

After half an hour of pounding the road, her consciousness registers the tarmac, its solidity, its homage to civilisation, and she resents it. A quarter of an hour later, she is glad when it thins, crumbles, and gives way to a mud track. The compounded earth is cracked in places as if it dried out quickly, spring breaking into summer, perhaps. After some time, the track, too, peters out as it grasses over, trodden flat in lines as if different people have taken different routes across it. Her pace slows and she licks her dried lips. She is thirsty.

Ahead opens out into a stony field, too open, too bare. She would feel exposed. But there, to the left, a break in the grasses where she can go into the orange grove. She takes it, playing out the need to keep moving.

The air becomes still under the umbrella of dark green. There's a hush, as if the world is waiting for something, a timelessness that grasps all possibilities. She passes a flat stone on the path, cigarette ends scattered around it. Maybe it is a shepherd's spot. Would they bring sheep into dark orange groves? She continues, but her steps have lost purpose. As she ambles, thoughts return, her head swims, and every emotion is played so loud it distorts, its meaning lost. Nothing takes shape except the pulse in her temple. Up ahead, searching for a focus, the trunks are interrupted by something reddish-brown rearing up vertically. Drawing closer, seeing more, it appears to be a small barn made from large bricks of dried mud. The corner facing her is weathered, the bricks eroded, carved away around the mud mortar, sculptural, dramatic.

At the front of the building is an area without trees, and sunlight creates a stage. A bark-bare trunk lies near the opening into the barn, the inner wood worn smooth and flat. Upon it lays a fork, tines up, and on the ground in front, a pan without a handle upturned next to a pit of charcoal. Sarah becomes still, trying to work out if the camp is still in use, but the pan and a single abandoned shoe look so old, it seems impossible. Besides, no one lives in such conditions these days. Her emotional pain subsides the more absorbed she becomes in the abandoned hovel. She pokes at a dirty cheap rucksack with her foot.

The barn has no door and inside, daylight streams between broken tiles, rods of light spearing the mud floor. A breeze whispers through the orchard and a plastic sheet on the roof billows and collapses with a crinkling sigh. The place looks as if it has been dismantled and half put together again. Some wide wooden shelves lie on the floor, others are secured to the wall. The one she steps on has been grafittied with pen and knife. She moves out of her own light to read. She can make out the words Azen, Behar, some dates, a carved heart, Sergiu, Aaman and in capitals JULIET. Perhaps Juliet from the village, but what would be her connection to this place? And there are lines, six straight, one crossing, like the marking of weeks, repeated again and again. It is all a little frightening, as if this has been a prison within an orange orchard.

A pair of boots sits side by side next to one of the shelves. There is movement and a man jumps down from a high shelf. He is dark skinned, white eyes. Sarah lets out a squeal and turns to run but the door is blocked by two men, one leaning either side of the opening.

One of her rings glints in a streak of sun that pierces the roof. Her hand jerks up to her necklace, the wealth around her wrists and studding her ears suddenly terrifyingly visible.

One of the men in the doorway is chuckling. He is very dark skinned, African maybe, with a Nike t-shirt on. The other looks European but the dome at the back of his head is flat and his forehead is very low. His clothes would stand up by themselves, the dirt is so ingrained. Sarah turns quickly to check what the third man is doing—the one who jumped from the shelves. He is putting on the boots.

Brave it, Sarah. Just push past and walk out. But the voice in her head is inconsistent. *They will rob you, kill you, or worse, and no one will hear. No one knows where you are, and Laurence is right, you are irresponsible.* She bristles with rage at her own thoughts.

Breaking into movement, she marches to the opening.

'Excuse me.' She looks the African in the eye and waits for him to move, but he doesn't. She turns to the European, who has a nasty scab on the bridge of his nose. He looks back but makes no movement.

'Excuse me. I want to get out.' She can hear the quiver in her own voice. Another man appears behind the two, out in the sunlight, and yet another rolls from a shelf behind her. Sarah stands motionless as, emotionally, she collapses inward. The situation is futile, but her fists clench and there is renewed energy in her legs. She will fight if she has to.

There are five of them. There is no chance to fight; it might make it worse. *Remain still, unmoving, don't respond, then it won't antagonise them. Or run, suddenly, push 'flat-head' out of the way, he is smallest, but then there is the man behind.*

'Whatchu wanting?' the man wearing the Nike t-shirt asks, the words rolling from his tongue, a quiver on the vowels as if the whole thing is amusing.

'I want to leave.' Sarah swallows. Sweat is running from her forehead into her eyes but she keeps her fists locked, her hands by her side. She blinks to retain clear vision.

'Nah woman, yous came in here for something. Whatchu wanting?'

Her heart is beating so strongly, they must be able to see it through her t-shirt. Flat-head is looking at her breasts.

'I was lost.' She turns again. The first man now has his boots on. He walks around her and leans with the others against the doorframe. He has a scar through one of his eyebrows; there is a leaping puma on his shirt.

'Lost is it?' Nike turns to Puma and chuckles as he speaks. 'She says she lost.'

'Lost and alone,' Puma replies.

Flat-head says something, but it is in a foreign language, and the other two ignore him. Spotting the divide, Sarah turns to flat-head, walks right up to him, and says, 'Move.' She raises her hand to push him.

'He don't understand the English, woman. He's from Bulgaria or Albania or somewheres.'

Sarah lowers her hand without making contact and steps back.

Flat-head steps forward. He is grinning, showing missing teeth. He takes another step and Sarah backs again. Nike and Puma are silent. The man who was outside now fills the space in the doorway that flat-head vacated.

Flat-head raises his hand. Sarah shrinks as his fingers touch her hair.

'Get off,' she snarls.

His hand thrusts around the back of her neck and takes hold of her hair, pulling her head backwards, a beam of sunlight on her cheek. The sharp pain from her hair tearing from its roots jolts her body into a spasm. Her arm flies sideways and one knee reflexes upwards. His grip releases and he collapses to the ground, his hand in his groin. Puma and Nike and the other man start laughing.

'She feisty, man. Too much for you,' Nike says, his laughter coming from deep in his stomach.

Sarah looks from one to the other to the prostrate man on the floor. If they see her reflexes as aggression ...

'Sorry. I am so sorry. I didn't mean to,' she says to no one in particular.

'Lady, don't you be sorry to him.' Nike laughs. 'He showed you no respect.' Nike regains some control of his laughter.

'I didn't know he had balls to hurt.' Puma is still laughing.

'So is you really lost?' Nike asks. He unfolds his arms, takes his weight from the doorframe and puts his hands in his back pockets. Puma pushes past him into the sunlight. The other man in the door steps back into the light and sits on the fallen tree trunk. Puma pees against a tree.

Flat-head starts to get up.

'You best stay where you is man, or she will flatten you for sure,' Nike advises. Flat-head crouch-walks to one of the shelves to sit.

'Lady?' Sarah turns back to look at Nike as he addresses her. 'Is you lost or is you from the government?'

'The government?' Sarah breaks eye contact with him and looks all around, trying to make sense of what he has just said. 'Oh, are you illegal?' Her hand seeks out the silver snake bracelet on her wrist.

'Ha. That is funny, you ask if we are illegal. What you think, woman? You think we want to live in a mud hut like this?' He looks at flat-head, who has now laid down.

'I am afraid I have no idea.' She looks at the shelves and the mud floor again. Someone has put up a calendar with a picture of a sports car. It hangs from a twig embedded into the mud brick wall. 'No, actually, I cannot imagine anyone choosing to live like this.'

'Nah, and you would be right.' He chuckles again. Sarah unclenches her fists. He wanders out into the sunlight. Sarah follows him into the sun. He heads into the trees where he stands, his turn to relieve himself. She could run now, but would it be an overreaction to the present situation? It may ignite a flame that is not yet lit. She thinks of all the films

Nicolaos has seen with willing victims fuelled with hope. She glances at the path again, best to run.

'Get up. The woman, she need a seat.' Nike pushes the man on the tree trunk sideways, and he stands and wanders to sit on a flat stone. 'Sit,' he encourages Sarah. The men move slowly, loosely, unthreatening, but with the wrong move from her, could it all quickly change? She sits.

'Where are you from?' She tries to ignite some neutral conversation.

'Nigeria. We came to make me fortune and now are living to regret it.' Nike chuckles again.

'I am from Ireland, have you heard of it? Next to England.' She can think of nothing else to say.

'I am illegal but I am not uneducated. What I always wondered though is why, when England, she has just the one good-sized island next to her, why she does not give it a good name? Like here, they have Mikonos, Sifnos, Siros, Thasos, Paros. They do get a bit stuck on their 'oses' but at least they have names and not just call them Island like England does.' He shakes with laughter. One of the men comes out from under the trees, smiling at the sound of him. Nike sits on the upturned pan, but whether standing or sitting, they are all gathered around a little too close for comfort.

Sarah smiles cautiously. 'It's not island as in *island*. It's spelt differently, named after a princess.'

'Ah, so what you are telling me is that you are from an island of princesses? We have a princess amongst us!' He laughs again. The man on the stone is rolling himself a cigarette. Flat-head staggers from the barn. Sarah glares at him.

'Perhaps I'd better go.' This response is natural, automatic. She stands and takes a step toward the track.

'No, lady, do not be put off by him. He showed you no respect and you put him right. My wife, she is the same, she has enough respect for herself to give herself a good life.'

'Oh, is your wife here or back in Nigeria?' Sarah stays, standing, and looks for the track around the end of the barn, judging the distance. It gives her confidence.

'Oh no, his wife and children are back in Nigeria.' Nike juts his chin toward Puma, who looks up sadly. 'But I am not married to my wife yet. I have not even met my wife yet, but I know what she will be like.' He thinks this is the funniest thing he has said yet. His laughter explodes in the clearing. It occurs to Sarah that in such a situation, miles from his home, illegal in his work, sharing his resting place with strangers, his sense of humour will be his only defence. It seems doubtful he will ever meet, let alone marry, someone. He has no job, no home, nothing. How little choice he has. She laughs although it seems inappropriate considering his possible future. She uses the jolliness of the moment to casually wave and heads towards the path she came in on. Nike continues to laugh and turns away from her to say something more to flat-head. She cannot hear these words now as she is on the other side off the barn, but she can hear more than one person laughing. Looking forward, she can see the end of the trees where the path joins the main track. If she keeps walking, increases her pace, she will be on the track within seconds.

A figure appears, turning into the trees ahead, but she keeps walking.

Chapter 23

The man walking toward her crosses Sarah's path just before she leaves the trees. He could be Indian or Pakistani. He smiles as he walks by and says 'hello' in English. His jumper is torn on one cuff and he wears trainers with no socks.

Sarah fixes her sights ahead and keeps moving.

Back on the tarmac, it feels safe. Sarah had not been aware of how shallowly she had been breathing, but now she takes big lungfuls of air. She strides out and makes some distance between her and the camp. How little they have, and yet they are surviving, with humour, and, to a degree, with dignity. She cannot imagine the pain Puma must go through knowing his children are growing up without him back home, probably not knowing when he will next see them, if ever.

But all she could feel with them was fear, her own fear for her life.

She laughs at the irony, but it is a dry and bitter sound. Nevertheless, it makes her think. If she had truly wanted to end it all in Liz's kitchen with a handful of pills and a glass of tap water, then would she really have cared at all what had happened back there in the illegals' camp?

She tries to recall the deep feeling she had back in Liz's kitchen, the desperation that pushed her to such an extreme. She shivers and the hairs on the back of her neck stand. It wasn't death she was seeking. It was control. Control over her life, control to make her own choices.

Looking behind toward the track, she reassures herself with the distance she has created for her safety.

The men have such limited choice. Choice of where they live, how they work, if they are with their loved ones or not. Choice must be mankind's ultimate freedom. She has never dared to grasp her choices. Again and again, she has given her power of choice to anyone who would take it. But now she is even prepared to try and kill herself to regain control. Stupid, just stupid. All she has to do is just take it. Make the choices and be prepared for the consequences.

The men are not even seeking choice; they act from the need for food, the need to provide for their families.

They are worlds apart.

Puma was probably the same age as Joss; Nike seemed younger even than Finn. The thought of her boys going away and not knowing when they would return is unthinkable. Besides, they are always only a Skype call away. But somewhere, Mummy Nike and Mummy Puma sit not knowing what has happened to their boys, whether they are alive or dead, all because they do not have papers and passports.

What freedom her passport gives her. The freedom to come and go anywhere she likes.

This thought gives her a little thrill of excitement. She may be under the dictatorship of Laurence, but the reality is, if she has the guts, she can leave. She can go anywhere she chooses.

For the first time ever, there is the glimpse of the possibility of breaking free, not just to move to Douglas on the Isle of Man or back home to Ireland but further afield, even to go somewhere exotic—alone. She shivers in the heat at the thought.

Some of the things Nicolaos said about choosing the meaning in her life are beginning to have power, although she cannot really say she completely grasps all he meant. Nike has shown her how privileged she is. Everything feels like it is shifting, creating butterflies in her chest rather than her stomach. Everything is coming into focus.

For so long, she has focused on what she could not do, the rules Laurence covertly introduced into her life that took away her choices. But now the question is changing. She is no longer interested in what Laurence is trying to stop her doing. Now her inquiry is what she can do! Nicolaos was right on that point, too! She has been one of those people who focusses on the bad and consequently blinds herself to the possibilities available to her.

Her eyebrows lift in surprise. She has always considered herself to be a positive person. The truth is, looking at her life positively, she can do anything, anything at all.

From the darkest place inside her, the weight shifts and, bubbling into her thoughts with it, quite unexpectedly, comes an explanation to her extraordinary reaction to Finn's wedding, why at some level she had not wanted it to go ahead, why it brought tears to her eyes and why the wedding would also release her from her sadness. Yes, that was it! Once her youngest son is married, both boys are safe. Safe in their life courses, leaving her all alone. Alone with Laurence. The thought pulls her mouth down at the corners, her nose wrinkling. But it seems the decision has already been made, the decision that terrified her, why Finn's marriage terrified her. The marriage is to be the turning point. It will be time to leave Laurence.

'Leave Laurence.' She says the words out loud to make them real. Such a terrifying idea, she has pushed it back and covered it over until it sat like a weight in the pit of her stomach, turning, churning over every time it tried to surface, pulling her down.

But now, the thought of Finn being married and the last apron strings undone, the weight in her stomach, the dark shapes, shifts. 'Leave Laurence.' She says the words again and the weight begins to lighten.

'Leave Laurence.' She whispers it, turning her face to the sky so the words are taken away on the breeze. She feels lighter and lighter. The dark weight bubbles into excitement. 'Leave Laurence.' She states the words which are clearly filling her with joy. She will leave Laurence, but instead of that being a fear for her, it now feels like freedom, the choice to do anything, make anything important. A new meaning for her life. Now she understands what Nicolaos meant. Whatever had she been so afraid of?

Her steps gain a bounce, her arms a swing. She hums to herself.

Compared to Nike and Puma and their friends, she has all the choices in the world. She could go to Africa, to India, Japan, Australia, anywhere she wants. Not only could she go, but she could call it home if she likes. There are always jobs if you are prepared to do what no one else will do. Nike and his friends prove it with their watches and bracelets. Back home, the newspapers always advertise a job or two, a gardener wanted or someone to make beds at the hotels on the seafront. What luxury such a job would appear to the illegals, but they don't have this choice. She does.

Other thoughts jumble for attention. The slap in the face that Laurence doesn't love her. So what, she will survive. Maybe free of Laurence, she can find love. Not another Torin; there'll never be another Torin. But then again, she isn't a teenager anymore and a boy in a Megadeth t-shirt would not interest her now.

She takes a breath. Her thoughts seem like blasphemy.

It will take time. She has been living her life based on a network of lies and beliefs. Lies and beliefs that are now shredded full of gaping holes, the structure of her world fragmenting with every thought, reducing the life she has been living from being painful to becoming ridiculous. She has been a fool, a fool for years, right from the agreement with Liz to go for a free lunch at the golf club. It will take time. Time to reassess. Time to forgive herself.

A dotting of houses announces the village. Returning to Laurence at this point is not a possibility. She can't. She needs to think more, work out what she is going to do. She stops, makes a decision, and takes the road that goes to Helena. She will go to the gully with the insects, the bees humming, a peaceful place where she can sit and think.

The gully is alive with nectar-seeking buzzing, the overhanging bushes providing some shade. Her stomach grumbles. The afternoon must be getting on; she still has had no lunch. The heat is relentless. If she is not careful, she will become dehydrated. There are no good-sized stones to sit on, so she sweeps a bit of dusty ground with her shoe, clearing away smaller pebbles to make the ground smooth. She will sit for a while and then she must go and at least find a drink. Not at home, nor at Liz's. She couldn't face that. How is she going to explain the empty bottles and pills all over the floor? There is hope that Nicolaos will clear them away.

She groans. She would rather he hadn't caught her. But then again, if he hadn't, maybe she would be lying on the kitchen floor by now with no choices left at all. Stupid, really stupid. If she had listened more carefully to the things Nicolaos had said, she could have got to this point without such extremes perhaps.

'No,' she says aloud. 'I will not do guilt anymore, either.' She looks up to the top of one of the bushes, where two white butterflies dance around each other. 'Nicolaos knows what he knows, and it is up to him how he deals with it.' The cicadas nearly drown her words. 'The question is,' she continues aloud, taking comfort from her own voice, 'what do I want to do and where do I want to do it?' She waits for an answer, but nothing comes to mind.

It was cooler when she was moving; the gully is a heat trap. Perhaps up in the field will be cooler, but she needs to apply some stealth in case Nicolaos is there. She is not ready to see him, either.

From behind the last bush, Sarah can see that the field is empty of both goats and shepherd. She steps into the open. Under the tree, halfway up, will be coolest place to sit.

'Well hello.'

Her head turns so fast, she feels slightly dizzy.

'Oh Frona. I didn't see you there.' Frona is holding a wooden frame and a dustbin bag with slats of wood poking from it as she stands in front of one of the old beehive boxes.

'What are you doing?' Sarah clumsily tries to forget her thoughts and make conversation.

'Just being here takes me back to happy days.' Frona looks at the broken frame in her hand before stuffing it into the bin bag with a sigh. 'Before we left, before the new house, when the old one stood there and it was just me and Nikiforos.' The old woman looks up the hill at what can be seen of the new house over the high fence.

'Was that your husband?' Sarah asks. Frona nods.

'Most of our income came from these bees and those.' She turns and points up the hill to hives beyond sight. 'He would come out here just to watch them, and when he returned, he would always ask how they knew.'

'Knew what?'

'The way home, which hive was theirs, which other bees were from their hive.' Frona picks up another broken frame and, between bent hands, breaks it into smaller pieces so they will fit in her bin bag.

'This hive and that one still have bees,' Sarah observes. This is the sort of place and the sort of conversation she would never find with Laurence. Talking about nature, the small things in life that bring the world so alive.

'Yes, such a shame,' Frona says wistfully. 'I have told him, you know, but he won't listen.'

'Who? What?' Sarah asks.

'Jim, my son, Helena's baba.' Frona looks up at her as if Sarah has not been listening. A look that holds Sarah back from asking what she told him.

'But he says, "you are too old to look after bees, too old to be here alone." But I say I won't be alone and then he always cuts me off.'

'You want to live here then?' Sarah picks up a broken frame, the corner still filled with wax comb. 'It doesn't look real, does it?' She pokes at the comb.

'It's not really. Way back, they started making the comb ready on the frame. It saves the bees some work so they make more honey.' She doesn't pause. 'Yes, I want to move back here, it is my home. America is too ... ' She searches for the word. 'American.' Frona sniffs, a noise of pride and defiance.

'Fascinating.' Sarah is still looking at the wax cast comb. 'I learnt a little about beekeeping at night school one year. They didn't even mention ready-made combs, such a good idea.' She looks at Frona. 'So why don't you just move back anyway?'

'Well, I guess it is Jim's house now the old one has gone. He built this new monstrosity and he is worried for me to be here without someone to watch over my moods. He tells me people do extreme things when they are depressed and alone.' Sarah shifts her weight as she listens. 'That, and he's frightened me into thinking I will get confused with the alarm system, or the air conditioning control or something. I think the real reason he doesn't want me to come is because he knows I will try and spend time with ...' She hesitates, looks quickly at Sarah and away again. 'There's a split in my family. It is all very sad.' Frona exhales heavily.

Sarah thinks of Pru and the situation with Finn and Helena. She can see how it could happen.

The old woman continues. 'But I think I would be happy back here, not so lonely as Jersey. Maybe I would keep bees again, maybe not. I wouldn't put the alarm system on.' She chuckles and struggles to break up a thicker piece of wood. After a try, she hands it to Sarah, who snaps it under her foot. 'Haven't got the balance to do that,' Frona says, watching her.

'I am thinking of moving abroad.' Sarah tries out the thought.

'From here? You aren't staying for the wedding?'

'No, I mean from the Isle of Man and the UK.' Just saying the names makes them seem so far away.

'You are going to move here?' Frona asks, her eyes lighting up.

'Well, no, well, I don't know. I hadn't really thought where. I just thought I could move.' She looks up the hill. 'Are you going to restore any of the hives?'

'Doesn't seem much point if no one's here? Why don't you move here, run the hives, in fact, run the house. Solution!' She almost shouts, as if saying *eureka*. 'I'll stay and you can run the house and the bees and Jim can't argue.'

'What a lovely idea,' Sarah laughs.

Frona gives her a hard look. 'I am serious.' Sarah recognises something in the old woman's eyes, the need to escape, the need to have control over her own life. He heart reaches out for the old lady, who physically reaches out and takes Sarah's hand and grips it with surprising strength.

She can't just up and leave her old life like that. She has a house with Laurence back on the Isle of Man full of her things. Sarah mentally scans the rooms, what would she miss, what would she want with her? There's things the boys drew and made when they were young. She couldn't part with those, but then, probably, neither could Laurence. But she can't stay for a clay dragon and a two-year-old's self-portrait, and she would be glad to leave her clothes. What else? There must be something. But nothing comes to mind. Her mother's wedding ring and her grandmother's book of psalms.

'You know, I could.' The words come out slowly as the realisation dawns on her.

'The old house was so much better, no stairs, not so many gadgets, simple. An open fire, no air conditioning, nothing that could go wrong that we couldn't fix ourselves. But if I were to stay, why would I go upstairs? All I need is my room and the kitchen.' Frona lets go her hand and looks back at the broken pieces of hive still on the grass.

'I suppose the pool needs maintenance?' Sarah offers.

'Jim has a pool man who comes once a week.'

The whole idea is very charming. She could do up the hives, make honey. She would need her computer so she could Google things she didn't know and Skype to call the boys. She is not sure if she is thinking seriously or having a little fantasy, not sure whether to encourage Frona about this idea or not.

It's a big house and very modern, beautifully finished and maintained. Ah, there is the catch. Jim will want rent and it will be way beyond her budget. How much would a small place be over here anyway? Maybe something less grand could be a possibility.

'What sort of rent would Jim want?' It sounds too cold and business-like, but it must be considered. Also, it will give her an idea of local rents, how small she would have to go if anything ever did come from this idea. Best to know now rather than start daydreaming and be disappointed if it ever does become real.

'Rent? From whom?' Frona moves down the line of hives to the one at the end and lifts the lid. 'Look!' She steps back but still has the lid up. Sarah peeps in. She cannot stifle the shriek as she leaps back. Frona chuckles as Sarah steels herself to move forward and carefully look again.

'*Boyas*.' Frona looks again herself. The spider cowers. 'I don't know the name in English.'

'It's so big. Do they come in the houses?' Sarah cannot bear to look and she backs away. Its body must be the size of a plum.

'Only seen a dozen or so in my life. I was told that they bite and that they are poisonous when I was a child, but they seem so scared, I cannot imagine either. Never seen one in a house. Rocky places usually, really hidden. When buildings are pulled down, they come out from between the stone work. I think we'll leave this hive. What were you saying?'

This time, Sarah falters. She is not sure it is a good place to move to if the spiders are that size.

'Oh yes, rent. Who would be paying rent?' Frona pushes some of the remains of the frames that litter the floor with her toe, lining them up before she slowly bends to bag them. Sarah hurries to help. She doesn't want to have an answer to her question now, it all feels a bit sudden. 'You mean you? Why would you pay rent? Jim would pay you as housekeeper more like. He is always saying how we should get someone so he can stop worrying about the place when he is not here, get it ready before he arrives. He had a room which he built especially for that purpose, at the back, with its own bathroom and a door to outside.' She stops what she is doing and straightens, looking at Sarah. 'What about your husband?'

Chapter 24

And there it is, the question Sarah least wants to think about. She cannot meet Frona's eye and she busies herself clearing more broken slats.

'Have you had a quarrel?'

'Not exactly.' Sarah draws the word out. If she says her thoughts out loud, they will become real, have power, demand action. 'We, or rather I, well, I have been thinking, how do I put it? It hasn't, well for some time really, been, not sort of working, for me anyway.'

'`Ah, that's sad. I did wonder when you came up to the house on your own. Do the boys know?'

'No. Actually, I don't think even Laurence knows. Fully.'

'Oh. Difficult. So it would be a bit of a shock if you were to tell him you were staying here?' Frona laughs, but Sarah can see that the tiny spark of hope she had in her eyes has extinguished. It makes her realise how desperate Frona must be to move back to Greece if she is hanging any hope on their conversation when these talks are in such a stage of infancy.

'Did you grow up in this village?' Sarah tries to lighten the conversation.

'No, I was born in Asia Minor.'

'Asia Minor?' Geography at school never really held Sarah's attention.

'Part of Turkey now. At the time, they wanted us out. My baba, he disappeared in the fighting when I was young, then they came for my mother.' She crosses herself three times. 'Into the house.' She puts the bag of wood down. 'I hid with my brother in the wardrobe and we watched through the crack between the doors.' She takes a sudden, short breath. 'They killed her.'

'Oh my God, how terrible. How old were you?' Sarah looks at Frona with new eyes. The old woman shrugs. Either she doesn't know how old she was or her age didn't matter. Sarah is not sure what to add. She cannot imagine losing her mother as a young child, but to watch her being murdered ... It was bad enough as a teen watching the cancer eat Mum's life away. She was seventeen when the disease won, and where was her father? Off in Waterford with that woman half his age, making excuses. He will be an old man now, if he is still alive. Sarah shakes her head slowly.

'I lost my mum from cancer when I was seventeen,' she shares. Frona crosses herself on Sarah's behalf.

'They put us in an orphanage and then we were shipped over to Greece in the population exchange. We knew no one. My brother, so young, had to find us shelter, work like a man to put food in our mouths, became a father to me.'

Frona takes out a water bottle from the folds of her skirt and offers some to Sarah. It is like liquid gold on her throat in the heat. She has to stop herself from drinking it all. Frona takes only a sip and puts it away.

'It sounds hard,' is all Sarah can think to say.

'It was. Nikiforos was just a bit older than Nikos, my brother. He had a family. We all grew close. His family took pity on us and we became their family, too. It was their wish I marry Nikiforos.'

'Oh.' Sarah's exclamation is sounded without thinking. The way Frona talks of her husband is as if he is her soul mate. Sarah closes her mouth firmly. She doesn't trust herself to say anything more. Guilt begins to raise its ugly head. If Frona stuck by her arranged marriage for all those years, it puts shame on her thinking of leaving Laurence.

'But we were already in love long before they mentioned it.' Frona giggles and Sarah can hear the girl she once was. It's also a relief.

'Would you think it terrible if I left my husband?' Sarah asks. It suddenly feels important to get this woman's view on her situation. She has been through so much and must have wisdom beyond anything Sarah could imagine.

'Is he making you unhappy?' Frona's voice is quiet.

'Yes, very.' Tears from nowhere prick her eyes and the world begins to blur before she blinks and waits for the reply. The waiting is like watching a tossed coin in the air. Which side will fall? Heads she leaves him, tails she stays.

'Life is very short, you know,' is all Frona says.

It's enough. The decision becomes firm.

'Frona?' Sarah opens.

'Yes?' The old woman looks around the bee hives. They have cleared a lot of the debris. It looks tidy now, cared for.

'Tell Jim I am willing to stay here with you.'

Frona stops looking around her and focuses on Sarah's face.

'You want me to do that, really? I don't want to put you off, but I want you to be sure. Don't do anything in haste.'

'It has been too long. It is time.' This is the truth, and the opportunity presented is like a gift falling from the Greek gods. Now all she needs is the guts to tell Laurence.

Frona takes both Sarah's hands in hers and now there are tears in the old lady's eyes. They look at each other for several seconds, checking, double-checking, reassuring themselves, each delighted in the escape they have found, the solution that has been presented.

Their trance is unbroken even by the sounds of goats and it is only when one passes them on its way to the bushes that their eyes unlock.

'Oh I must go.' Sarah pulls her hands free. She is not ready to meet Nicolaos yet and surely where the goats are, he is not far away.

'No, no, please don't go.' Frona's grip tightens.

'Really I must.' Sarah's back is to the hill but she can picture him striding down, crook in hand.

'Just stay a minute.'

'Really, I must go.' Sarah tries to sound kind, but she is just a little desperate. Another goat passes her, towards the bushes. He must be sitting under the tree by now or even closer if he is coming their way.

'Please?' Frona begs and Sarah begins to wonder why.

'Ti kaneis?' The low voice can only be Nicolaos'. Frona releases her grip and opens her arms. Sarah turns and stands opened mouthed as Nicolaos bends into the old lady's open arms and kisses her tenderly on the cheek.

'Sarah, this is my younger son, Nicolaos.'

Sarah can feel herself frowning and she consciously raises her brow as she looks from one to the other.

'The cast-out black sheep.' Nicolaos extends his hand to shake hers as if they have never met. Sarah shakes, but he is not eager to let go and her fingers remain longer than necessary.

'The estranged brother?' Sarah asks and then it all falls into place: the caustic wife that Jim would have nothing to do with, the Australian link, so obvious now, she wonders why she didn't put two and two together before.

'Jim is such a jealous boy, we do not tell him of our meetings, or our letters. It is our secret.' Frona's hand reaches out for Nicolaos' arm, her love evident in every look, every motion.

'So you must not give away our secret.' His eyes twinkle as he speaks and Sarah knows he is really promising to keep her own.

'Absolutely not,' Sarah answers, and she is sure she can see his father's face in Nicolaos' own features, the boy who befriended Frona and her brother. The man who vowed to care for the old woman.

Jim looks more like Frona, that's for sure.

'We have another secret,' Frona tells Nicolaos, who finally lets go of Sarah's hand and puts an arm around his mother. 'I am going to stay here. No more New Jersey.'

'Oh Mama, *auto einai fantastiko.*' Nicolaos sounds excited. Maybe *fantastiko* means fantastic; he looks pleased. *'Alla ti lei o Jim?'* Sarah picks out the word *Jim*. His face is serious now.

'Aha! That is the secret. Jim's argument is he does not want me here in the house on my own.' She sighs. 'He is still denying your existence.' Her eyes search Nicoalos' until she returns to the subject with energy. 'So Sarah is going to stay and be my companion and the housekeeper.' Frona sounds triumphant. Nicolaos turns from his mother to Sarah and stares.

'Really?' he asks.

Sarah nods. His look is penetrating. His lips move as if to ask a question, but he shuts his mouth again and turns to his mother. 'You have told Jim?'

'Er no, not yet.'

'And you have told your family?' He turns to Sarah, who feels a heat raising in her neck, creeping up her cheeks. She cannot answer.

'We have only just come up with the plan,' Frona steps in. Nicolaos frowns slightly and says no more. Sarah can see Frona deflating.

'Nicolaos, do not spoil this.'

'Not for a million drachmas, Mama, but I know how stubborn and proud Jim can be. He will not want to back down.'

'There is no backing down. It is a decision. He might like to think the house is his, but until I die, the land it is built on is mine and if I want to stay, I will stay. Besides, having Sarah by my side gives me courage, and now he has no reason to object.'

'And your family?' Nicolaos turns to Sarah.

Sarah's not sure what to say. Finn will stand by her. He and Laurence get on, but Finn is, and always will be, a mummy's boy. And she will be staying with Helena's grandmother. He might even like the idea. The gelling together of the two families.

Joss will shrug, maybe sulk a bit, but he has always seen people as individuals even when they are in relationships. Like this argument with Pru and Helena. It never crossed his mind that anyone might connect Pru's behaviour to him, or that either of their behaviour could be connected to Finn. In his eyes, that would be ridiculous. No, he will deal with it pragmatically, ask when will he see her, moan a little about the long journey from the US to Greece, and no doubt suggest a meeting point—London, maybe. She could stay with Liz.

But Laurence. She has no idea how he will react. He seemed pretty adamant that she will continue to be there when he gets home after a stint of work. He seems to find the thought of anything changing unthinkable.

When he asked her why she was making his life difficult that first time she suggested going with him on one of his trips, he was harsh. Hard, even. Back then, she had no idea what he was and was not capable of, and she has no greater idea now. He is a closed book.

'The boys will be fine,' Sarah finally answers.

'And your husband?' Nicolaos' head is slightly tipped to one side, his eyes moist. He knows the pain of separation.

'I think once the deed is done, he will be reasonable, fair. But honestly, I have no idea how he will take it.' Sarah cannot miss the anguish of his own divorce in Nicolaos' face. She must tread gently telling Laurence it is over. There is no reason to cause unnecessary pain.

The shepherd does not look away from her. He is wanting her to say something more, but what more can she say? That it will be fine, that Laurence won't care? She doesn't know that. She has no idea what his reaction will be, but she suspects the main emotion will be anger.

'Right.' Nicolaos finally breaks his gaze. 'Here Mama, or up by the tree?'

'Oh, by the tree.' Frona sounds sure. 'Sarah, will you join us?'

Nicolaos turns his back to show her a rucksack. 'Picnic lunch.' He smiles now and Frona takes her arm, and the three of them climb to the shade. Frona has the flat stone as her seat, Nicolaos and Sarah sit in the warm dust, and the food is spread. Foil is peeled away, tupperwares are unlidded, forks are passed. Feta, fresh bread, olives, a ceramic pot of yoghurt, tomatoes, a small bottle of olive oil and a jar that Frona tells her is fresh oregano as, after she pours a little oil on her bread, she sprinkles it on top before taking a big bite. Nicolaos is dipping his bread into the yoghurt.

Sarah takes the water bottle and drinks her fill. Frona twists the cap off a plastic bottle of local wine. There are only two plastic mugs, but Frona gives one to Sarah.

The goats munch their way towards them until Frona is the one to throw a pebble at their feet. The action is as thoughtless as breathing, and it is easy to see how ideal her life must have been with Nikiforos in those early days.

'Where do you live then?' Sarah asks Nicolaos.

'He has a lovely house over the other side of the hill. The one with the stone arches,' Frona interrupts. Sarah frowns.

'It is rented out at the moment to friends of yours, I think?' Nicolaos glances at her as he breaks off a lump of feta.

'Oh, that place is yours?' Sarah sounds more incredulous than she means to and tries to redeem herself by adding, 'But if you rent it out, where do you live?'

'The back field there with the really old house on it. Nice place, no stairs, everything simple, like the old one here used to be.' Frona jerks a yogurt-covered thumb over her shoulder.

Nicolaos smiles at his mother. 'You'd still be living in that house if you had your way.'

'I most certainly would. Some modern things save time, but so much just makes life more complicated. If you can't fix it yourself, you have no business having whatever it is.' Frona is emphatic.

Nicolaos chuckles and Sarah grins. Frona is one of those women she just can't help but like. Everything she does and says makes her smile.

They slowly eat their way through the food, talk of the possibilities of Frona and Sarah's plan, what to do with the beehives, and where to get more bees. Frona says Nicolaos should move into the new house and let her have the old cottage. Nicolaos laughs, telling her how dirty and basic it is, how her memory is not true to reality and that she would not like all the work of keeping the dust at bay and no air conditioning in the summer and the damp in the winter. Frona says she lived before air conditioning, that people have gone soft, and on they banter until the leftovers are either thrown to the goats or packed away again. Nicolaos stands and stretches.

Sarah picks up a round, smooth pebble and tucks it in her pocket.

'Mama,' he groans with his hands above his head. He exhales and they drop to his sides. 'I, too, have something to tell you. But you are not to be sad. It is for the best.' He sounds nervous.

'You have sent her the divorce papers?'

'How did you know?' Nicolaos' motions freeze, his eyebrows arch.

'For years, you have been carrying the weight of that woman. Today I can see a weight has lifted from you. It is a natural conclusion.' Frona does not smile.

'But, I ...' Nicolaos stammers.

'That, and you have a proof of postage receipt in the bottom of your rucksack.' Now she grins, her eyes twinkling in the same way Nicolaos' do.

'You are cross?' Nicolaos moves again, breaking into his own broad grin.

'How can I be cross? You moved here two years ago, alone. I have had plenty of time to get used to the idea.'

'Will you tell Jim for me?'

'Why don't you tell him yourself? It might help.'

'Because he will think that he has won.' Nicolaos sets his mouth in a hard line.

'For the love of Christ, you are not children anymore. It is not a competition, and you are grown men. It is time you started acting like them.' Frona takes his hand and pats it.

'Tell him for me, Mama, and ask if I can call round? I would like to be there for Helena's wedding,' he looks at Sarah, 'to this lady's son.'

'Ah, so you know who she is?' Frona narrows her eyes.

'Actually, we have met once or twice when I have been out walking and Nicolaos has been herding the goats,' Sarah interrupts. She should have said this when she was first introduced. She doesn't know why she didn't.

'You kept that quiet.' Frona looks from Sarah to her son to Sarah and back again.

'Come on, Mama.' Nicolaos yawns and stretches again. 'I need my *mesimeriano* sleep.'

'Me too.' Frona struggles to her feet.

Nicolaos has turned to go up the hill; Frona has turned towards the side gate of her house. Sarah suddenly realises she must decide what she is doing next.

'Well, I'll be off then,' she says, with no idea of where she is off to. A sleep would be good; it has felt like a long day so far.

'So I will talk to Jim about the companion/housekeeping idea and let him know your news.' She turns first to Sarah and then her son. 'Life's never dull, is it.' She chirps and begins her slow shuffle to the gate.

'I'll walk you to the gate, Mama.' Nicolaos catches up with her and waves to Sarah, keeping eye contact for a split second longer than necessary. Sarah heads back down the hill.

Now what? Does she go home and tell Laurence before she knows if Jim agrees to their plans, or should she wait to hear what Jim says, with the risk of the children getting to know first through Helena and then spilling the beans before she has had the chance to explain everything to Laurence?

Perhaps she should talk to Laurence first. But if Jim vetoes the plan, will there be any going back?

'Don't be stupid. You won't want to.' Sarah speaks aloud as she turns into the gully between the bushes down the road. Her fingers caress the smooth pebble in her pocket as she takes in the hum of the insects in the afternoon heat.

As the gully meets the road, she heads home to face Laurence.

Chapter 25

She turns into her lane when her phone pings. It is a text from Finn.

'So happy. Wedding back on.'

Sarah lets her head drop back and she smiles. 'Just let everything come together,' she asks the blue sky. A cat runs down the lane to greet her, and it winds around her legs. It is one of Juliet's. The animal arches its back to meet her caress and makes a noise between a meow and a purr. They walk together up the lane. The animal provides enough distraction that Sarah does not think about Laurence, nor does she look up from the cat until, in her peripheral vision, she notices that alongside their hire car is Neville's. That's all she needs. His and Laurence's voices come from inside, through the open door to the kitchen and beyond in the sitting room. Confident that she cannot be seen coming through the gate if they are in the sitting room, she passes noiselessly onto the decking and tiptoes into the bedroom. She really could do with a nap.

The cottage is built solidly of stone, but the muffled sound of Neville and Laurence's laughter permeates the layers. Cool to the touch, Sarah leans against the dividing wall, her cheek and hands against the stone. In one particular sandy recess, she can hear their words filtering through distinctly.

'I swear that machine does more to the gallon than my Audi,' Neville brags.

'But you haven't really been anywhere. Did you check the odometer when you started?' Laurence replies.

'No, but you get a feel for these things when you do as much driving as I do.'

It's the same old drivel. Neville bragging in his passive-aggressive way, Laurence competing. Pulling herself from the cool of the stone and lying on the bed, she deliberates the best way to tell Laurence. Perhaps not directly at first. Maybe even say she is staying on to get to know Helena's family. Laurence will not want to stay on with her, she feels certain of that. Besides, he has work. But then, if she does not tell him face to face before he leaves, she will have to tell him by Skype, or email. That's not good.

Laurence's laugh filters through the stones. It grates on her every nerve. Her decision seems to have made her less tolerant even to his voice. What really will she lose if she goes?

There's her home, of course, but the house is in his name anyway, as are the cars. She will lose the ease of never worrying about money. That's hard, but it is not as if she gets the chance to indulge in designer clothes or has racks full of shoes. Laurence buys all those sorts of things for her anyway. She doesn't need the hairdresser; she can manage to do her own hair, manicure her own nails and, on a reduced income, she would be happy to eat less meat. In fact, she would be happy to not eat meat at all. Well maybe, or perhaps that is just a reaction to Laurence's *meat with every meal* policy.

If she divorces him, maybe, surely, she has a right to a settlement. The papers are full of women who gain vast lump sums from people they have been married to for just a few months. Her twenty-six years is a lifetime compared to them.

Maybe she would have got her life together and trained in something if she had not married Laurence? Maybe she would have something to offer to the world by now? But she chose to marry him, so she cannot really lay that at his door as though that is his fault. But in a settlement case, surely the cooking and organising, the cleaning and hostessing for him all these years, that must be worth something? If she had been paid for it, would she have saved much? But the truth is she has no idea how divorces work.

Her laptop lays closed by the bed. The screen springs to life as she opens it. She isn't sure what to type in, what she is really looking for. Just typing in *divorce* brings up a host of legal firms offering quick solutions. But there is also a link to a divorce and separation calculator.

'What ever next?' Sarah whispers to herself as she shakes her head and clicks on the link. The majority of the questions are around Laurence's income, which she does not know the answer to, but as she moves down the list of questions, with growing irritation, it seems there is no value to the daily work she does around the house and Sarah clicks away in anger. Back on Google, she thinks what to type, something, anything to show that her time is valuable. She types in *Housekeeper weekly wage,* not really expecting anything useful to appear.

Several sites offer information on hiring home help. One of the link for housekeepers suggests a weekly amount that is way beyond whatever she could have imagined and she exclaims 'Good grief!' out loud. Clicking open the calculator tool, she multiplies the weekly figure by fifty-two. With her bed and board taken care of there, would be very little else she would have to spend her money on. Her own clothes if she had the choice, but in this light, she could regard the clothes Laurence bought for her as a uniform. Her eyebrows drop. If her clothes he bought her are uniforms, what was the uniform of the Saturday night dinners? Laurence's taste in evening dresses was frills around a plunging neckline and high heels. Who would wear a uniform like that? With a grimace and her eyes half-shut she looks up *Escort rates* out of curiosity. A site with a rather dubious photo at the top offers a list of prices on its front page. Prices for dinner based on hours and location, but nearer the bottom, there are additional prices if there will be an overnight stay. Here, there is discreet link to *further individual preferences,* but Sarah does not feel brave enough to know more. It's another world. The figures are mind boggling. One Saturday night three-hour dinner would earn double the weekly wage of a housekeeper.

With this taken into account, she is sure she could have saved all her wages as a housekeeper if she had been employed by Laurence all these years. Bringing up the calculator, she multiplies the weekly housekeeper's wage by the number of years she has been married. 'Oh ...' She holds in an expletive. She could have bought their large house with its extensive gardens and the one next door outright by now! Looking at the stone wall behind which Laurence and Neville continue their laughing and talking, Sarah closes the laptop and reassesses her position.

The laptop will not go back on the bedside table without moving her purse, which she puts on her knee. Settling back, she opens her purse and looks at the picture she keeps there of the boys. So young. Joss was about ten when that was taken, Finn only eight. Finn still looks the same. Bless them. There can be no price on them. Behind the picture of the boys is a photograph of her and Laurence on their wedding day. She looks so young but awkward in the dress, which cost so much, it had scared her. She wouldn't have the same reaction today—she is used to wearing these sorts of clothes now. So much has changed. In the picture, Laurence holds his arm up for her to link with him, his other hand over hers. The gesture looks tender, as if he had sworn to take care of her. Which he had, and does.

Maybe things would have been different if she had not met Laurence. But maybe her sinking into despair over Torin's death would have continued, spiralled out of control. She was on the edge of just not bothering to go into work; what if that had happened? She would have lost her job and Liz would have had to pay for rent and food for them both. Poor Liz. There was no way she could have managed. What would have happened? She wouldn't have had the money to go back to Ireland. Besides, she would not have left Liz. Would she have become homeless, sleeping on cardboard at the end of the alley where her and Liz's pokey, damp flat was? Who knows?

Standing and taking her purse and picture to the wall that divides her from her husband, she leans against it. Maybe he has been her knight in white armour after all. Maybe she is being too harsh on him. Perhaps he deserves better. After all, what has he done, really? He married her, bought her clothes, and gave her an easy and luxurious lifestyle. What had he asked for in return? Not much, really. They had two beautiful boys which she gladly and willing raised, but since then? Well, dinners out, and dinner cooked when, or rather, if he came home. He seldom complained about anything, although he made it clear what he expected, and that kept her busy. Quality cooking, a fully stocked larder and wine cellar and, ultimately, not to have to think about the upkeep of the house or gardens. If a drain was blocked, Sarah must call a plumber; if something heavy needed moving, she had to wait until the gardener came. Laurence wanted his world to run smoothly with no thought at all in return for the lifestyle he gave her. It wasn't such a bad deal.

But does it rule out her right to want change, her right to move on?

Her hands drop, still holding picture and purse, and her head inclines against the stone wall, her cheek revisiting the cool. She has no idea what is right and what is wrong in this situation.

Neville is laughing hard.

'Do you remember that car you bought from me?' He seems to think this is funny, but Laurence is not laughing.

'The green one,' Laurence replies. He sounds a little drunk. Sarah looks at her watch. Well, it is late afternoon. 'That BMW. Scrapped it quick as I could. It nearly got me killed,' Laurence slurs.

'Did it? You never said.' Neville's laughter subsides.

'Just after the TT races. I was due over in Jurby—you remember that airships company that took over the disused RAF base up there for a while? Well, I knew one of them. Can't remember what he wanted from me. Anyway, I was in the Albert when he called. Bob was it, Robert, or Regi, can't remember now. Asked could I pop over, he asked, needed some information from a pilot. Good money involved for such a short trip out, I seem to remember, but it meant leaving the pub.'

'Which is a crime in itself,' Neville guffaws.

'Anyway, taking the A18 was the obvious choice, cut straight across.' Laurence is speaking quietly and Sarah can only just pick out the words.

'Hell of a journey using any another route by Isle of Man standards.' Sarah recognises Neville's idea of humour. He sniggers at his own joke.

'The A18 was re-opening from the races later that day, so I ignored the closed signs, drove straight past them. Damn fool thing to do, nearly got killed.' Laurence is trying to cut off Neville's laughter.

'Clear roads encourage anyone to drive too fast,' Neville replies, sympathy replacing his mirth, his over-expression suggesting how much he had drunk.

'Wasn't that! It was a fool of a boy on a motor bike, came careering down the road, no helmet, no control, one foot off the foot plate, hardly got himself round Craig-ny-Baa corner and headed straight at me.'

'You never told me.' Neville's voice is genuinely sober now.

'Quick reflexes got me out of that one. Steered around him last minute, straightened up just in time to take the corner. Damn fool. Hit the sump tank on something, bent a wheel rim. When I got to Jurby, I was still sweating. That was first and last time out with that pile of rust. Decided the car was bad luck, so I sold the thing to a farmer up there in Jurby.' There is a pause. 'He only wanted the engine. He said the car body could rot in his field for all he cared. Funny old bloke. Still spoke the Gaelic.'

‘Sounds like a near thing,’ Neville replies. ‘Ice?’ he asks, his voice quieter, presumably from the kitchen.

‘Make it neat this time,’ Laurence says.

Sarah absorbs the conversation, the picture of their wedding day slipping from her fingers, fluttering to the floor. Mechanically, she lifts her purse, her fingers exploring the pocket behind her driving licence until she pulls out the picture of Torin.

‘And I bet the biker drove on completely unaware,’ Neville continues, his voice growing louder again.

‘Well, I saw him wobble a bit. I think he might have come off, but to be honest, served him right; shouldn’t be on the roads if he had no control. Nearly killed me,’ Laurence clips.

He knew. He knew Torin came off and he didn’t stop. No wonder he sold the car to the farmer in Jurby. No wonder the police couldn’t find it, didn’t find it trying to leave the island on the ferry. The cold sweat on her brow runs down her temple. Her hands are shaking so much, she can no longer hold purse or picture. She puts them both on the chest of drawers next to her and grabs its edge as her legs feel like jelly. She sinks, sitting on the bed. What kind of man is Laurence? To hit and run could be fear. it could even be instinct, but to cold-heartedly get rid of the car the same day is calculated awareness. He knew, all right.

There is a ringing in her ears and flashing brightness before her eyes. She closes them to see Torin's body hurtling through the air and the man in the green car look away from her, looking around at the bike on the ground. He saw Torin, saw him sail over the fence. As she ran, the car came to a halt before speeding off. She opens her eyes again. There is a good chance she is going to be sick. The salt in her mouth makes her salivate. Her forehead feels ice cold, her throat constricts, there is nothing but the taste of salt, saliva. The muscles in her neck twitch. She grabs the wastepaper bin, hugging it on her knee. Her stomach contracts and she retches, expunging her horror, her shock, her disgust, her loss until she is gasping for air and there is a stinging in the back of her nose. The father of her children killed her soul mate. She heaves again and pants furiously, holding back the urge to vomit again. But there is no holding back. The beautiful picnic lunch returns as burning acid. One hand across her stomach, her muscles ache, she pants again, and the spasm quietens.

She lifts her head, looks out of the window at the blue sky and the lush fig tree. The back of her nose is on fire. Putting down the bin, she grabs for a tissue from Laurence's side of the bed. Blowing her nose does not help. She spits in the paper and wipes her mouth before throwing it in the bin.

Chapter 26

Perhaps it's her duty to tell the police? Would they believe her? The car will have rusted into the ground by now. Laurence would deny ever having the conversation she just heard, and no doubt Neville would back him up. Sarah looks out of the patio windows to the decking and chairs at the front of the house where she had sat holding her boys' hands. The bottom line is does she want her sons to have a father in prison and a mother who put him there? Sons with wives, maybe one day, grandchildren. How would having a grandfather in jail reflect on them? The incident suddenly seems a long time ago.

But of one thing she is now absolutely sure: she is not going back to the Isle of Man with Laurence. Back to his house that she has always struggled to call home. She will never load that dishwasher looking through the side window across the lawn as Laurence's car pulls out of the drive again. She will never pull his shirts from his stop-over bag after a long flight again, never check the pockets of his trousers for change before stuffing them into the washing machine in the utility room. There will be no more chats with Mrs McGee, watching biscuit crumbs gather around her mouth between slurps in her coffee break, duster still in her hand. No more lonely afternoons sitting in the conservatory waiting for the crunch of Laurence's tyres on the drive, just glad he is home for the sake of some company.

Maybe she should feel joyous, but, looking in the mirror on the chest of drawers, all she can see are the lines, the wasted years in her eyes and her loveless existence. The man who vowed to love her all these years is the man who killed the only person with whom she had ever really known love.

No, she will not tell Laurence that she now knows, nor will she tell him her plans. She will not tell him anything ever again.

Her phone rings. It's a Greek number. Nicolaos springs to mind, but she casts the image away before it is truly formed. It could be someone calling from a land line—Helena, Finn, even Joss from the hotel.

'Hello.' She speaks quietly. Laurence is only next door, and she has not made her presence known yet. While she packs, she would like to keep it that way.

'Hi Sarah? Jim.'

Sarah lets go of her suitcase, which she is pulling from under the bed, and stands straight.

'Jim, hi.' She waits. Has Frona said something already or does he want to talk about the wedding?

'So tomorrow the big day, eh?' He sounds cheerful.

The days have flown. Surely it cannot be the wedding tomorrow already! The date on her watch confirms Jim is right.

'Oh, the days have passed so fast, I have almost lost track of time,' Sarah says and then worries it makes her sound irresponsible.

'Greece does that,' Jim replies as if it is the most natural thing in the world for her to forget her own son's wedding day. 'Mama tells me you two have been cooking up a plan?' For some reason, Sarah is nervous to reply. She looks at her feet shuffling on the bedside rug. He continues, 'She seems very keen. You know she has been suffering from depression, right?'

'Yes, she mentioned it.' Sarah straightens and looks out of the back window to the pool and the fig tree.

'Well nothing seems to have worked, it did occur to me that I should come over here with her, have a sort of long holiday to see if being in her Greece would help, but, really, there is no way I could take the time off work. But if you are really willing?'

'Absolutely.' Sarah breaths more easily. He has a pleasant nature. The way he pronounces some words, she now notices, is like Nicolaos. His accent is a mix of American and Greek, but still with a hint of an Australian twang.

'I have given it some thought and I am still not decided if it is the best for Mama. As for you being a housekeeper for the place, if you are serious and having Mama here is not one of your conditions, let's discuss it in more detail after the wedding. I cannot, for love nor money, find someone I feel comfortable leaving the place in the hands of, but if you have half the ability of Finn, I couldn't wish for anyone better, so I feel very hopeful.' Jim's voice is soft but something in the confidence behind the words shows all the traits Sarah would imagine of a hardened businessman.

'I had not thought of being here without Frona,' Sarah begins. 'But, well, I will give that some thought, too. After the wedding would be a good time to thrash things out.' Maybe 'thrash things out' is a bit of an over-the-top turn of phrase; after all, it is only a housekeeping job, hardly 'thrashing' material, but the last time she discussed her employment was when she and Liz took the jobs in Douglas. It all feels very alien.

'Ha!' His laugh is light, as if he has taken her comment as a joke. He also audibly breathes out and it occurs to Sarah that maybe finding a housekeeper weighs more heavily on him than she has imagined it could. 'Yes, let's beat the terms and conditions into submission after the wedding.' He laughs again. He will be an easy person to discuss the idea with. 'But now, about tonight,' he adds.

Grabbing her handbag from the chest of drawers, Sarah pulls out her diary and thumbs to today's date. Nothing. No note, no scrawled reminder. 'Tonight,' Sarah half-asks and half-states, hoping Jim will fill in the rest.

'I have found a gun for your husband and rice enough for everyone, so just come as you are.'

'Ah!' Sarah has no idea what he is talking about but if anyone is having a gun, it will be her.

'So just to let you know to come when you are ready, really. There is enough food for the whole village.' He chuckles as he speaks. 'See you soon.' And the line is dead.

Texting Helena seems the best idea. Happy to let the rice and guns reveal their purpose during the evening, she simply asks what time. She is rewarded by an instant response. 'Whenever you are ready.' So unhelpful.

In a second text to Joss, she asks what time he is going, and importantly, where he is going, and this time she gets a more concrete answer. 'Helena's about eight or whenever Pru wakes up.' Eight seems about right to be eating and presumably they will be staying up late, too, enlivened in the cool of the night air. A sleep now would be a good idea, let her mind shut down for a bit, calm her thinking. Her stomach turns as she recalls Laurence's words and with it come the images of Torin's death.

Searching through pockets, she finds her four pebbles. She rolls them through her fingers, feeling each one in turn. One from the still warmth of the gully surrounded by thousands of humming bees, one from her late night chat with Finn by the pool under a million stars—such a special night. One that Nicolaos threw at her feet like she was a goat, cheeky man. She gives this one a squeeze. The fourth one from the picnic on the hillside with Frona and Nicolaos still has some traces of red earth on it. She rubs at it with her thumb.

Tucking them under the cool pillow with her hand on top, she calms her mind and tries to look forward. 'I will have enough pebbles a year from now to fill a bucket.' Her eyes close and she drifts into sleep.

The sky is still light when she wakes. She cannot have slept long, but she feels refreshed until the overheard conversation rushes back to her and the room loses some colour, but the memory of the conversation with Jim quickly follows. Twisting her wrist, she checks the time and relaxes. There is time to change and walk to Helena's. She can still hear voices next door. What does she do about Laurence tonight? Does he even know they are due to go to Helena's? It would be adult and responsible of her to tell him tonight's arrangements, and Finn would want her to, but a part of her would enjoy leaving him out in the cold. Ignore him. He deserves nothing from her.

Taking her time to shower and dress, she hears Neville making all the noises that lets her know he is leaving. He and Laurence are now standing on the decking, their backs to the bedroom patio window. Laurence is complaining that she is missing, and something about her being irresponsible. Neville asks if she will have forgotten about the gathering tonight, to which Laurence replies, 'Probably'.

'Well, I'd better push off, get Liz in gear. Takes her an age to get ready,' Laurence responds. Sarah sees an opportunity, and the two men jump as she pushes open the patio door. The outside heat has dropped, but it is still very warm.

'I'll come up with you, Neville. Give Liz a hand.' Sarah walks around them both and climbs into the passenger seat of Neville's car.

Laurence's mouth is open, his eyes wide. He begins a sentence, 'Where have you ...' But seeing Neville's smirk, twisting his keys between his fingers, he acts as if her behaviour is the most natural thing in the world.

'See you later, then. Come up to ours and we'll all go together,' Neville says as he climbs in beside Sarah and gives a brief wave, then cranes his neck round to reverse down the lane. Laurence is coming out of the gate, his mouth shut now. He is waving but frowning. It won't be long before he follows them up to Neville's villa.

'You look awfully pretty.' Neville drives with one hand on the wheel, the other, nearest the passenger seat, remains on the gear stick. Sarah shifts her knees towards the door. She does not answer him. Does she tell Liz what she heard Laurence say? Would it help Liz if she knew, or would it just open old wounds? Really, everyone should know what an evil piece of dirt Laurence is, but to what end? To upset Finn and Joss? To renew Liz's pain? After all, Neville is Laurence's cousin. That's not going to feel great to Liz, her own brother killed by a blood relation of her husband. But then, why should Sarah be on her own with this?

'You're very quiet. Everything okay?' Neville takes his hand from the gear stick and reaches across towards Sarah's knee.

'I hear you are moving your ex-wife in with you. Was it not enough that Liz looked after your mother all these years?' Neville's hand hovers before he withdraws it to the steering wheel.

'Well, I think that's a bit strong.' The colour has drained from his face. His eyes are glued on the road. Sarah's hands are trembling. What is possessing her? She interlocks her fingers. Can she retract her words, shift the meaning, smooth out the harshness? She tries rephrasing the sentence in her head but before she has finished, she is speaking again.

'Do you? Imagine how it is for Liz after all your talk of the things you were going to do together.' But at that moment, Sarah cannot recall anything specific except the sailing, and she cannot remember which islands Liz said they dreamed of sailing around. She closes her mouth and stares out of the side window. Liz is going to kill her; she is way off the 'not discussing each other's husbands' rule.

'Well, things change,' Neville defends himself as he puts his foot down on the accelerator, his knuckles white as he grips the wheel. They crest the hill and Liz and Neville's villa becomes visible. Nicolaos's villa, Sarah corrects herself. She manages to hold her tongue but as the tyres crunch to a standstill, she hears more words hissing from her own mouth, sharp but calm.

'You owe her.' She slides out and slams the car door hard before marching into the house. 'Liz, you there?' she calls loudly. She calls again once inside.

'Out by the pool' There's a sound of splashing, 'Bring the martini, oh, and some ice. Glasses are by the sink if you want one.'

The side door is open, but the back door that Nicolaos barged in by is closed. Sarah's eyes are drawn to the floor, searching for tell-tale pills. It's clean. Gathering the requested items, she makes her way outside. The cicadas are deafening.

'Wow, you look nice,' Liz greets Sarah as she walks round the poolside, bottle and a glass of ice in her hand. 'I haven't even thought about what to wear tonight. What is it exactly, sort a pre-wedding do? Where's Laurence?'

'Laurence wasn't ready; I got a lift with Neville. I'm not really sure what tonight is about. Where's your glass?' Liz, floating on a rather deflated-looking lilo points to the far end of the pool. Sarah pours a generous measure and tops it with the warm lemonade that is sitting in the sun next to the empty glass.

'You not having one?' Liz asks.

'I think it will be a long evening.' The words sound brittle as they resonate through her. She does not know where she will go after the party, but she will not be going back with Laurence. A streak of black humour tells her there is always a worn board to lie on at Nike and Puma's hut.

'You okay? You don't quite look yourself.' Liz paddles towards Sarah and the refilled glass. Liz's hat is so wide, she has to tilt her head back to meet Sarah's gaze. If Sarah is going to tell Liz that Laurence killed Torin, now would be as good a time as any.

'I need to tell you something.' Sarah tries to hold Liz's gaze. Her friend suddenly looks fragile as she breaks eye contact.

'I know,' Liz states but still looks away.

'What?' Sarah screws up her eyes, partly against the sun that is making its way to the horizon and partly from lack of understanding. Her legs stiffen, keeping her rigidly upright.

'Neville made a pass at you, right? On the way here, in the car.' Liz sounds tired, bored almost, rather than accusative.

'Oh no! God no!' Sarah loses her frown, exhales. Her shoulders drop and her legs become her own again. 'No, no.' Her words are emphatic. It helps the decision: she will not tell Liz about Laurence and Torin. Why add any more pain to Liz's life?

'What then?' Liz demands. Sarah searches for something to fill the gap.

'I'm afraid I got cross with Neville in the car, told him a few home truths.' Sarah needs to tell her this anyway.

'Such as?' Liz takes a sip of her drink and pushes off the side with her foot.

'I told him what a good wife you've been and that he owes you.' Sarah is not sure how Liz will respond.

'A double whammy!' Liz chuckles. Sarah frowns but before she can ask for an explanation, Neville's head appears round the side door.

'Ah, Liz my dear, don't you think it's time to start getting ready? I think they are expecting us by eight.' and then he disappears just as fast. Liz turns back to Sarah.

'I told him I was leaving him when he took me out for lunch today.'

'What!' Sarah was about to sit down on a woven cane sunbed but now jerks up.

'I told him that he can pay for a nurse for his ex-wife coz I'm off.' She paddles her way around to face Sarah. 'You remember that waiter with the lovely eyes?'

'Oh, no Liz, what? What's a waiter got to do with this?'

Liz puts out her free hand so Sarah can pull her to the poolside, where she struggles to replace the lilo with solid ground. Once by Sarah's side, Liz takes a long drink of her martini and then reduces her tone to a whisper. 'Nothing. I just made it clear if Neville wants a nurse, he should get a nurse and when he smirked—you know that horrible smirk he does—and said what would I do without him, I just happened to mention Costas.'

'Costas. Is that the waiter's name?' Sarah can feel her temple in her pulse.

'No idea. I'd had one too many, I saw this old dear on the table next to us dribbling her lunch down her chin, and I just thought there was no way I could go through all that again. So when Neville was looking, I winked at the waiter and made the rest up on the spot.'

'You never?' Sarah looks through the open side door to check Neville is not eavesdropping.

'I was really a bit too far gone to know what I was doing, truth be told. But you know what?'

'What?' Sarah thinks the heat must be affecting them all.

'We finished our lunch and Neville held my arm as he walked me back to the car. It seemed a lot further than the way we came and then he pulled me into a jeweller's.'

Sarah checks Liz's ears and neckline before pulling at her hands.

'You won't find anything.' Liz tries to mount the stairs. 'He wouldn't even tell me. I had to look away.'

'I don't understand.' Sarah guides her into the house but Liz just puts her fingers to her lips and Sarah gives up trying to make sense of what is being said. Liz leads the way into the main bedroom. Neville pokes his head out from the room next door.

'Anyone want a coffee?' he asks, his eyes on Liz but his head turned to Sarah.

'Might be an idea.' Sarah follows Liz, who shuts it behind her.

'What are you wearing?' Sarah opens her closet door.

'The gold!' Liz is slurring her words badly.

'Not sure if it is a gold occasion.' Sarah pulls out the shimmering gold skirt of a full-length dress.

'It had better be.' Liz looks to the closed door, beyond which Neville can be heard descending the stairs. 'It better be something big and bulky and gold, preferably,' she struggles with the word, repeating herself, 'preferably with inset diamonds.' The bed groans as she sits and Neville opens the door wide enough to pass through a full mug. 'Hot,' he says as Sarah takes it and he closes the door.

The coffee helps and after a few false starts, Liz decides on a white floor-length dress with a gold belt.

'He will surprise me with whatever he bought tonight.' She taps her nose and drinks her coffee, sipping it like a cocktail. Sarah tries to put on Liz's makeup as she fidgets about. Sarah chastises her in an un-heartfelt way. Liz recalls an anecdotes from their school days, which brings laugher and they lose themselves in meaningless banter. Within minutes, they could be in their bedsit in Douglas, fresh off the boat from Ireland.

'We need whiskey,' Liz suggests.

'No you don't. What is all this drinking about anyway, Liz? Has it just been since Neville's mum died? Are you just kicking loose?'

Liz breathes in and out, long and hard through her nose. 'Since the plans.' Sarah tells her to hold still whilst she finishes her mascara. 'When Miriam was on her last legs, we began to plan more and more what we would do. We would giggle like children at our plans, Neville would sit with his calculator doing the sums. We would share a bottle of wine together. It was nice.' Liz slumps and Sarah gives up on the makeup and tries, instead, to pin up her hair.

'You nearly ready, girls? You want more coffee?' Neville shouts up the stairs. Both of them turn and look at Liz's yellow silk kimono that hangs on the back of the door. Neither of them answer him.

'But when she died, the cozy bottles of wine stopped, the planning stopped, and I knew it was all just dreams.'

Sarah thinks of Nicolaos' wisdom. Some dreams are never to be realised—they are just to give us hope. Fat lot of good that did Liz.

'So I continued the planning and drinking on my own. I wanted him back. I wanted the dreams, the closeness, the oneness. When I drink, he pays me more attention, he worries, he helps me if I overbalance when I walk. It forces him to be close.'

'Girls, we should really go now.' Neville taps on the door before opening it.

'I don't think I can stand.' Liz hiccups. Neville is by her side, taking her arm, lifting her from the bed. She turns to look at Sarah and winks.

'Oh is that Laurence's car I can hear?' Neville escorts Liz down the stairs.

Chapter 27

'You know, I think I'm going to walk.' Sarah beats them down the stairs and gives a half wave from the patio. Liz looks up, grins, and waves. Neville shouts he is 'coming', to a knock at the front door.

Sarah hears the tone of Laurence's voice as she ducks into the olive grove but she cannot make out the words, nor does she care. She is no longer accountable to him.

The light is draining from the sky. The view is paling to pinks and blues, the olive trunks black in the fading light, and the evening whispers through the leaves. It is magical. A crack of dried twigs turns her head but there are no goats, no sheep, no Nicolaos. It is probably late for grazing the herd. Something scuttles, unseen, through the dried grass. There is the smell of warm earth.

Would she tell Nicolaos about Laurence if he were here? Probably not, but she would tell him that she had spoken to Jim. If she does stay and become housekeeper, Nicolaos will be in the field next to the house every day. In a way, that's a disconcerting thought. She has shared so much with him she cannot remember all she has said. But now there is a possibility that she might stay, it dawns on her that perhaps she only confided so much in him because she thought she would never see him again once the wedding was over and they had packed to return home. Hurrying out from under the trees and onto the track, she wraps her arms around herself. It is not cold but she feels suddenly exposed. How must Nicolaos see her? Probably as someone who is pretty foolish. Someone who chased after ease and riches and threw her life away in the process. Stumbling through life, allowing those around her to dictate how she lives and spilling her heart out to strangers.

Out on the road, she turns towards Helena's. In the darkening sky, a halo of ambient light above the trees indicates the house. It will be too dark to go up through the gully and in at the side gate. Sticking to the road, she still wishes she had worn flat shoes. Her heels are low, elegant, but still not suitable for hiking. She takes them off, the tarmac warm even though the sun has set now.

A firework cracks above the house, a dog barks, another responds from across the village. Then the silence falls again, with just the rustling of branches by the roadside in the slight cooling wind. The sky so large, the stars go on forever. As Sarah stares into the expanse, smaller stars emerge between the brighter ones, and then dimmer ones again between those, layer after layer. So vast, the pettiness of her own life seems infinitesimally small. The universe does not care if she is joyful or miserable. Mankind will not alter its path by either her happiness or her sadness. In short, it makes no difference to anyone anywhere, so she might as well choose. She picks up a stone. She cannot see its colour in the fading light. If it is white, she will be happy to the point of selfishness from now on; if it is black, she will continue with her plans and if happiness comes, that will be a bonus, not a decision. She tucks it in her pocket, a secret stored for later.

The gates to the house are open and a car passes her as it pulls up the drive, forcing her to step to one side. As she nears the bend, Sarah puts her shoes back on. Neville's car is there already, in front of one of the garages. A Jeep has hemmed it in, making it look small. This pleases her.

In between the garage and the house, a bonfire has been lit. In the floodlit garden on the other side of the front door, two barbeques provide gathering points, and lines of linen-covered tables fill the lawn, being lifted to the heavens by clusters of white and silver helium-filled balloons. Men stand around, some smoking, one with tongs in his hand, two with white tea towels tucked into waistbands. Jim is there, laughing, as the man who holds the tongs points them to the sky; a story is in progress.

The orator briefly breaks away to turn whatever is cooking on the grill.

'Dogs hate it.' The teenager, Jenny, comes from behind the garage. The same girl who opened the door for Sarah when she came to see Frona. 'It's the noise, but no one thinks about the dogs.'

'Grab them a sausage each and they will forgive you everything,' Sarah suggests.

'I'm going to get them a steak each.' And off she goes, winding her way between the people who are thronging in front of the house. Beyond the dressed tables and the barbeques, at the far end of the lawn, a stage has been erected and, in front of that, a wooden dance floor. A man plays the bouzouki, and he is accompanied by a guitar. The speakers whistle and crackle to the sound check.

'*Ena, dyo, ena, dyo, ena, ena, ena.*' The man strums his long-necked instrument and the guitar picks up the tune. The group by the barbeque raise their glass to the men on the stage, who begin to perform in relaxed earnest. The guitarist wedges his cigarette in the strings above the neck and sings a guttural warble into his microphone. The music speaks of ages past, a culture that has remained steadfast for centuries despite invasions of the Turks and, more recently, the E.U. Sarah knows that if she was Greek, she would be proud.

'You know, you should be inside with the women.' The teenage girl is back, a big raw steak in each hand.

'Really, why?'

'They are doing the rice and child thing in a bit. They are all clucking like hens inside.' Her accent is American, but her olive skin and dark hair are all Greek. She throws a slab of meat to each of the dogs and they sniff without much interest. 'I'm gonna watch a video. Beats all this.' One side of her upper lip lifts into a sneer but her words and this action are awkward, a brave attempt to look composed when really she has no idea how to act or what is expected of her. Joss was morose at this girl's age, Finn painfully shy.

'Good idea,' Sarah agrees, and the girl gives a self-conscious wave as she leaves.

Spitting grit from its wheels, an opened-backed truck comes to a halt and a man shouts as he leaps from the cab. One of the men by the barbeque goes in the house and returns with two rifles. Sarah drops back into the shadows by the dog cages, keeps in the shadows as she follows the wall and finds herself around the back of the house where she enters by a door that opens at the far end of the swimming pool. Silk water lilies are clustering around the filter. Slowly, they are sucked into the stream of returning water from which they are suddenly jettisoned, bobbing and spinning back to the centre of the pool. A dragonfly, fooled by the colours, hovers over them. The window that dissects the pool at the front of the house has been raised and the hall is open, neither inside nor out.

A group of women comes from the direction of the kitchen with stacks of circular basketwork trays in their hands. Seeing Sarah, they smile and beckon, bustling up the stairs. Sarah is given several baskets and a bag of rice. The women gabble at her in Greek. The baskets are filled with red silk petals.

Giggling and talking over each other, the women lift skirts and hold tight to the hand rail as they ascend to the first floor. The lady at the rear waits for Sarah, who has stopped to look up through the skylight as a rocket explodes. Noise seems to be coming from every direction. Music and talk from the front of the house, fireworks above, the echo of laughter and shrieks from inside the house. The whole place is filled with excitement but emphasises Sarah's loneliness.

The group collides with more women, and one or two men who are trying to keep their dignity in the throng. Everyone is jamming into one room. The squash of people propels Sarah along and she finds herself next to a large double bed strewn with rose petals. A child of about six reaches up to try and grab some petals from the baskets Sarah has forgotten she is holding. Handing the girl the whole basket, more hands reach and Sarah hands out all she has but is offered one back. Taking a handful, she follows suit and throws the petals on the bed. The packet of rice she brought is split open and that, too, is spread on the bed. The older woman, with sun-browned and work-worn fingers, stirs the mix, coating the bed evenly. The men, who had taken a step back from the central point, now reach over the throng and throw bank notes onto the counterpane. Some flitter though the stirred air, people snatching at them before they become lost amongst the feet, and they are thrown again to lodge between rice and petals.

The rice and petals seem to be finished now, but the money keeps coming. Everyone is laughing, talking and excited, their traditional magic a heady brew. Men keep pushing into the room, throwing notes, outdoing their friends. As they leave, new faces arrive. The twenty and fifty euro notes that began the ritual are now replaced by hundreds and then five hundreds. One man in a shiny suit drops a note that says it is one thousand euros. Sarah is not even sure if such a note exists. The man lights a cigar as he ambles from the room. A group of children come in, screeching and shouting. The smallest girl, in a lace dress with a large ribbon at the back, is roughly grabbed by one of the old ladies in black.

With effort, she is picked up and thrown on the bed, but the child squirms and runs away. Another willingly offers her services and climbs by herself into the central position. With all the attention on her, she awaits instruction. She is to roll, roll amongst the money and the petals. Many hands assist her.

'May they be blessed with many children,' someone calls in English and is answered in Greek. Liz puts her head around the door. Sarah lifts her hand to attract her attention, but she is gone. Neville's head appears. He studies the room, watches the other men. Someone pushes past him, slapping him on the back as he throws his own note. Someone else pulls Neville into the room, encouraging him to join in. The child has had enough of rolling and wriggles from the bed and runs away. Neville pulls out a twenty and tries to be casual as he lets go and it floats down onto the bed. Laurence is behind him now. His eyes dart around the room, trying to make sense of what is going on. Sarah bends her knees, glad that the woman in front of her is tall. Between shoulders, she watches as someone gesticulates, trying to explain what is going on to Laurence. He is offered rice; someone else takes out his own wallet and shows Laurence what is expected.

Sarah could tell them that Laurence will not join in. He will see the encouragement as bullying, expecting him to conform to something that is not in his culture. Gritting her teeth, she waits to see how he will handle it. She hopes he will not make a fuss. The man who is trying to be helpful taps him on the shoulder and points to the bed, his eyes alight at the game they are playing. Laurence shrugs the man's hand off and takes a step back. Two men are facing Laurence now, their smiles gone. Liz reappears and talks in Laurence's ear. He turns and is gone. Well, at least there was no fuss, but how mean can you get? It is his own son who would benefit.

More baskets of petals arrive, the floor underfoot now crunchy with grains of rice. Gently pushing past people, Sarah heads for the door. As she passes the bed, she takes a fifty euro note from her handbag and pushes her hand through the mass of people and lets it drop. For a second, she is part of it all.

Back in the hall, the fireworks ring above. She has seen neither Joss and Pru or Finn and Helena, nor has she yet met Helena's mother. It would also be polite to say hello to Jim, and where in all these rooms and in all this crowd is Frona? Maybe in the kitchen.

Spotting Laurence in the hall, she leaves through the back door she came in by. For a second, there is calm, quiet, but as she turns the corner back towards the bonfire, the noise is heightened by some of the men pointing rifles in the air and shooting at the sky. In the shock of the sudden sound, Sarah runs and finds herself in the shadows on the dog pen again. The dogs' heads rest on crossed paws; she is more alarmed by the gunfire than they are. After each round of shots, there is laughter, and more men come to join in the celebration. Jim is at the centre of it all, loading and handing out rifles. The men cheer with the cracks, and occasionally, the trees that line the other side of the wall rustle as they are hit.

The man in the shiny suit with his cigar in his mouth saunters around the pool. Behind him are Laurence and Neville. Liz hangs back, glass in hand, looking at the silk water lilies. Jim greets Laurence loudly as they are absorbed into the throng of men. The man with the shiny suit is handed a gun. He looks at it with disinterest, steps to one side to let others gather around Jim. Holding the shotgun in one hand, he concentrates on his cigar with his other, drawing out the last few puffs.

Someone from the barbeque area shouts, first something that sounds like 'Eh Timmy' and then another voice bellows, 'Food's ready.' No one responds except the man in the shiny suit. He grinds out the last of his cigar, props the gun against the dog cage, and, pulling up his trousers from their waistband, hurries his steps towards the waiting food.

He does not see Sarah.

The gun waits.

Laurence is being shown how to hold a rifle by Jim. Neville has returned to Liz. There are many people shooting, so much noise. Jim leaves Laurence to assist another man. Laurence stands still as he takes his aim.

In all this chaos, who would know how it happened?

Sarah picks up the rifle.

Chapter 28

The gun is heavier than she expected. The metal is cool to the touch, the wood smooth. Laurence is still standing there, trying to figure out what to do, where to aim. Sarah acknowledges his attempt to join in, but it is a discriminating choice. He did not choose to join in with a gift of money, rice throwing, or petal scattering; he chose the gun. A weapon of destruction. Metal and engineering. Capable of taking a life in the wrong hands. Just like a car can.

Fireworks scream and explode above the house. Children run. The musicians are singing and playing with gusto and, here and there, men and women, arms across each other's shoulders, dance with cries of '*Opa!*'

A lone boy, unheeded, is in amongst the men with the guns. He can be no more than nine or ten years old and firing shot after shot into the air, his little body jerking with each recoil. He laughs at his game.

Sarah puts the butt of the gun she is holding against her shoulder, to see how it feels. It sits well, if heavily. Looking down the shaft, there's a V-shaped notch where the wood turns to metal and at the far end of the barrel, a lug of metal. Aligning the lug to fit in the V, Sarah finds she is focused on Laurence's left knee. The macabre thought crosses Sarah's mind that with just one little squeeze, or a sudden cough, a jerk of her hand, there would be an accident. Laurence lame for life, his neat little world blow open. No driving, no walking, no strutting. But at least he would still have his life, which is more than he granted Torin.

Her breathing becomes laboured, her sight bleary.

Laurence and the people around him seem to be moving in slow motion, their next steps predictable, obvious. The boy with his head back is frozen in mid-laugh as he fires his pistol. The seconds elongate to minutes, the fireworks hang motionless and noiseless in the air, the music is silent, the laughter suspended. There is just the lug of metal in the V and Laurence. She raises the barrel. The action pushes her shoulder against the dog pen, which lends support.

The sight lines up with Laurence's stomach. If the Hollywood films are to be believed, that would be a slow and painful death. Internal bleeding, mincemeat of his organs. She could rush to him, pretend she is heartbroken and watch him groan and writhe until, slowly, the light goes out of his eyes, just as she watched the light go out of Torin's eyes.

But maybe it would not ensure death. Maybe the films are not to be believed.

Up a little.

Chest.

Through his arm and into his heart. Huh! What heart? Her finger twitches on the trigger.

Laurence still hasn't moved.

Up.

Head. Right in his temple, and that would be the end of him. Wiped from the planet.

Sarah shifts the sagging weight of the gun up into her shoulder and lowers her head so her cheek is against the polished wood. Taking aim, she steadies herself.

'Squeeze,' she whispers. She heard that advice somewhere, or read it. A film or a book maybe. 'Squeeze the trigger. Do not pull or jerk.'

It feels as if there is no give in the metal. She tightens her grip and readies herself to squeeze.

Something appears in her peripheral vision, over her left shoulder. Time speeds up again and Sarah loses control of the moment. The fireworks explode. The gun is pushed forward and up and is lifted from her grip. Laughter and shouting echoes from the buildings. The weight of the wooden stock skims down her dress, the barrel pointing skywards, and the whole gun is taken out of her hands, out of her sight to her left. It happens so fast, she has no control. The arms enclose around her, holding her so she cannot move. Twisting her head, she tries to see who it is, a glimpse of gold reflects around a neck. The grip releases just enough to allow her to turn. A firework lights up his face in green and then orange.

'These shotguns have a kick like a donkey.' He does not smile. Behind him, the side gate is still open.

Anger brings a tremor to her limbs. How dare he interfere? Her mouth tightens into a line and she turns and twists. His grip remains firm.

'And a kick like that can wipe away your future.' Fear flickers in his eyes and there is no releasing his grip, no choice but to stay still. He smells of soap and the sun, with just a trace of goat. Hairs poke over the unbuttoned neck of his shirt. She doesn't like hairy men. The only movement that is possible is the turn of her head. Lowering her chin and twisting it sideways, she avoids the hairs and rests against his shirt. In one ear, she can hear all the rumpus of the party, the music and the guns, the laughter and shouting. In the other ear, faint at first but as she concentrates, it becomes clearer. A reassuring rhythm, a meter of strength, the steady beat of life, his heart. Taken for granted, the muscle that is a miracle maker. When it stops, everything is lost. But this heart, so close, sounds strong, assured, determined. Something that could be trusted to throb on and on until time, naturally, takes its toll.

What on earth possessed her? To even think about stopping another person's heart, what right had she to do that? Laurence being dead would not have solved anything. In fact, it ... She blanks her mind. She cannot bear to think about it: the boys' father dead, their mother in jail.

'It would be nice to think that you have a future here.' As he speaks, Sarah can feel the brush of his chin, or is it his lips, against the top of her head. She turns her face upwards. His chin is tucked in to look down at her. A trace of sweat on his brow belies his calm. His lips are parted and she can feel his breath on her skin.

'Explain?' The voice comes like a roar; even the fireworks cannot drown it out. The arms around her fall away and they turn in unison. Jim stands, legs apart, a gun, broken, over his arm.

'You'd better take this, or fire it, or something. It's loaded.' Nicolaos calmly picks up the gun he rescued from Sarah's grip. Jim accepts it without comment but still waits for an answer to his question.

'I have come to wish your daughter a happy marriage, to spread petals on her marriage bed, and to wish her everything in her marriage that I never had.'

Jim looks at Sarah, his eyebrows lowering, his mouth twisting, perplexed, before looking back at Nicolaos.

'If you do not want me to do it in person, then perhaps,' Nicolaos fumbles in his back pocket and draws out a wallet.

Over Jim's shoulder, coming out of the house, Sarah spots Frona shuffling towards the bonfire, towards the men still firing guns.

'I think your mother is looking for you.' Sarah points over Jim's shoulder. He turns. It is apparent that Frona has not seen them and there is no haste in her steps. She is looking for no one. Jim turns back, ignoring Sarah, his steady gaze on Nicolaos. Maybe she should have kept quiet.

'Jim, is that you?' Now Frona has seen at least Jim, who is not in the shadows.

'I'll be with you in a minute, Mama,' Jim shouts over his shoulder. A rocket whizzes into the heavens and explodes. The musicians finish their song and the people applaud. Looking first at Nicolaos and then at the open gate behind him, it is clear what Jim wants, but then he looks at Sarah. It must have appeared to him as if they were in each other's arms, which they were, only not for the reason he must be thinking. But she cannot explain it without explaining about the gun.

'Jim?' Frona is still moving towards them. Sarah steps out of the shadows. 'Ah Sarah,' Frona exclaims as she spots her, too, 'I was wondering where you were.'

Nicolaos leans half into the light. A shower of cascading sparkles fills the sky and a hissing noise accompanies the display, lighting all three of them up. Frona does not miss a step but her eyes widen at the sight of Nicolaos. She scans across to Jim. 'Ah how lovely,' she begins, but she pushes her sleeves up to her elbows as if preparing herself for hard work—or a fight.

'Mama, go back to the house. I'll be with you in a minute.' Jim does not take his eyes from Nicolaos.

'No Jim.' Frona stands her ground. Now Jim looks at her. 'Nicolaos has been excluded from this family for too long.'

'He knows why.' Jim does not seem to be an international businessman to Sarah at the moment; rather he is a small, angry boy. Nicolaos puts his hands in his front pockets and stands tall.

'Perhaps you should ask him how his marriage is, Jim. Perhaps you should think about who you care about most: his wife or your brother.'

'There is more to it than that.' Jim scowls.

'Yes, Nicolaos saved you from the life he led, which has not been a happy one.'

'Karma,' Jim snarls like a sulking teenager.

'Oh grow up, Jim,' Frona spits. 'She has gone now anyway. Nicolaos has sent her the divorce papers to sign. You have no more excuses.' Frona takes a step nearer him. She looks ready to slap the back of Jim's legs.

'Is that true?' Jim asks Nicolaos. His face is hard to see. There is a pause in the fireworks and the floodlights on the lawn behind him are bright. The blaze makes his expression indiscernible, but his voice has lost its edge.

'Haven't seen her since I moved here two years ago. Sent her the divorce papers, just waiting for the Decree Nisi.' Nicolaos shows no emotion. Sarah wonders if she should sidle away. It feels like an old family argument and it is hardly her place to be there.

'I thought you guys would be for life.' There is a softness to Jim's voice now. He takes the cartridge out of the cocked gun over his arm and, closing it with a snap, he leans it against the dog pen, putting the cartridges in his pocket. He then cocks the armed gun and, pocketing the cartridge, he leans that next to the first. Once his hands are empty, he puts them in his front pockets. The two brothers, mirroring each other's postures.

'Thought wrong then, mate.' Nicolaos lets his Autralian accent out. 'Wouldn't have a beer, would you?' It is spoken to suggest there is more meaning than the simple words, a repeat of history perhaps, an old private joke maybe?

Jim hesitates.

'Oh for the love of God almighty.' Frona crosses herself. 'Enough. Hug and make up,' she demands and pushes Jim by his elbow. Nicolaos takes his hands from his pocket and, opening his arms, takes a step and engulfs Jim, who looks neat and small inside his brother's bear hug.

'After all, we cannot have Helena married without me. I am her godfather.' Nicolaos releases Jim and slaps him on the shoulder. 'Now, where's that beer?' Jim gives Sarah one last quizzical look before taking his brother, who has an arm around his neck, toward the drinks. They cover no more than a few feet when Jim introduces him to a guest, first one and then another. At first, he sounds tentative but as his introductions begin to flow, he becomes sure and then proud. He introduces Nicolaos to one person after another and they make no ground at all.

'Ridiculous,' Frona says to Sarah. 'They don't talk for years, and then all it takes is the want of a beer.' She huffs and takes Sarah's arm. 'Have you just arrived? Can I get you a drink? Oh and Jim says yes, by the way—to our plan. Told him I was not going to the wedding until he agreed.' Frona thinks this is funny and cackles, her hand going to her mouth, her head lowering as if she has been caught doing something naughty but fun.

They reach a long table covered with bottles before Jim and Nicolaos, who are side-tracked with introductions. The bartender asks Frona and Sarah what they would enjoy, first, presumably, in Greek, but in the same breath, also in English.

'You look very nice all dressed up. We'll have champagne.' Frona makes the bartender blush. In doing so, he loses all traces of manhood and it shows him for the boy he is. He hands them a glass each and Frona smiles.

'Known his mother since she was a baby.' They turn to face the party.

'So, to my united boys and to a united us.' Frona lifts a glass. Sarah hesitates. 'What is it?' the old woman asks.

'I have yet to tell the boys. And Laurence.' Sarah can see Laurence with Neville inside the hall, looking at the lilies on the pool. Liz is still leaning heavily against the doorframe, drink in hand.

'Ah yes.' Frona sighs. 'After the wedding, I think.'

The bouzouki player has begun again, and Frona turns to watch.

'Do you know all the Greek dances?' Sarah asks as she watches one or two people form a line.

'Vevea,' Frona says. Sarah presumes by the way she has said this word it means *sure* or *of course*. 'Come on, I teach you this one. It is easy.' Frona gives her half-full glass back to the bartender. Sarah puts her empty glass on the table and Frona leads her to the area cleared for dancing. There is a line of people snaking around the space but Frona ignores them, puts an arm around Sarah's waist and begins to shuffle, first two steps forward, then a half step back, then forward. It is not clear what she is doing, her feet move so little. Sarah looks to the younger, more energetic dancers to see where her feet should be and between Frona and watching the other dancers, she finds it is indeed very easy. Her movements gain a spring as she grows in confidence. After a couple of minutes, Frona pushes Sarah to the main line of

people and goes to sit down. 'I am too old for all this,' she calls. 'You dance for us both, Sarah.'

The energy of the musicians propels her feet, her arms over the shoulders of the person before her and the person behind. Someone shouts '*Opa!*' and the person at the head of the snake turns under the uplifted arm of the person behind him. With his lead hand, he waves a handkerchief. The lady in front of Sarah breaks away and the man in front of her beckons Sarah to rejoin the line. It is the man in the shiny suit, with no cigar. The steps are becoming known, anticipated, automatic, the lightness in Sarah's step joyful. Frona claps to the rhythm as she passes her.

Sarah looks out into the crowd. The shooting seems to have stopped. There is a crowd around the tables laden with food, and children are still running between everyone's legs. Someone breaks into the line behind her, and she turns to find Nicolaos already lost in the music, his eyes glazed over as he looks skyward. Someone breaks into the line in front of her. It is Jim, who smiles and for a moment looks just like Frona. The next time around, the dance area, Frona shouts '*Opa!*' as her two boys with Sarah in between pass her, and then the leader takes a turn off the dance floor and makes his way lacing through the crowds. The pulse seems to be quickening and Sarah is enlivened as she tries to keep up. Ahead, she can see Liz sitting at a linen-covered table, a plate in front of her, and Neville with a forkful of food poised before his mouth as he talks, and Laurence next to him, staring straight at her. The eye contact is penetrating. Jim shouts something to her, and breaking the gaze with Laurence, she turns to him.

'Sorry, what?' Sarah asks.

He repeats it, but it is in Greek and he is speaking over her head to Nicolaos, who looks at her, laughing. She does not want to look back to see Laurence's reaction. Between the two brothers, she feels appreciated, liked, part of something. She could dance on forever. But before the music stops, Jim pulls away to talk to some new guest, so when the bouzouki player finally stops for a drink and a cigarette, there is only Nicolaos to ask if she is hungry. She glances over all the tables. There is no sign of Laurence, Liz, or Neville.

'I haven't seen Finn and Helena yet, nor my other son Joss and his wife.'

Nicolaos is loading his plate. 'They are under the tree.' He spits out the pit of an olive and helps himself to salad.

'Tree?' Sarah looks around. There are many that border the property.

'You know.' He inclines his head toward the side gate. It takes Sarah a moment, as in the same direction, beyond the barbeques, are cars, the bonfire, and, behind the garages, the dog cages.

'Oh right. Our tree.'

Nicolaos stops piling his plate and looks at her.

'You know what I mean. It is where we have sat ... with Frona. The picnic,' Sarah stutters. He purses his lips and nods, eyebrows raised.

'So Jim has said yes to Mama staying here with you,' he states, offering her a spoonful of, well she is not sure what it is, roast vegetables perhaps. Sarah's stomach turns. The food looks delicious, so she is not sure if her response is fear or excitement.

'Frona said she refused to go to the wedding unless he said yes.' Sarah shakes her head. She is not sure if she wants to eat at all right now.

'Sounds like Mama.'

'Why has Jim got such a big say in everything, if you don't mind me asking?' She picks at an olive and takes a slice of feta.

'No, I don't mind. It is just his way. It is what got him his big business and it is how he runs his life.'

'But Frona lets him and you have stayed away?'

'Mama and I are two of a kind: anything for a quiet life. No fight is worth the stress. Have you tired the *kolokithia*? They are so good.' He lifts something from his plate and puts it on Sarah's. For some reason, it seems like an intimate act and Sarah becomes aware that there are just the two of them helping themselves at the buffet. She hasn't even spoken to her husband tonight and she has yet to meet Helena's mother. Inside her head, the sound of Laurence saying she is irresponsible rings true. What would her boys say?

'You know, I think I will go and find the boys.'

Nicolaos looks at his full plate.

'No, you're alright. You finish your food.' With which she puts her plate down, picks the feta off with her fingers, and nibbles away at it as she heads towards the side gate.

Chapter 29

It is hard to see if anyone is under the tree, even though the moon whitens the ground around it and the fireworks cast colour every now and again. Then she hears Pru's voice murmuring.

Sarah counsels herself to not be so selfish, but the voice inside her head repeats: *Tell them. Get it done with. Just tell them and be free.* She must put her own thoughts and troubles to one side until after the wedding. It is very tempting to spill it all out, lift the weight of it all from her chest. But that is not what is best for Finn.

'Hey Mum!' Finn stands.

'Hi guys. I wondered where you lot had got to.' Apart from her boys and Pru and Helena, there is one other person there, sitting on the stone, her knees neatly together, her hands in her lap. No one introduces her. Sarah smiles an introduction, which is reciprocated, but there is a cautiousness in the woman's eye contact, a nervousness. Sarah recognises a reflection of part of herself in the woman's demeanour, the part of her whose sole purpose was the washing machine filler and dinner maker. This immediately warms her to the woman, an understanding. It is the part of her that is quickly shrinking away but until she stands up to Laurence, nothing has really changed, certainly not in his mind, and that matters!

'Joss is going to make the world's worst best man speech.' Finn laughs as Helena hugs onto his arm.

'Right, that's it. I rescind my position as best man.' Joss keeps a straight face but Sarah recognises his humour. Pru is only visible by the glowing end of her cigarette, her face in the dark as she leans her back against the tree.

'So why are you all out here?' Sarah asks.

'No reason,' Helena replies. 'Just came to look at the stars.'

'They give such hope,' the un-introduced woman says.

'Greece is such a beautiful place,' Sarah confesses.

'I just love it. You know, Mum, Helena and I have been trying to figure out ways we could work from here,' Finn says.

'Really? I would love to live here, too.' There, it's out. Sarah keeps her eyes fixed on the stars. She cannot meet anyone's gaze having just said that. Why can she not keep her mouth shut?

'The problem is work,' Finn says.

Tell them the plan. Let it all out. Have a clear conscience for the wedding. No, that's not fair. It is the kids' day tomorrow. There should be no worries in the back of their minds.

'It would be amazing, though, to come out here, live the dream, or at least to spend some time out here.' Sarah tries to sound light, dismissive, not really telling them anything.

'You should, Mum,' Finn says emphatically.

It feels like such an opening, it would be so easy, just let it all tumble out.

'Ha, what about your Dad?' Sarah feels like a traitor to herself as she hears her own words.

'Do him good, a spell on his own,' Finn sniffs and puts his hands in his front pockets.

No one says anything. They all continue to look at the stars.

'So have you figured a way to stay out here, then?' Sarah addresses Finn. Even just to talk about it feels exciting, satisfying.

'No, we both need to be in London really, or maybe New York. Joss says there are loads of opportunities there.' Finn squeezes Helena to him.

The subject seems closed. The fireworks have stopped now and the field is darker without the occasional shock of coloured light. Pru leans forwards and stubs out her cigarette and then takes hold of Joss's arm to pull herself up.

'Why don't you, Mrs Quayle?' Pru brushes down her skirt.

'Sorry.' Sarah feels thrown by the question.

'Do it. Stay here. Live a bit. See if you like it.' Pru's tone is flat, but Sarah can sense there is a little dig in there, the implication that she does not live by Pru's standards.

'Oh, I ...'

Finn's head turns from the sky, watching, and she meets his eye. He looks at her hard. The top of his cheeks are lit by the moonlight, his white shirt glows. He nods. It is such a small movement, it is almost imperceptible. Helena, who is still wrapped around his arm, looks up at him and then at Sarah before her mouth tightens into a sideways smile that looks decidedly wicked. She raises one eyebrow. It feels like a challenge, a dare, a collusion.

'Dad couldn't manage.' Joss breaks the silence. It is a long time since she has heard Joss call Laurence *Dad*. Clenching her teeth, she is aware of why he has decided to use the term now.

'Don't be silly, Joss,' Pru says. Her tone could not be more dismissive as she takes control of the group by leading the way back towards the house.

The two couples go ahead. Sarah finds herself walking beside the woman.

'Greece does that,' the woman says.

'Does what?'

'Filters out the important things in our lives, shifts priorities.'

Sarah chooses not to answer. As they reach the house, Helena waits for Sarah to catch up and, grabbing her hand, she pulls her towards the dance floor. The un-introduced woman goes with them and the three of them dance to the next two songs. Pru sits, smoking. Then Helena pulls Finn in. He struggles to be let free but her grip is insistent. Once dancing, he seems to know the steps.

The warmth and the dancing, arm in arm with Finn, feels joyous to Sarah, and she forgets about everything but the moment. Finn pulls Joss into the line, who, surprisingly, does not resist. With their dark hair, they could be Greek; they certainly fit in. After the next dance, Sarah needs some water. Returning from the bar, she finds Nicolaos between Finn and Helena. Finn's head is turned, talking to him. Joss is between Helena and the woman. By the way Helena and the woman move, the twist of their hips, the turn of their feet, it is apparent that this could be Helena's mum.

Sarah is only standing long enough to finish her water when Jim links her arm as he passes her and pulls her back into the line.

They seem to dance on and on. The rhythm changes and the steps become more complicated. To her amazement, Finn seems to know these steps, too. Sarah watches with Joss and Pru until Pru suddenly stands and grabs Sarah's arm, pulling her nearer to the house and demands that Sarah teach her the simple steps she knows. They laugh as their feet get tangled, but Pru's tenacity makes the lesson short.

Within the half hour, they are all dancing to shouts of '*Opa!*' There seems to be no specific timing to these calls; it just seems an explosion of happiness, a release of euphoria.

The songs merge one into another. When one musician tires, another takes over and, as they perform in rotation, the dancers strut on and on until, slowly, the lawn thins of people and the revellers lose their energy. Pru yawns and Joss uses this as his cue to bid them all farewell, scooping her into his arms. The horizon lightens and the top of the hills burn orange as a slither of intense light peeps over the hills. As the sun creeps from its rest, there is now a slight chill to the air and the cicadas are, just for this hour, silent. A bird song whistles across the relative quiet as the musicians put their instruments into cases and the stage lights are switched off.

There is no sign of Laurence, and Neville's car has gone, along with most of the other vehicles. Looking towards the dog cages, Sarah catches sight of Nicolaos leaving through the side gate.

'I guess it is bedtime.' Finn is grinning at Helena. 'Where's Dad?' He looks over at the garages, searching for the hire car.

'I think he's gone,' Sarah says. Her dress for the wedding is back at the holiday cottage, so she will need to go there to change, but she wants to avoid Laurence as much as she can.

'Oh stay here.' It is Helena's turn to yawn. The waiters are beginning to tidy the drink tables. The food table has been cleared. 'Maria,' she addresses one of the people who has been serving. 'Are any of the guest rooms free?' The woman nods. 'There, sorted.' Helena leans on Finn as they all slowly make their way into the house.

The next morning seems to pass seamlessly. Someone knocks on Sarah's door to let her know breakfast is available. New caterers stand bright eyed and ready to serve them in the beautiful sunshine. It seems many of the guests stayed on. The man in the shiny suit is there, looking rather creased. Helena is full of life and shows no tiredness at all. The woman Sarah was not introduced to is by Helena's side, and in the light of day, there can be no mistaking their relationship. That and Helena calls her *Mama*, but the time has passed for formal introductions.

Finn is nowhere to be seen, nor is Jim. It seems they are maintaining tradition and the groom is not allowed to see the bride.

A whole fleet of cars leave the house around mid-morning, and Sarah is bundled into one them in the same dress she wore to the party. Sliding in next to her is Helena's mother, Nicolaos, who looks amazing in his morning dress, and the man in the shiny but now crumpled suit. The smell of cigars accompanies his slamming the door closed.

As they drive around the village in convoy, more cars join them as they snake through the lanes. Sarah hears a light ringing and only after a minute does she recognise her phone. By the time she has pulled it out, it has gone to voicemail, but there are several text messages from Laurence and one from Liz. She reads Liz's.

'Where are you?' is all it says, sent today, about an hour ago.

'With Helena's family, see u at the wedding.' *There, Liz can tell Laurence if she wants.* And with that thought, she snaps her phone shut and looks out of the window at all the passers-by waving. Behind them, the convoy of cars seems to go on forever as they leave the village.

By comparison to the preparations, the service, in a very large and central church in Saros town, is a sedate affair. Conducted in Greek, Sarah finds herself looking around the church for a great deal of the time. Helena's mum spends a lot of the time gazing up to the ceiling, too. Maybe she doesn't understand Greek, either. Maybe Jim met her in Australia. Helena looks amazing. Her dress has a fitted lace bodice and, as Helena suggested, it is sensational. Maybe even slightly too sensational for a white dress. Finn and Joss also look amazing in their grey morning suits. Flowers cover every corner of the church, and hanging from the ceiling are brass chandeliers under an icon-covered ceiling. Everywhere glints with gold and brass, incense hangs in the air, and all corners glow with candles. The priest, in white robes embroidered in gold thread, begins to sing in monosyllabic tones. A thrill runs through Sarah and she shivers slightly. The priest sings on and on. After half an hour, it appears that nothing is really happening. No one has moved and the priest continues. Not wanting to look behind and meet an angry glare from Laurence, Sarah contents herself with imagining Finn's life ahead of him. Surely Helena will want children? It is becoming apparent Pru will not be having any and Joss seems happy with that, but Finn will make such a good father.

A movement breaks her daydream. Joss steps behind the couple. It occurs to Sarah that there must have been rehearsals but instead of feeling left out, which is what she would have expected, she feels nothing but happiness: that her boys have each other, that Finn is marrying. Everything in the world seems perfect. The priest has taken a step back. A man with a microphone drones a religious script in a monotone that is halfway between a chant and a song. Outside, a dog barks, as if in accompaniment.

The priest steps forwards again and the chanting stops. The dog outside continues. The heavy, embellished robes of the priest rustle and swish across the tiled floor as he moves to face the couple, where he begins his own chant over two intertwined thin metal crowns that he uses to bless Finn and Helena before placing them upon their heads, a ribbon joining the two. He then steps away and Joss takes his place behind the couple, lifting the crowns. He crosses his arms and the crowns switch heads. He repeats this two more times and then the crowd stirs.

Children push to the front with baskets of rice. Modest handfuls are taken by the guests and then eager young men elbow forward, taking as big a handful as they can. Helena, Finn, and Joss—behind them and still holding the crowns—begin to circumnavigate the altar. The priest retreats and the guests throw handfuls of rice, the young men with as much force as they can. Helena and Finn duck, Joss dips his head below his arms. With their faces bent to the ground to withstand the stinging onslaught, they try to sedately walk the full circle. The young men in the crowd push for second handfuls and some receive halting hands on their wrists to curb the competitive play. The priest continues his drone and Sarah looks at the sun pouring in through the coloured glass windows. Suddenly it is all over and people are leaving the church. Moving with the throng, it occurs to Sarah that she could have been more involved, maybe studied up on Greek Orthodox weddings before she came, understood what was going on a bit more, and she is not sure why she didn't. She almost falls into feeling guilty but decides the day is too perfect for such thoughts and as she leaves the church, she is given a silk bag of what looks like sugared almonds by Jenny, who is lined up with several other children, all handing out these gifts.

'It called a *koufetta,*' Jenny states in her monosyllabic tone. 'The bittersweet of the almonds represents life itself but we coat them with sugar in hopes that the married life will be sweet. So I guess they give them to guests to pass on some of that sweetness.'

'Oh, do you think that is where the word confetti comes from?' Sarah asks. Jenny shrugs and picks up another couple of bags to hand to the guests behind Sarah. She moves on so as not to be in the way.

A horse and carriage picks Finn and Helena up and the guests wander after the carriage along to one end of the waterfront, where waiters in cummerbunds eagerly greet them, and Sarah enters the shiny foyer of a large hotel. This could be anywhere in the world; all Greekness is lost.

The room is as lavish as a setting could be, with linen and flowers competing with the silverware and glass in abundance. A board in the entrance maps out the seating arrangements. As expected, she has been placed on the top table. It is also inevitable that she has been seated next to Laurence.

Chapter 30

Hanging back, Sarah waits for the tables to fill. She uses the time to find that Liz and Neville have been seated by one of the floor-to-ceiling windows. Outside, the sun's brilliance on the sea is mesmerising. It seems a shame to be indoors; the lunch will go on all afternoon with a dance in the evening. At least Finn and Helena will spend some time in the sunshine. Jim has arranged for them to be flown by helicopter from the reception to a destination of his choosing. No one, not even Finn and Helena, know where they are headed for their honeymoon. Maybe the helicopter will take them to the airport, or maybe to a nearby island. Either way, it is very romantic but right now, Sarah just wants to go outside, sit by the water's edge, and soak up the sun. Actually be in this country, not in some characterless hotel.

More guests are filling the room and discrete music is being channeled through unseen speakers. Finn enters with Helena on his arm. Sarah has never seen Finn so happy. Joss is right behind him; he, too, looks lost in the moment. Laurence is with them, and Joss turns and speaks to him, smiling. Maybe now would be a time to meet Laurence; with all the attention on the newlyweds, it will feel safer.

Slipping between tables, she approaches the group to address Helena.

'Congratulations, daughter-in-law, or should I call you Mrs Quayle?' Sarah kisses Helena on both cheeks.

'Oh my face hurts from smiling so much.' Helena squashes her cheeks together with both hands, her bouquet getting in the way.

'Oh very attractive,' Finn teases and leans in and kisses her.

'Hello.' Laurence addresses Sarah, the muscles around his mouth tense.

'Hi.' Sarah replies briefly. 'Congratulations Finn. No longer my little boy now.' Helena lets out a chortle.

'Always your son, Mum, but husband to Helena first now.' He kisses Sarah on the cheek and then Helena on the mouth.

'As it should be.' Sarah reaches for Helena's hand and puts it in Finn's.

Joss steps forwards and puts his arms around Sarah and pulls her in to him. He is smiling at something Finn said that she missed. Taking the hand that dangles over her shoulder, she gives it a brief kiss, knowing he will not tolerate any more than that. They all glide to their places and it is only when they are sitting that Laurence hisses, 'Where were you? I have been worried to death. You are so irresponsible.'

This is it, the moment she must make her stand.

With no lowering of her voice, she says as calmly as she can, 'Not now, Laurence.'

To her relief, this one confrontation is enough to keep him silenced during the wedding lunch. He does try to hold her hand as they all file out to see Finn and Helena off to the waiting helicopter. But Sarah shakes free, refusing to lose the last moments with her youngest son.

Then Finn is gone. Joss pats her on the shoulder and walks back inside with her and Pru. Laurence gets separated from them in the crowd. A live band has set up in one corner of the room and Jim, with his wife, is on the dance floor. He gently sways with her, arm in arm.

Sarah looks around for Liz. She had caught her eye over the dinner, when Liz had been grinning from ear to ear. They had raised a glass to each other from a distance but now, she must let her know she is going. With relief, she spots Liz being taken onto the dance floor by Neville. Nicolaos is dancing with Frona. The man in the shiny suit is dancing with a thin lady in a low-cut dress who looks pale and fragile. The floor is rapidly filling.

Liz and Neville glide towards her.

'Look.' Liz breaks free of Neville's hold. She needlessly lifts her chin to the ceiling; the necklace and earring are so dazzlingly ostentatious. Liz tosses her hair and looks back at Sarah. 'And.' She leans in as if to tell a secret. Sarah smells the whiskey. 'He doesn't want a divorce, so his ex is not moving in. Indonesia, here we come!' She taps her nose to Sarah as Neville pulls her back to dance. He holds her tightly, and round and round they go.

'Round and round,' Sarah says to herself and, seeing Laurence marching her way, she heads off to the cloakroom. Bypassing the front doors, she hurriedly follows a maid pushing a linen truck down a corridor. Sarah leaves the hotel through a service door which comes out between rows and rows of refuse bins. The heat of the sun after the air conditioning is thrilling. Without a glance behind her, she walks slowly to the end of the bins where she can look around the building and see the sea.

With the jumble of thoughts demanding her attention, it is not easy to enjoy the view. Laurence will be expecting her to drive with him up to Athens tonight, as their flight home is first thing in the morning. Their cottage rental ends this evening, so it would be a good idea to get back and see if Juliet can let her stay on for a day or two whilst she makes arrangements with Jim. She cannot expect to move into the housekeeper's rooms the day after the wedding. Besides, it would put her in a weak position. If she seems needy, she would have to take whatever terms were offered. If she stays independent, they are more likely to agree to something that was mutually beneficial. She quite likes all the independence. It gives her a feeling of power.

The taxi drops her at the end of the lane. There is no cat to greet her and the walk feels like a bit of a dream as the momentousness of what she is doing begins to become a reality.

Juliet is not on the patio, but the door is open. Sarah steps in and calls her name. There is no answer. *Surely she wouldn't leave it open and go out.* A noise from the garden takes her around the side of the house to find Juliet lying on her back on the curved bench around the twisted old olive tree. It doesn't look all that comfortable.

'Are you off?' Juliet pushes herself to sitting and puts a olive leaf in her book as a mark.

'Actually, that's what I wanted a word about.' Sarah begins. 'Do you have new people coming tomorrow?' She intertwines her fingers in front of her.

'No the day after. Everything okay?' Juliet stands and stretches. 'Was the wedding beautiful?'

'Oh it was amazing.' Her fingers unlock, her arms relax. 'Helena looked stunning. Jim, that's her father, has flown them off to a surprise honeymoon. The whole thing was so romantic.'

'Oh lovely. So now it's your turn to go.' She looks Sarah up and down, frowns briefly before sitting down again and nodding to the seat next to her. For no reason whatsoever, Sarah feels on the edge of tears, but considering what she is about to do, maybe it is not surprising. It is bound to all feel stressful until she finds her feet.

'I was just wondering, if it is not too much trouble, if I may keep the cottage on for the night.' The cat slides round the corner of the house and approaches them purring, flopping onto its side before it reaches them.

'Sure, why not. Everything okay? Your flight still running?' Juliet asks.

'No, yes, the flight's fine.' She straightens her back. 'Well, I suppose you might as well be the first to know I am not going home.' She stresses the *I* and looks Juliet straight in the eye as she does so.

Juliet does not move, nor does she say anything. They sit for what feels like minutes until Juliet says very quietly, 'Are you sure?'

Sarah nods. The image of the green car with Laurence's head turned away flashes through her mind. She is absolutely sure.

'Well, of course you can stay tonight, but after that, I am afraid it is booked. Have you any plans? Where will you go?' Juliet sounds cautious.

'Just tonight is fine.' Actually, just the one night should be enough, and there is always the hotel in Saros. 'I have been offered a job. One night, should all work out just perfectly.'

'A job, how exciting.' Juliet's moment of caution is gone. She springs into excitement.

'Yes, just up the road.'

'Is it permanent or just for the summer?' Juliet leans her back against the twisted bark.

'Permanent. You know, I think I might just go and take a shower and change. I kind of made a night of it last night and some clean clothes would be very welcome.'

'Oh sure, sorry. I didn't mean to hold you back. Besides, if you are just up the road, there will be loads of time to chat.' With which Juliet stands,

Sarah follows suit, and, after both of them pause to watch a swallow dive for water over the pool, Juliet picks up her book and heads to her house and Sarah heads to the cottage.

The cottage is, of course, locked.

'Oh for goodness sake.' Sarah flops onto one of the chairs around the patio table. She would rather have showered and maybe even have gone out when Laurence returns. She must face him today, but does she want to do it in the cottage? Maybe meeting somewhere else would be best, somewhere public. She could also do with more sleep. Leaning over the table, she puts her head on her arms. An upturned dish is in the way and, as she moves it to one side, it suddenly occurs to her why it is there.

The key for the cottage is under the dish. Just the sort of thing of which Laurence would think. She hadn't come home, he didn't know where she was, he went out to Neville's maybe or straight to the wedding, so he left her a key in case she came back. 'So responsible and predictable, Laurence,' she tells her absent husband.

Lying in the bath, Sarah watches the afternoon light turn to early evening, a pinkish hue. The fig tree through the window looks beautiful. She can see the beauty and feel it; the world is a wonderful place. Dipping beneath the water and opening her eyes, the blue ceiling ripples. Her adventure is about to begin. If she stays calm with Laurence, it could just be a very adult conversation, reasonable.

Pulling herself out of the water and wrapping a towel around her, she pads to the bedroom. Whilst she dresses, she hears the car on the lane.

Without hesitation, she strides from the bedroom to the sitting room, pulling up zips and tucking in as she goes, and sits neatly on the sofa and waits.

The engine stops but the cooling fan of the car keeps humming. The gate clangs shut. The kitchen door opens.

He stands in the sitting room doorway, twisting the car keys between his fingers, looking at her. Waiting.

Sarah tries to slow her breathing, consciously relaxing her limbs. The prickling heat starts on her neck; she can feel it rising to her cheeks. She expected to feel nervous, to feel a little fearful even, but all she feels is anger. Raw anger.

'Well?' Laurence hisses.

'Laurence, there is no easy way to say this, so I am just going to say it. I am not going back with you. I am staying here.' The relief is enormous and her hands un-interlock and her elbows relax from digging into her sides.

'Don't be so ridiculous. Are you packed? I suggest we leave in about an hour.'

'If you don't like what I have to say, fine. Don't listen. But I won't be coming with you.' Sarah doesn't move. Her fingers find each other again and her arms re-pin themselves to her sides. She remains silent.

Laurence is winding up his laptop charger. After gathering all his things from the sitting room, he disappears into the bathroom and comes back out minutes later with a bulging ablutions bag.

'Come on,' he snaps as he passes her on his way to the bedroom.

How much clearer can she be? She doesn't move; she waits.

Laurence returns for the bedroom and stares at her. 'Okay, we haven't really got time, but what's this all about.' He sits on the chair opposite.

Stay calm.

'I am staying. You are going. I cannot make it any clearer.' Sarah realises that he probably won't send on her mother's wedding ring or her grandma's

Psalm book. Maybe she can phone Mrs McGee and ask her to send them.

'Okay Sarah, look. Everyone feels like that at the end of a holiday; it's just the way it is. No one wants to go home. If they did, what sort of holiday would that be? I see it all the time: they fly out laughing and fly back silently. It is the nature of the beast. Come on or we are going to have to navigate Athens in the dark.' He stands. Sarah remains sitting. One of Laurence's legs begins to jiggle, a muscle in his cheek begins to twitch, his hand in his pocket agitates the coins that are there. 'Come on.' This time, his words are firm. He is holding back.

Chapter 31

The shadows lengthen and the sun slips behind the fig tree. The garden is still but the cicadas maintain their incessant love song. A bat skims across the pool's surface; another follows it. In the dark, one flies very close to her face but instead of flapping her hands and shrinking, Sarah doesn't even flinch. She is spent she has nothing left.

Laurence's hire car pulled away about half an hour ago but since walking to the pool's edge, she has not moved.

If only he had shouted, got upset, it would at least imply he felt something. But no, once he realised she was serious, he became quiet, reflective. Then he shrugged his shoulders and went into the bedroom to finish packing.

'Are you not even bothered?' The anger wanted to overflow as she followed him, and it took a great deal of self-control to keep it in check. Reminding herself that Juliet would hear if they began shouting, she dug her nails into her palms.

He didn't even make an effort to reply. She stomped from the bedroom to the sitting room, seething, but then returned, determined he would feel something before he left.

'I know why you sold the green car.' She introduced the topic with no intent to follow through to find justice. She just wanted to cause him pain, make him feel unsettled, or even afraid of subsequent possible consequences, anything other than his blasted calm.

At her words, he looked up. 'What green car?' He appeared unfazed but looked in a drawer he had already emptied.

'The one you drove the wrong way on the closed TT race track.' She waited.

Laurence hesitated in putting a pair of socks into his case. 'No idea what you are talking about,' he said as he smoothed the pair flat on top of the shirt he wore for the wedding. Sarah had bought him a set of three pairs of white socks from Marks and Spencer for the trip. Socks were one of her regular purchases; he was hard on them. But now she would never buy him socks again, never wait for the electric doors of that shop to open, never struggle to park on the quayside, never listen to Manx Radio as she drove to Douglas, never feed the ducks behind Rushen Abby in Ballasalla village with the leftover toast from breakfast before that drive. Those trips were done.

'I have no idea what you are talking about.' He continued his packing. 'Nor do I think it matters.

You have made your decision, so that is that.' He snapped his suitcase shut.

It might not matter to him, but Sarah needed some display of emotion, if not for herself, then for Torin.

'The green car you killed the boy on the motorbike with.' Her fists tightened. She felt such power coursing through her muscles.

Laurence stopped lifting his case. He slowly looked up at her.

'You may have seen me, too. The girl on the corner.' Her voice quivered.

'I think you are mistaken.' He cleared his throat after speaking, lifted his suitcase off the bed, and headed for the door.

'Just before you go, Laurence, I want you to know what it is like to lay face to face with a man who has a wooden fence post through his chest, whose arms and legs are broken and whose stomach has been gouged open with barbed wire. The light in that person's eyes burns with the need to live, his every breath a determined struggle to hang on and even ...'

Laurence's eyes narrowed in response. He made a move to the door. Sarah positioned herself between him and the outside.

'Even as he took his last gasp of air, just in those last few seconds, he lived more than you have done in twenty-six years, and his last words proved it.' She waited. Would he ask? Would he dare to hear the words Torin spoke?

'Go on, then. You are dying to tell me.' His voice was harsh but Laurence blinked rapidly. Sarah hoped he was envisioning the crushing reality of that last minute of Torin's life before his actions killed him. He blinked again. He knew alright.

Sarah leaned towards Laurence, nose to nose. 'He told me that he loved me.'

His face muscles relaxed and grew slack, the corners of his mouth pulled downward, all his hardness dropped away. His eyes softened and he whispered, his lips only inches from her own, 'And who denied *me* love?' With which he walked out into the sunshine.

Slinging his suitcase in the boot, he got in the driver's seat and without even a last glance, turned his head away and reversed down the lane.

Sarah stood for a long while, watching the dust from the car swirl in decreasing circles just above ground until it settled and dispersed. Then she pivoted on the spot and, unable to face the empty interior, she walked to the poolside and stood motionless, blindly staring at nothing until the bat took her attention.

He was gone. She was alone. Torin was still just a piece of her history and twenty-six years of marriage were finished in what felt like a petty point-scoring spat.

Swallowing hurt her throat, it was so dry.

Even faced with someone witnessing that he had killed a man, Laurence showed no emotion. He maintained his impenetrable wall and showed no feelings. If he could hide all that, how much more of himself had he kept hidden all those years? What other secrets did he have? Had she ever really known him at all?

Another bat flies close by her, the wind from its wings lifting one or two of her hairs over her face. The need for sleep suddenly engulfs her, extinguishing all thoughts but providing the motivation needed to propel her to the cottage and into bed.

The heat wakes her and the emptiness of the double bed brings her to full consciousness. She is tempted to turn over and seek the release of more sleep, but as her limbs stretch to wakefulness, an excitement begins to build. Out there, beyond the door of the cottage, her new life is waiting for her. The emptiness of the bed becomes a joy and she rolls, reaching into every corner, the space all hers.

Standing, the excitement rushes energy through her limbs. She dresses quickly and starts to sling all her clothes into her suitcase. On the top of the dresser is the box containing the string of pearls Laurence gave to her all those years ago, and next to that, her jewellery box full of gold and diamond trinkets he has bought her over the years. It would have been a nice finale to have given him the pearls back before he left yesterday, complete the task she should have done all those years ago.

Picking up the box, she hinges it open.

'I don't believe it.' She puts the empty box down and picks up her jewellery box. 'Bastard!' How could anyone in the emotional heat of splitting up from two decades of marriage have the presence of mind to empty the necklace box and her jewellery case? Not only empty it but ensure that he was not seen doing it. When? In the split second she had left the room after accusing him that he wasn't even bothered. It must have been; there was no other time.

'Unbelievable.' She sits on the bed, the jewellery box on her knee. It takes a few minutes to recover herself. Shaking her head, she drops the empty box in the bin, searches through the drawers for anything she might have left before going to the bathroom. Laurence has taken all the bottles of shampoo and everything he lined up at the end of the bath, but it is with mixed emotions that Sarah finds his Jacob and Co cuff links in the soap dish. She snorts her brief, hollow mirth—they are worth more than her entire collection of jewels and pearls put together.

That's it. The cottage is empty. Half a bottle of red wine sits by the sink and in the fridge there is some goat cheese and an open box of crackers. Clearing everything out, she wipes the fridge clean. She does not want to make work for Juliet.

It all feels a bit unreal. She wanders to the pool and back inside, then from the sitting room to the bedroom. The bathroom is a recheck where she takes the time to look out of the square window at the tree and the pool. Eventually, she settles on the hammock and tries to read her book, but she is fidgety. Back in the bedroom, she unpacks and repacks everything, this time folding her clothes carefully and putting clean things at the bottom and those that need a rinse through at the top. When she is settled at Jim's, she will spend her first wage on new clothes and burn this collection of Laurence's choices. When she has finished, the open case seems very empty and she wonders what is missing. It is only by chance that she spots her and Laurence's dressing gowns on the back of the bedroom door. She feels a little smug that she is not as forgetful as him. She leaves his hanging.

Outside again, the book is no more entertaining. She walks to the pool but does not fancy a swim although it is lovely just to stand there and watch the light sparkle on the surface. Maybe she could ring Jim. Back in the house, she searches through her handbag for her phone. Checking her received calls, she tries to recognise his number. Jim's household, however, will be upside down today in the aftermath of the wedding. Some of the guests will still be there, and the last thing she wants to do is push him when he will have so much to think about. Tomorrow morning is soon enough. Let things settle a bit, move from here to the hotel in Saros and get to know her surroundings. She should buy a Greek phrase book, start to learn the language.

With an enormous sigh, she goes back in the kitchen and, taking the goat cheese and the crackers, she returns outside. The cat appears and meows incessantly until Sarah gives him some cheese. A lizard stands motionless on the smooth dust where yesterday, Laurence's car stood, and a moth, or a fat butterfly, so big Sarah mistakes it for a hummingbird, hovers by the bougainvillaea, its proboscis dipping deep into the flowers.

'This is it, Sarah girl. This is the pace of your life from now on.' The words produce a shiver down her spine. Does she take out her laptop and start reading up on beekeeping or ...

Her thoughts are interrupted by her phone.

'Oh hi, Jim. I didn't expect to hear from you today.'

Chapter 32

Walking through the bee-buzzing gully is different today; no longer something precious to hang onto, it is now going to be part of her daily life. Nevertheless, Sarah loiters before leaving the enclosed path, and when she does enter the rough grazing ground, she takes the time to look over the hives again.

'I am a beekeeper,' she says to herself. She is not sure she has ever had a title before, except as Laurence's wife. 'Beekeeper.' She says it again as if introducing herself to someone.

The rough ground is empty of sheep and goats and so she heads straight for the side gate. 'And housekeeper.' She fills out her improvised introduction to an imaginary person.

Unlatching the gate, she cautiously opens it; the dogs might be free. They are out of their cages but on long chains. If she sticks to the wall, they cannot reach her. The ground is littered with gun cartridges and Sarah briefly recalls her moment of craziness, and then the moments of embrace with Nicolaos. They will be living next door to each other.

'Ah, that was quick. You didn't have to come straight away.' Jim is fishing something from the pool with a net. 'I have just ordered some coffee. We were going to have it up on the balcony; will you join us?'

Sarah presumes, when he says *we*, he means himself and Frona and she looks about for the old woman, but they are alone.

Jim puts down his net and leads Sarah up to the balcony. When they are nearly at the top of the stairs, Jim says, 'Did you met Rudolph and Maria? Maria is my second cousin and her husband Rudolph.'

They have come out onto the balcony and rising from the sofa and offering his hand to shake is the man in the shiny suit, his cigar clamped between his teeth.

'How do you do,' Sarah responds formally. The wife remains sitting. She looks very fragile, and she nods and says 'hello' in a small voice. Sarah smiles.

'Please.' Jim offers Sarah a seat. 'Ah here is the coffee.' The maid arrives and puts a tray down.

'So, as so often in life, things have changed a little, Sarah, but I think it could be for the better, give everyone a little time to gather themselves.' He sits next to Maria and he puts his arm around her. 'Maria here has been a little under the weather as of late.'

Maria puts her hand over her mouth and gives a weak cough in response. Jim looks at her with concern. 'The area of Germany they live in has high pollution so, last night, I talked Rudolph into taking a little time off work to come out here for Maria's sake.' Sarah looks at Rudolf, who leans back and takes a big lungful of cigar smoke and smiles like a caring husband as he exhales.

'Oh,' is all Sarah can raise herself to say. Does Jim want her to act as maid for these people or is it something more complex? What does he mean by 'giving people time to gather themselves?'

'Obviously, things cannot run themselves in Germany,' Rudolph says with an American twang that does not disguise the German accent, 'but I think I can give my Precious six months of clean air.' He looks over to Maria. Jim takes his arm from around his cousin to pick up his coffee cup.

'Coffee?' He indicates for Sarah to help herself. Rudolph takes a cup and gives it to Maria before taking one for himself.

'So I thought it best to introduce you to each other, as it is probably best if your time crosses by a week or so. Rudolph can bring you up to speed on everything and it gives you,' he says, looking at Sarah, 'what, say a full six months, Rudolph?' Rudolph nods whilst sipping his coffee, his large hands awkward around the small cup's handle. 'How does that sound, Sarah?'

'You don't need me for six months?' Sarah's coffee cup rattles in its saucer, so she hastily puts it back down.

'That'll give you time to pop home, tie up loose ends, and gather yourself. Sounds perfect, doesn't it?' Jim takes a sip of his coffee and Rudolph nods. Maria's eyes are on Sarah. Sarah's throat has become tight and she can hear the throb of her blood being pumped. She cannot stay in a hotel in Saros waiting for six months. Her limbs seems to have gone to sleep; her back is rigidly fixed. Trying to focus on her situation is causing her mind to go blank.

'Sarah, don't you think?' Jim repeats something Sarah has not heard.

'Sorry?'

'Six months is a perfect length of time to sort everything back at home. I know if it was me, I would need longer but then, I have never really come to terms with running a house. Give me a shipping company and I am at home. Give me a home and I am all at sea.'

Rudolph seems to think this is very funny and puts down his coffee in fear of spilling it with his belly laughs.

'Did Frona show you the housekeeper's rooms?' Jim asks.

'Er no.' Sarah cannot remember if she did or she didn't. Right now, her thought processing seems to have hibernated, and she wonders if Frona has agreed to this change of plan. 'What does Frona say about the six months?' Sarah asks, beginning to dislike Jim. Okay, so they didn't have a contracted agreement, but they had agreed to talk it all over and it seems now he has decided to cast her aside for his cousin. Obviously his cousin is more important to him than she is but, even so, the way he has gone about it all is rather tactless.

'Frona says it would be good. She is going to close up the house in Jersey. She might even sell it, she tells me. Well, she said two or three months, but I think she can see how six months would mean she doesn't have to rush.' Jim finishes his coffee. Sarah hasn't even started hers. She stands. She will not be a pawn any longer.

'Well, very nice to meet you Rudolph and I hope you feel better soon, Maria.'

'Are you going?' Jim stands.

'I think it's best.'

'Please let me walk you to the door. We can go by the housekeeper's rooms, chat about the terms and conditions.' He gives a weak laugh. Sarah does not stop him.

The rooms, as it turns out, are plain, large, and light filled, and Sarah could not wish for anywhere nicer to stay. The pay he is offering is also higher than she anticipated, but she has no idea what she will do from now till then. She cannot return to Laurence.

'I am not sure what I will be doing in six months. Can we be in touch nearer the time?' Sarah hears her voice and is impressed with how calm she sounds.

'Oh.' It is Jim's turn to sound thrown. Good. 'Well, yes, if it would suit you better, but I really was hoping ...' He trails off.

Sarah does not give him any reassurances and she leaves not having seen Frona, either.

Deliberating on whether to march quickly down the drive or take things more slowly through the side gate, she realises she has nowhere to go and nothing to do. There is no point in marching anywhere even though she has recognised her feeling of anxiety and a good march would unwind her.

The side gate creaks open and Sarah walks looking at the ground. Why had she counted on this job when nothing had been decided? How stupid. Irresponsible, Laurence would say. Maybe she isn't fit to live her life on her own after all. Maybe she is not able to!

'No, that's just stupid,' she tells herself.

'Who's stupid?'

'Oh, Nicolaos, I didn't see you in the shade.'

'Why so sad?' He seems quite animated and steps out from under the tree into the sunshine.

'I think I have made a bad choice again.' Sarah cannot find a smile.

'What do you mean *again*? You are not condemned to repeat the same negative thought patterns, you know.'

'Right now, all I need is a "there, there" and a little sympathy. I don't need to know that I am thinking wrong as well as doing wrong.' Sarah is sharp, but she looks at him to make sure she hasn't offended him. He still seems very buoyant.

'There there ...' He steps towards her, puts a hand on her shoulder, and looks deep into her eyes.

She pulls away. 'Look, life will make you unhappy. But if you expect a cure to come from a pill or from someone else providing the answer, you will be even unhappier when it doesn't happen,' he says.

'Can you stop being philosophical just for today?'

'Sure.' He shrugs and his hand falls from her shoulder. 'But I need to ask you something.' His hand takes her hand as he speaks. It is an intimate act and Sarah looks down to their intertwined fingers. 'You are staying, right?' Sarah has no idea what to answer. What on earth does her future hold? But he does not wait for a reply. 'Do you think that over time, living so closely that you and I ...' He pulls her gently into his arms, his head bowing. Their noses touch, his mouth so close to hers she can feel his breath on her lips. Her body responds and yearns for him, her hips moving forward, their bodies moulding together.

She pulls away sharply. If there is one thing she is not going to do, she is not going to let a relationship determine the course of her life again. First she must decide what she wants to do and then she can get involved. If she gets involved.

'What? Was I so wrong?' Nicolaos's eyes are wide, his palms upwards towards her. Sarah sees the hurt in his expression; she wants to rescue him, tell him that despite herself, her body said yes. But that would lead to another embrace, she would be lost, and their relationship would make all her choices for her. That was the old her, but right now she would like to think, no matter how hard it seems, she has upgraded her personality. She must make herself act independently.

What matters right now is that all her thoughts are aligned to her autonomy and that her actions are aligned with her thoughts. It all feels very grown up somehow, but there is no other way to get where she wants to be.

Just thinking this seems to give her some peace. Her internal struggle subsides and she knows she cannot give in.

'Nicolaos, you are not wrong. But for once in my life, I must make a self-determined thought, not one based on a relationship I am in, or could be in.'

'Oh.' His face loses structure and she can hear beads clicking in his pocket. She looks up at him, her eyes creasing up in the sun's glare. She steps sideways into the shade of the tree, and he does the same. 'I got a letter back today, from my wife.' He takes a deep breath that sounds tired and sad. 'She says if I go back, we can try again.'

Sarah understands why he tried to kiss her. It seems he, too, makes his decisions based on the relationships he is in. 'Oh.' She says it kindly. 'What will you do?'

'Well, if I thought there was any chance ...' He looks at her, searching her eyes, looking for a glimmer of hope.

'To be truthful, first I must find my feet, alone.' Sarah has never said anything so brave in all her life. She clenches her teeth.

'My wife has invited me for her birthday. If I want to make a go of it, I would have to fly the day after tomorrow to be there in time.' He hardly blinks as he looks into Sarah's eyes.

Sarah says nothing. His face is so full of expression, his lips so quick with a smile, so easy to make tremble. He is a sensitive man. He is so sensitive that after Laurence, it is a little bit scary. She would be so responsible for his feelings, his comfort, his happiness. But surely that is better than an emotionless lump like Laurence? But it is scary.

Nicolaos takes a step backwards in the silence. 'Okay. I see. I understand.' He waits for her to contradict him, but when she doesn't he adds, 'Tomorrow, I will find someone to take the herd, the day after I will fly. If you change your mind, I am in the cottage just over the brow of the hill.' He seems to wait for her to stop him as he takes another step backwards. Everything in her screams to reach out and take his hand, to stop him going. But if she does not stand on her own two feet now, today, in this moment, she probably never will. Her vision blurs. He takes another step away.

Chapter 33

The holiday cottage echoes with Sarah's footsteps. Her phone has one message waiting. It is from Joss, who wishes her safe travels and says he is at the airport himself. She didn't even say goodbye to him. It is one thing to walk out on her husband, but she should keep it together enough to remain a good mum. It goes straight to voicemail when she tries ringing him; he must be in the aeroplane already.

The sun streams in, but it brings her no cheer, her thoughts replay her walking away from Nicolaos. Her breath comes in shallow gasps. Has she just made the biggest mistake of her life, or has she just taken the most self-reliant step possible? The clock on the wall in the kitchen tells her it is time for her to vacate the cottage and as she ponders this, she hears Juliet's voice. She must leave but she is reluctant.

'Hello? Sarah, are you there? Oh there you are. Are you off? Have you found a place to stay for your job or are you still on the hunt?'

'Not decided yet.' It is as vague as Sarah can manage whilst remaining truthful.

'Well as soon as you are settled, come back and we'll open a bottle of wine together and wish you "*kaloriziko*."'

'*Kaloriziko*. What does that mean?' Sarah asks, but just at the moment, she has little real interest.

'Literally it means "Good Roots." May your roots here spread and grow strong so you cannot be moved.' Juliet is all smiles.

'I will definitely drink to that.' Quite spontaneously, Sarah hugs Juliet, whose return embrace is warm and heartfelt. It is with a sad heart that Sarah pulls her wheeled luggage down the lane. Now she is officially homeless. A tramp. She snorts over this thought, but it is short-lived mirth because she really has no idea where to go or what to do. If she checks into a hotel in Saros, she can imagine the days passing until she runs out of money, so it sounds dangerous from the start. At the village square, she rolls her bag to the bench and sits down. If she is going to Saros, she will need a taxi.

'Hey, hello. Was the wedding good?' Stella steps from behind the kiosk awning with a bottle of water. 'You want some?' she asks, twisting the cap off.

'The wedding was beautiful.' Sarah shakes her head at the water.

Stella looks at the suitcase. 'Oh you are going now?'

'Yes, I guess so.' The first time she meet Stella seems an age ago even though it is only days. At that time, a dark weight used to live in her stomach. Sarah smiles, almost laughs. Things may be bad, she may have no job and no home and no husband, but there is no sign of that darkness, no feeling of futility or pointlessness. But there is a churning in her stomach, a feeling of excitement.

'Well, it has been lovely to meet you and if you ever return, you must come to my house and we will eat together. Agreed?' Stella says.

'Agreed.' Sarah stands and Stella hugs her, kisses her on both cheeks before bouncing away. The warmth of Juliet and Stella gives Sarah the sure feeling she will survive. This, in turn, dispels the hint of remaining anger she recognises. She is holding anger towards Jim.

'He never promised anything,' Sarah tells herself and with this thought, she sets off to see Frona before she leaves. Also, going up to the house will give her an excuse to, once more, go up the heat trap gully, hear the insects and see the beehives. 'One day,' she tells herself. 'Maybe in six months.'

Her bag rolls easily, if noisily, until she turns off the tarmac and onto the gorse-bordered path. The suitcase is too heavy to carry but, much as she would like to, she cannot just leave it. The plastic wheels jar and snag as Sarah drags the bag a little way off the road and then, once hidden from view between the gorse, it becomes her seat. Relaxing all her limbs, she soaks in the buzzing and the scents of the flowers and her head rolls as the warmth overpowers her.

She tries to recall where she put that last pebble, the one she picked up after looking into the stars on the way to the party the night before the wedding. If it is white, she will be happy to the point of selfishness from now on; if it is black, she will continue the way she is and if happiness comes, that will be a bonus not a decision. It seems a strange pledge now, a decision to be happy placed on the colour of an unseen pebble. It is not in the suitcase pocket with the other stones. It must still be in the pocket of her dress. Unzipping the bag, it seems too hot to start foraging in her clothes. She zips it up again. The next time she goes in the case, she will find it. In fact, the next time she goes in her case, she will throw away all the clothes she neither likes nor wants. It is crazy to be lugging around Laurence's choice of wardrobe.

Rousing herself and pulling her bag, she enters the open field to take a last look at the beehives .

'I think it should work out well, don't you?'

Sarah turns towards the beehives, where Frona is busy with a can of paint and a brush. No one ever seems surprised to see anyone here, but Sarah still feels caught unawares every time, although it is becoming less so as the days pass. This time, she is calm enough to pretend she was expecting Frona.

'Not sure,' Sarah answers.

'I am going to sell up in America and then Jim cannot give me a reason to go back. Six months is more than enough time but poor Maria, she is in such bad health, I don't suppose she will live to see Germany again if they stay.'

'Oh really? I hadn't realised she was so bad.' And there she had been thinking only of her inconvenience.

'Slow but expected.' Frona continues to cover the hive in paint. It is running down the sides, dripping off and pooling in the grass. She is making a bit of a mess of it. 'What will you do for six months? Travel? Go back to your husband?'

'No, definitely not that.' Sarah picks up a twig and rescues a beetle from the paint in the grass, putting it in a gorse branch, which it promptly falls off. 'I am not sure. I also don't really trust myself to make a good decision,' Sarah confides, scanning for the beetle, which has disappeared into the longer grass.

'Ha, do any of us make good decisions or do we just make the decision we are faced with and have no choice over?'

Sarah frowns as Frona seems to be making no sense.

'You know, to survive, I have done many things, and some of them do not make me proud. Out of fear sometimes, I have not spoken up when I should. Out of plain laziness, I have wasted days, a year, a decade even. To save my own skin, I have harmed others.' Frona has stopped painting and looks beyond the horizon. Sarah wonders if she is talking about the war, her evacuation from Asia Minor. 'But at least I know I have never gone against my prime directive, which is to stay alive.' She sighs. 'Maybe I feel guilt, but I get to live long enough to do it better next time.' The old woman resumes her painting.

'You always have to *do* something,' Frona says as a matter of fact. 'This has been the one thing that is always true in life. You goal may even be spiritual, but you still have to actually *do* something.' Sarah is not sure she is following Frona or if, indeed, the old woman is being coherent, but she continues to listen.

'What do you do if you have followed a belief for years and then you find it is fake? What do you risk? You can ask a friend. You can get counselling, you can sit and look at a blank wall and not move, and this may help you to know how to think. It might even give to you the best way to see the event, but none of these are going to give you the answer as to what you are going to actually physically do next and there, very often, is the problem. So, unable to make a choice, get swept along the easiest route and call it a decision.'

Sarah has no idea what Frona is talking about and wonders if something specific has happened that she is referring to or whether the old woman is showing signs of ageing.

'Right, I am done. That will last them six months.' Frona leaves both paint pot and brush by one of the hives. 'Well, whatever you decide to do, have a wonderful, adventurous six months doing exactly what you want to be doing where you want to do it, and then you can't go wrong. That's my advice.' With this, she kisses Sarah on each cheek, looks her in the eye as if transferring some secret, and walks away up the hill.

Sarah watches her go through the side gate and then the field is empty, all hers. The sun is almost directly overhead. If she is going to stay in the field for any time, she should at least be in the shade. The suitcase bumps over the rough ground, twisting in her grip until she makes the shade of the tree.

Sitting on the stone, she looks over the village. She traces the roads and tries to commit the sight to memory. The tops of the gorse obstructs the view of the entirety of the village, so she stands. Pulling resentfully, the bag trundles to the top of the hill where she lays it flat and uses it as a seat.

Now the valley is fully spread before her. The world is at her feet. She could put her shoes on and walk for six months. That is something she would like to do. This makes Sarah laugh quietly, as she is not sure if she really has the energy for such an adventure. What she would really like to do is sit in the insect-laden gully or this field without a care in the world. That is what would give her peace. That is what she would like to do and where she would like to do it. Sit for six months or longer in peace and safety until she finds her feet and her vitality.

Her spine straightens. the hairs on the back of her neck prickle. She stands and raises both hands to the sky, clasping them together and then relaxing them to rest on the top of her head. She has absolute certainty where she can find that peace. She knows exactly what she will do.

Grabbing the bag by its handle, she crowns the hill and, with gravity forcing the bag into the back of her legs, she gains momentum as she careens down the other side.

Releasing the bag, she takes a breath as she comes to the flag area outside of the tiny cottage. Everything is still except the *baa*-ing of sheep from a nearby pen.

Regaining her breath, she taps at the door. There is no reply. She taps again. Nothing. She unzips her bag and delves into her clothes, looking for the fifth pebble. It will be white; she is certain it will be white. She grasps it and as she withdraws her hand, the door opens. Nicolaos in his vest stands with a piece of toast in his hand, opened-mouthed. Hastily finishing the snack, he wipes his fingers on his work trousers and steps to one side, waving her in as he swallows.

'Sarah!' He seems delighted to see her. 'Come in.'

The sun caresses Sarah's back, melting away tension. She can smell the geraniums planted in pots either side of the door. The place exudes peace and calm.

'No I won't come in just yet. I just want to ask one question.'

'Ask anything. The answer is yes. For you, it is yes.' His arms are open and he steps towards her. Past him, within the shaded interior, she can just make out a flagged floor, pale blue walls, basic, rustic, charming, dusty. A suitcase neatly waits by a pair of shoes.

She pauses, looks at her clenched fist, the pebble held within. She turns and throws it as far as she can across the field. Straightening her back, she faces Nicolaos. 'My question is,' His face is expectant as he watches her form her words. 'Does the cottage come with the job of goat-herding?'

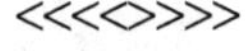

22072319R00265

Made in the USA
San Bernardino, CA
18 June 2015